CW00971904

lost with me

~

"Look at them," he says, turning me around so that I'm looking down into the grand room, at the people touching and kissing and petting. I watch, my blood heating as I do, and my breath coming faster as Damien's hands stroke lightly over my back and then down to cup my ass.

He bends forward, and I feel his breath on my neck, then I gasp when I realize that he's used his teeth to tug the bow free. My blouse falls, attached only around my waist, my breasts now completely bare. "Mine," he says, then starts to tug up the back of my skirt.

~

The Stark Saga
by
J. Kenner

novels
release me
claim me
complete me
anchor me
lost with me

novellas
take me
have me
play my game
seduce me
unwrap me
deepest kiss
entice me
hold me
please me
indulge me

For all of JK's Stark World and other titles,
please visit www.jkenner.com

Praise for J. Kenner's Novels

"PERFECT for fans of *Fifty Shades of Grey* and *Bared to You*. *Release Me* is a powerful and erotic romance novel that is sure to make adult romance readers sweat, sigh and swoon." *Reading, Eating & Dreaming Blog*

"I will admit, I am in the 'I loved *Fifty Shades*' camp, but after reading *Release Me*, Mr. Grey only scratches the surface compared to Damien Stark." *Cocktails and Books Blog*

"It is not often when a book is so amazingly well-written that I find it hard to even begin to accurately describe it . . . I recommend this book to everyone who is interested in a passionate love story." *Romancebookworm's Reviews*

"The story is one that will rank up with the *Fifty Shades* and Cross Fire trilogies." *Incubus Publishing Blog*

"The plot is complex, the characters engaging, and J. Kenner's passionate writing brings it all perfectly together." *Harlequin Junkie*

A sizzling, intoxicating, sexy read!!!! J. Kenner had me devouring Wicked Dirty, the second installment of *Stark World Series* in one sitting. I loved everything about this book from the opening pages to the raw and vulnerable characters. With her sophisticated prose, Kenner created a love story that had the perfect blend of lust, passion, sexual tension, raw emotions and love. - Michelle, Four Chicks Flipping Pages

lost with me

J. KENNER

Lost With Me Copyright © 2018 by Julie Kenner

Cover design by Michele Catalano, Catalano Creative

Cover image by Annie Ray/Passion Pages

ISBN: 978-1-940673-85-1

Published by Martini & Olive Books

v. 2018-10-19-P

M&O

1

I stand on the wooden patio of my beachfront bungalow, the lively notes of Mozart's *Rondo Alla Turca* filling my head, the quick tempo of the hold music at odds with the relative calm of the Pacific spread out before me. I press my fingers to the earpiece, settling it more firmly in place as I wait, then once again grip the railing in front of me as I look out to the sea and breathe in the beauty that stretches to the horizon and beyond.

At just past ten, the sky has already lost the orange and purple hues that defined the morning, and it spreads out like a cerulean blanket over a dancing sea that sparkles in the brilliant light of the climbing sun.

I'm no stranger to fine art—how can I be, married to a man like Damien Stark, who appreciates the arts and has the money to buy what he loves? And as I look out on this incredible vista, two thoughts are clear in my mind. First, that no painting or photograph could ever truly capture the majesty of this view. And second, that I am more blessed than I ever expected to be, and I'm grateful every day for the life I now have, so different from the horror that was my life back in Texas.

I have my children. My home. My work. My view.

And Damien, I think with a delicious frisson of delight. Most of all, I have Damien. My husband, my lover, my heart.

I exhale slowly, intentionally enjoying the moment. It's a good day. An easy day, and I feel like it's my due. After all, during our trip to San Francisco a few months ago, there'd been a chasm between Damien and me. Not deep—I don't know that there could ever be one that is deep or uncrossable between us, and if there ever were, the pain of that separation would kill me. But he'd been keeping secrets. Trying to protect me.

An ironic smile tugs at my mouth. I understand why he did it, but secrets between us never really work out. And now, of course, he owes me a do-over of that particular trip.

I'm considering when we could both squeeze out time for a jaunt back up the coast, when Abby bursts back onto the line with a breathless, "Sorry! Sorry! I didn't think I'd be away so long. Debugging this code is going to be the death of me."

My company, Fairchild & Partners Development, designs and implements corporate software as well as web and mobile device apps—both business and entertainment related. Today, Abby is tearing her hair out about Mommy's Helper, a deceptively simple app she conceived that incorporates parent-related reminders, appointment scheduling, audio and video monitors, direct messaging with babysitters, and other similarly useful parental tidbits in one place. We've been in beta-testing the last two weeks, and our official release day is just around the corner.

Naturally, the closer we get, the more glitches appear, but Abby's brilliant at programming, and she's tackled each challenge as it's come up. If she's having trouble now, this string of code must really be a beast.

"Travis wasn't any help?" I ask, referencing our newest employee.

"Not really." Silence hangs between us, and she rushes on. "I mean, he's got so much on his plate that I didn't ask him."

I press my palms together as if in prayer and tap my chin, debating between silence and speech. Silence is easier, but this is my company, and I need to be the grown-up even if my employees aren't.

Partner, I correct. She's only got a ten percent stake, but Abby is now my partner. I brought her in when I was juggling the pressures of being a business owner and a new mom, and I don't regret it. Not only is she one hell of a programmer, but she also doesn't bullshit. If she says she can do something, she can. If she's not sure or screws up, she lets you know. And she doesn't play stupid workplace games.

Or she never has before.

With a sigh, I take a seat on one of the cushioned, outdoor chairs. I'm wearing a black bikini with a sheer blouse and a large scarf tied around my hips as a makeshift sarong. It opens as I sit, revealing bare thighs, both ridged with scars. Roughly, I cross my legs, shifting the scarf as I do to cover the exposed skin. Then I force myself to think about Abby. Not about my past and certainly not about the speech I'm delivering tomorrow morning.

Just Abby.

"So, I'll shoot you the code," she says. "And you can work your magic, okay?"

"That's one option. Or you could pull in Travis. Unless I'm misremembering, debugging code is a major part of his job description." I can hear the mom-tone in my voice, but can't seem to dial it back. "And since you haven't asked for his help already, that makes me think that you're either too proud—which isn't going to fly at this company—or you can't get past this dark cloud that's shoved its way between the two of you. And that's not going to fly either."

"Oh, *hell*." She mutters a long string of nearly unintelligible curses, presumably not meant for my ears, then draws a fortifying breath. "Nikki, I'm sorry," she says, once again sounding like the professional I know her to be. "I didn't mean for our personal crap to spill over into work."

I run my fingers through my hair, thinking. I'm certain I saw sparks flying between the two of them during his first weeks on the job. Now, those sparks have been replaced with an unpleasant tension and, apparently, an inability to work together.

Reluctantly, I push myself out of the chair, knowing what I have to do, but not liking it at all. "I don't know what happened between you two, but I do know that it's affecting your work. Yours, Abby. As far as I can tell, Travis is doing the work assigned to him. But I brought you in as a partner because I thought you could handle it. And that means getting past whatever happened between you two."

"I know."

"We're so small I never thought about setting out rules for dating inside the company—"

"We should never have—"

"—*and* I don't think we need rules like that now. But I might change my mind if you two don't work this out."

In the grand scheme of things, I'm not that much older than Abby, who's twenty-five. But right now, the chasm between the two of us seems wide. I've experienced so much —good and bad—and in many ways, Abby still has a small-town girl sheen, despite coming to LA years ago as a freshman at UCLA.

"Can you work it out? Or do we need to cut Travis loose?" I bite my lip as I wait for her to answer, hoping she won't call my bluff.

Thankfully, her answer comes quickly. "No—no, he's an asset. And it's probably my—never mind. I mean, I'll see if he can help with this section of code."

"What's he working on now?"

"He's running through all the support requests we've received this month on the smartphone apps and assigning code fixes to our freelancers if it's a legitimate bug. But he should have time to help. And you're right. He's as good as they come. Chances are he'll see the solution."

My body goes limp with relief. I haven't had to face too many management issues since I started my business— probably because I was a one-woman shop for a long time —and I give myself a pat on the back for successfully navigating this one.

Honestly, I shouldn't have let the tension between them get to this level. But that's the downside of working out of this bungalow—I spend less time with my co-workers than I did when the office was in Studio City, and that means I'm less tied in to the various nuances between my employees.

The upside, of course, is that I'm closer to the house. Just a few steps away, in fact, since the bungalow that I've been using as an office for almost two years is situated at the lowest point of our Malibu acreage.

When we first started going out—or, technically, when Damien first paid me a million dollars to pose for the nude portrait that now hangs in our third-floor open area—he was almost through with construction of the stunning hillside mansion that is now our home. Then, as now, the only flaw that I could find in the place was its distance from the beach. Situated on the slope of a hill, the house has a breathtaking view and every comfort imaginable, from an infinity pool to a helipad. But if you want to walk along the beach, you have to first traverse a serpentine, crushed stone path. No stepping out the back door and onto the sand, because even though the *property* is technically beachfront, the house isn't.

Enter my husband, who worked with an architect to design the bungalow as a gift for me. And though it originally served simply as an extension of our home, I've been using it as my office, a wonderful arrangement that allows me to be close to our daughters, Anne and Lara, even when I'm knee-deep in a project.

That, however, is coming to an end in just a few days, as Abby reminds me with her next question. "So, I'll meet you at the office?"

"That's the plan. I want you and Travis and Marge to make sure you're happy with your offices." I'm meeting a journalist at a nearby bakery for a quick profile piece in just over an hour. Then I'm going to lunch with my best friend, Jamie, before running a few more errands, including heading over to the new office space to go over the final punch list.

"Sounds good," she says. "You know, I thought I'd be bummed as we got closer. After all, no commute and working in my pajamas is great, but I'm really excited about being in an office again. I'm starting to talk to my dust bunnies."

"Keep your unconventional pets at home," I tell her. "But maybe we can negotiate a casual dress code."

Abby rewards my attempt at humor with an unladylike snort. "I'll send you over the list of all active projects as soon as we hang up," she promises. "It's a massive list—which is good because it means we're doing fabulous."

"We are, aren't we?" That fabulousness is part of the reason why we're leasing office space. I'd sold my original space not long after Anne was born when I decided to start working out of the bungalow. Back then, it was just me, Abby, and Marge, our office manager/general assistant/everything else. Abby worked primarily from home, and Marge split her time between working remotely and coming to the bungalow.

Now Anne is almost two, our client list is growing, we have a solid team of freelancers, and we're looking to hire at least one other full-time programmer, a marketing exec, and a client development manager. Even more important, revenue is not only up, but on a pretty sharp trajectory.

"Wow," Abby says.

"What?"

"I'm not sure I remember how to put on make-up."

"Liar," I say, making her laugh. "You put on makeup to go to the grocery store."

"Um, pot. Meet kettle."

I can't argue. I've worked hard to unlearn each and every lesson from The Elizabeth Fairchild Manual For Life, but on that count, my mother won; I've never managed to walk out of my home without looking my best. "I guess that's why we make a good team."

"Wednesday," she says, referring to our first official day in our new space.

"We'll have cake," I promise.

"In that case, I'll make sure I'm on time."

I roll my eyes. Which, of course, she can't see.

"Should I ask Travis to work on the Greystone-Branch

updates?" Abby asks. "Or do you think we should wait until we bring in a new person?"

"It can wait a week. Let's see how Thursday and Friday's interviews go." We've had feelers out for a while, and five potential programmers are scheduled to come for interviews in the new space, along with applicants for the other positions as well.

"Sounds good. Oh, and Marge and I are both coming to the brunch. Travis, too. We're all so excited."

"That's great." I swallow, a little guilty that I hadn't personally invited them. I'd agreed that the Stark Children's Foundation should send all my employees an invite—after all, the company donates to the SCF regularly—but I hadn't let myself think about the fact that they might actually be in the audience when I give my speech.

The prospect is daunting, and I slowly lower myself back into the deck chair, once again afraid that I'm making the wrong choice. That Saturday is going to go horribly, horribly wrong.

"Nikki?"

"Sorry. The connection went bad. You said you're all coming together?"

"We can't wait."

"Me, neither," I lie. Or, at least, it's a partial lie. I *am* excited. It's an honor to speak at the Foundation's annual brunch. But I'm also scared to death.

I'm about to wrap up the call, when she clears her throat and says, "Actually, there is just one last thing."

Something in her voice makes me cringe, and I hesitate before saying, "Okay," in that long, drawn-out way that suggests bad news is just around the corner.

"No, no," she says hurriedly. "It's no big deal. I just wanted to let you know we got a new resume in today for the programmer position. Brian Crane. You used to work with him, right?"

I make a face, and I'm immediately glad she can't see it. Brian worked with me at C-Squared, and my distaste for that company stems from the fact that the company's owner, Carl Rosenfeld, was a total prick. It's only by proximity to him that my co-workers were sullied. Brian was a solid programmer back then, and I can only assume he's gotten better. "Forward it to me, and I'll take a look. If nothing else, I'm curious what he's been up to."

She assures she will, then hangs up, and I draw a long, slow breath. *Brian Crane.* The man holds no particular interest to me, but Carl raises all sorts of emotions, with vile dislike being right there at the top of the pile.

But maybe I'm being unfair to him. After all, if it weren't for Carl, Damien and I might never have gotten together.

My phone rings, and I tap the earpiece. "What did you forget?" I ask, certain that it's Abby.

But it's not Abby. It's Damien.

"Forget?" His voice, strong and sensual, fires my blood, making my body tingle with at least as much awareness as if he were standing right beside me, his dark eyes skimming over me, taking my body to full awareness. I realize I'm standing, as if the force of his voice lifted me to my feet. "I don't think I've ever forgotten a single thing about you."

"That's good to know, Mr. Stark." My voice sounds husky, laden with desire. And as the cool ocean breeze teases my now-heated skin, my nipples contract into tight beads inside the bikini top.

Even after so many years together—even after two children and sleepless nights and toddler tantrums—it only takes a word from Damien to melt me. Sometimes I wonder if the desire that boils between us will ever calm to a simmer, but I don't really believe that could happen.

"Tell me what you're thinking."

I close my eyes, imagining him standing in front of me, tall and lean and commanding. "I was just thinking about you," I admit. "You ought to know I'm always thinking about you."

"Then that's another thing we have in common, Ms. Fairchild."

"That's *Mrs. Stark*, thank you very much." I'm confident he can hear the smile in my voice.

"Yes, it is," he agrees. "And I like the sound of it very much. What exactly were you thinking?"

"About that first night at Evelyn's house. And how even though Carl is a vile little worm, if I hadn't been working for him that night, we might never have gotten together."

"We would have," he says, his tone leaving no room for argument. "As soon as I learned that you were in LA, I would have sought you out. Count on it, Mrs. Stark. We're part of each other, Nikki. We're inevitable, you and I. And Carl Rosenfeld was merely an extra on the stage of our life together."

I hear the truth in his words and sigh happily. He's right, of course. Somehow, we would have found each other. "What were you thinking about?" I ask.

"That it's been over sixty hours since I've seen you, and by the time I get home tonight, we'll be pushing dangerously close to seventy."

"That's far too long," I agree. Damien left for Chicago early Tuesday morning. It's now Friday. And although he flew back to LA this morning, he went straight to the office.

"Fortunately, I have a very active, very visceral imagination."

"Do you?" My mouth has gone dry in response to the heat in his voice. "What were you imagining?"

"My wife, naked and panting and desperate in our bed. The way my cock hardens as I watch her lips part and her back arch when she's about to explode. The way she grinds against my face as I eat out that beautiful cunt."

"My God, Damien." My voice is so heavy with need I almost can't push the words out, and I squeeze my legs together in a futile attempt to quell the desire pulsing between my thighs.

"I want you waiting for me. Not at the house, though. I want you to myself."

I nod wordlessly, which is ridiculous since he can't see me.

"I'll come to you at the bungalow," he says. "I want you naked, your body bent over the railing as I fuck you from behind, my hands on your breasts and my face lost in the silk of your hair. I want to feel you tremble beneath me, your skin on fire. I want to draw it out, to take you close but never over. Not until the moment when the sun finally slips below the horizon, and as that last glow of orange and purple explodes in the sky, I'll make you explode in my arms."

My legs have turned to jelly, and I lower myself back into the deck chair. "Christ, Damien. I think I just did."

I'm rewarded by his soft chuckle. "Three days is too damn long. I'm claiming you, Nikki. Marking my territory. Tonight, I'm taking what's mine."

"Yes," I whisper. "Thank God, yes."

"And after we can both breathe again, I want to walk hand-in-hand with you to the house so that we can go see our girls."

"They've missed you," I say, happiness wrapping around me like a warm, safe blanket.

"I've missed them, too." He makes a raw noise in his throat. "I used to enjoy traveling. Now it's like cutting off a limb every time I go away."

"For us, too," I say. "Of course, I make do." I add a lilt to my voice. "Like last night, for example. I wasn't alone in our bed."

"Is that so? Did someone negotiate her way into my side of the bed?"

"Just like her Daddy," I say. "That one's going to broker big business deals." Our oldest, Lara, will turn four in a couple of weeks, and already she's a prime manipulator. "She said she wanted to keep me company so that I wouldn't be sad that Daddy was away. How could I say no?"

"You'd be stronger than me if you'd managed. I wouldn't have been able to deny her either." For a moment, he's quiet, the silence weighing heavy. "I missed all my girls this weekend."

"We missed you, too. Desperately. Do you have to go back next week?" I try to keep my voice neutral, but I fear I already know the answer, and it's not one I like. He'd come back to LA because of a series of meetings that couldn't easily be moved. But if the Chicago crisis hasn't been resolved, I have a feeling I'll be kissing Damien goodbye at the Santa Monica Airport come Monday morning.

"That's one of the reasons I'm calling, actually. To give you fair warning that I'll want my side of the bed back next week. I'm afraid your bedtime companion may be disappointed."

"That Daddy's home? Not a chance." I feel a thousand pounds lighter knowing he won't be leaving again, and it's only when I realize that my wide smile actually hurts my cheeks that I fully acknowledge how much I was dreading Damien leaving again come Monday.

"What are you doing now?" he asks.

"Other than talking to my husband? I wrapped up a phone meeting with Abby right before you called. At the moment, I'm just enjoying my view."

"What a coincidence," he says. "So am I."

I picture him standing in front of the floor to ceiling windows that make up one wall of his penthouse office at Stark Tower. His body long and lean, his midnight black hair gleaming in the morning light. A modern gladiator in a tailored suit surveying his domain.

"You're so damn beautiful," he says, and it takes a minute for my mind to shift gears. He's not looking out his window. He's looking at me.

I turn, putting my back to the ocean so that I can see inside the bungalow. But he's not there, and when I frown in consternation, his low chuckle ripples over me.

The security cameras.

Deliberately, I turn so that I'm facing the one mounted at the corner of the roof. I tilt my head and rest my hand on my hip. "Aren't you supposed to be running an empire?"

"It's on today's agenda. Right now, I'm getting in the mood for some world domination."

He stresses the last word, and I stare boldly into the camera. "In that case, Mr. Stark, I look forward to seeing you this evening. Although…"

"Although?"

I smile innocently. "I'd planned to take a quick walk on the beach before I meet Jamie for lunch. Get a little sun, a bit of relaxation. You know…"

"Sounds like an excellent way to unwind."

"It does," I agree, then turn so that he's looking at my

back, "But I'm not sure that's the kind of unwinding I need anymore."

As I speak, I unbutton the loose blouse that I'm wearing, then let it fall to the deck, revealing my bikini top.

"Nikki..."

"You shifted my mood, Damien. Wound me up even tighter. Got me craving a different kind of heat." I reach back and unfasten the clasp that hits between my shoulder blades, then I use one hand to hold up my shoulder-length blond hair while the other tugs on one of the ties at the base of my neck. The bow comes loose, and I release the string, letting the bikini top flutter over the rail to the sand.

"Better," I say, as Damien simply breathes. "But not good enough." I'd intended to walk in the surf later, and I dressed accordingly. Now I untie the knot at my hip and let the scarf drop to the wooden deck.

"Nikki." His voice is rough. Tight.

"Hmm?" In contrast, I'm all innocence as I wriggle out of my bikini bottoms, then step daintily out of the puddle of material that has collected at my feet. Now I face the ocean, completely nude, my back to the camera, the open sea in front of me. Not to mention yards of thankfully empty beach. That's one of the benefits of this location. Lots and lots of privacy. "Isn't this how you wanted me?"

"Christ, Nikki. I have a meeting in fifteen minutes."

I force myself not to smile as I turn to face the camera. "Slacks fitting a bit tight?" I ask, my voice full of earnest innocence as I slide my hand slowly down my abdomen until my fingers slip between my thighs. I've been thinking of Damien, and so of course I'm wet, and I can't help the little gasp of pleasure that escapes my parted lips.

I close my eyes and dance my fingers over my slick core as I lift the forefinger of my other hand to my mouth. I suck gently, then skim my fingertip over my nipple. I'm already wildly aroused from the knowledge of what this show must be doing to Damien, but the sensation of the ocean breeze against my dampened areola sends shivers of pleasure coursing through me.

"I missed you," I say. "And even though you're back, you're still too far away."

"I can be home in forty minutes. Less if I take the helicopter."

I laugh. "Tempting," I say. "But I need to put some clothes on, then hit the road. Jamie's expecting me."

"How unfortunate," he says. "I suppose I'll have to wait."

"Anticipation, Mr. Stark."

"Tonight, baby." The words are rough. Raw.

"Every night," I counter.

"Yes." He draws in a breath. "I'll be home by six. Until then, imagine me, touching you."

I close my eyes and nod as he clicks off.

I always do.

2

I hum to myself as I stroll the path that leads from the bungalow back to the main house. It's almost eleven, so I'm going to have to change and put on makeup in a hurry if I have any chance of making it to my interview on time. But I can't head out until I see the girls. So instead of taking the outdoor stairs all the way up to our third-floor bedroom, I enter the house on the first floor from the pool deck.

I circle around the floating marble staircase that is the focal point of our home's entrance hall, then make my way to the second of the three guest suites located on this floor. Damien and I have already talked about letting both girls move into their own suite when they hit their teenage years. By that time, I figure we'll appreciate having a little space between us and our teens.

Right now, though, the kids are coming on two and four respectively, and we're content to have them share the bedroom located behind our master on the third floor. Originally intended as the smallest of our home's four guest suites—five, if you count the actual guest house located beyond the tennis courts—it shares a wall with the master closet and is plenty big enough to house two little girls. Even little girls as rambunctious as ours.

In a nod toward keeping their room tidy—and because Damien has a habit of buying them sizable gifts—we decided to dedicate one of the first floor suites as a playroom, which better holds the walk-on keyboard, tumbling mat, and five foot tall plush elephant that Damien swears he couldn't resist.

I've repeatedly told him he's going to spoil the girls rotten, but he doesn't seem too concerned. They're his little princesses and spoiling them is a daddy's job. Or so he tells me.

I hear them before I see them. Or, I hear Lara, anyway. Her drama-filled voice announcing, "No, no, Anne. I'll show you." And Anne's soft giggles suggesting that she'll eagerly do whatever her big sister orders.

Our nanny, Bree, flashes me a quick grin as I step into the room, then turns her attention back to the lunch she's setting out on the low toddler table. Lara is oblivious to the PB&J sandwiches, apple slices, cookies, and milk. She perches her hands on her hips, then pulls her mouth into a pouting moue as she focuses on her blonde imp of a sister who stands wide-eyed beside a squat plastic table covered with crayons and half-finished drawings.

"You watch me, okay? Eyes on me," Lara adds, mimicking one of my mommy-phrases in a tone so like my own that I almost lose it.

"See?" Her silky black hair is pulled into a pony tail that hits below her shoulder blades, and it bounces as she puts her hands over her head, then turns a wobbly circle on tippy-toes, her feet encased in tiny pink ballet slippers. Just seeing that brings tears to my eyes, because it wasn't that long ago that she was post-surgery and forbidden to be on her feet at all, much less on tiptoes.

Lara was born with polydactylism, a condition we were aware of when we found her picture on the website of a Chinese adoption agency and started the process to bring her home. We adopted her at twenty months, and she still had the extra two toes, one on each foot, when we arrived in LA after the long trip back from China. Since the extra toes were large and positioned in such a way to prevent her from wearing shoes, one of our first challenges was the removal surgery.

We didn't want her first memories of her new life with us to be shrouded in pain and fear, so we waited a few months before scheduling the procedure even though she was already past the recommended age for removal, as most kids with the anomaly have the extra digit removed before they start to walk.

We don't regret waiting, but kids grow fast, and that meant she was older and more active right about the time the doctor insisted she be sedate. Hard enough for an adult, but a nightmare for an active toddler. Things were stressful for a while, what with balancing Lara's post-op toddler tantrums with Anne's baby needs.

Now Lara is fully recovered, Anne is an active toddler, and the exuberant chaos that fills this room never fails to put a smile on my face.

"Mama!" Anne calls, something else that always tugs at my heart. She's wearing a fairy princess outfit and now she lifts her hands like Lara and twirls. "I dancing! I dancing!"

"Good, Anne!" Lara says seriously. "That's real good." She turns to me, her smile both wide and smug. "I taught her!"

"You did great," I say, squatting down and opening up my arms to embrace my two little angels. "Both of you."

"Missed you, Mama!" Anne clutches my leg, almost throwing me off-balance. I compensate by grabbing her around the waist and letting her hang upside down as I rise.

"Can we play Memory?" Lara begs. "Please, Mommy." The card-matching memorization game is her current favorite. "Pretty please."

"I can't right now, precious," I say, giving her my free hand as I flip Anne down so that her feet hit solid ground. I walk the rest of the way with both girls trotting alongside me. "I wanted to come in and see my girls, but now I have to go do a work thing and then meet Aunt Jamie for lunch."

"Jamie!" Anne claps her hands.

"You'll see her soon, precious," I promise. "In the meantime, I bet Miss Bree would play Memory after your lunch. It looks yummy. I'm jealous." I really am, too. About the chocolate chip cookies, anyway. Since I've gotten more serious about working out, I've also been eating better. I've only dipped into my stash of frozen Milky Ways once this month. And that was when I was missing Damien.

"Memory?" Bree says absently from where she's crouched on the floor. "Oh, yeah. Sure."

"Bree?"

With the meal set out, she'd moved on to laying blue painter's tape on the floor. Now the colorful line forms part of the perimeter of a rectangle that extends out about five feet from the wall, and I can't help but wonder if this project —whatever it is—is what's distracting her. Because she definitely seems distracted.

"Sorry," she says, her familiar sweetness returning. "Mind wandering. And of course Miss Bree's happy to provide lunch for all of the Stark women. Or just cookies for the adult Starks," she adds with a grin for me.

"Tempting," I admit. "But no."

"Cookies!" Lara says, clapping wildly. Which, of course, encourages Anne to do exactly the same.

I get them settled at the table with stern instructions to eat the meal before the cookies, and they both dig in as Bree peels herself up off the floor, then shoves a lock of long dark hair out of her eyes. The daughter of a Cherokee mother and a Jewish father, Brianna Bernstein is stunning, with olive skin, sharp cheekbones, and dark eyes that seem to reach back into infinity. Even on a day like today, when she's smeared with colored chalk and has been crawling around on the floor, she looks put together and on top of things.

As far as nannies go, I'm convinced that Bree is as good as it gets. We lucked into her, and I dread the day when she leaves. A sad day that's fast approaching. Exciting for her, as she's going back to school. But it sucks for me. Bree's not only brilliant with the kids, she also helps out around the house. Most important, she's become a friend.

I have no idea how I'm going to replace her, and I've been procrastinating in my search. Probably because I'm neck-deep into denial.

"So what exactly are you doing?" I ask, mostly to distract me from my thoughts.

She'd been adjusting a line of tape, and now her head snaps up. "I'm not—" She cuts herself off with a shake of her head. "Sorry. The floor. Right."

I frown. Bree's always at the top of her game, and yet today she seems off. I almost stay quiet—after all, everyone has bad days—but I hear myself saying, "Listen, are you okay?"

"Oh, yeah. Absolutely." The words sound a little too

perky. "I'm just frazzled." Her eyes dart to Lara, and as I watch, Bree seems to forcibly gather herself. "Our leading lady is getting ready for her grand debut after dinner. Apparently, I'm the stage manager. And my boss is running me ragged," she adds with a teasing smile

"Miss Bree!" Lara's voice rises. "It's a secret."

"Oops. Sorry." She blushes, and I frown. She's been with us since before Anne was born, and in two years I've never once see her overstep the rules of any game she's playing with the kids.

"Mama! Don't listen." Lara claps her hands over her ears.

"Listen to what? I didn't hear anything." I aim a huge smile at my little girl, but my thoughts are still on Bree. I tell myself it's silly to worry. Of course she's frazzled. I only have to find a replacement nanny; she has to uproot her entire life, move across country, and dive into the unfamiliar waters of academia. Who wouldn't be a little off?

Certain I've found the explanation, I push my concern away and focus on Lara. "Don't I get a clue about what you three are up to?"

Lara shakes her head regally, her chocolate-smeared lips pressed tight together as she clutches the rest of her cookie. Anne, on the other hand, claps and squeals, her blonde ringlets bouncing. "Dancing! We dancing!"

Lara rolls big brown eyes, her expression so exasperated that I have to keep my head down and my focus on my shoes to keep from laughing.

When I'm sure I can hold it together, I lift my head and smile at my oldest daughter. "I just came for hugs before I get back to work. Come give Mommy a kiss." I kneel down, and they both scamper toward me. I gather them close and cover them with kisses and tickles until both my girls are squealing and giggling.

They're so different in appearance and personality, with fair-haired, fair-skinned Anne tending toward quiet and calm, with only the occasional moment of toddler mania mixed in to keep us on our toes. I can imagine her all grown up, maybe running a laboratory and shouldering great responsibility while exercising both concentration and patience.

In contrast, Lara has the dark hair and yellow-brown skin that reflects her Chinese heritage. More outgoing than Anne, I imagine Lara will grow up to be an actress. Or a politician. Somebody who's out there in front of the world, confident and strong, and completely comfortable with all that attention.

Right now, my girls get along great, presumably because they complement each other. And Damien and I are crossing our fingers that this congeniality never lets up.

I lean back so that I can look at both their sweet faces. "Okay, my princesses. Who's going to be good for Miss Bree today?"

They both raise their hands, and I give them high-fives, then grin at Bree, who no longer looks rattled. "You need anything before I head out?"

"Nope. We're doing great. Aren't we girls?"

Lara nods, then throws her hands up and executes a wobbly pirouette. She stops, takes a bow, then grabs Anne's hands and drags her to the play mat, where they fall into a wriggling, squirming, giggling heap.

Bree's smiling eyes look into mine. "Wish me luck. The chocolate might have been a mistake."

"Could be." I can't keep the laughter out of my voice. "And good luck with the insanity." I sigh fondly at the sight of my kids. "I'd take over, but I've got that interview. Plus, I haven't seen Jamie in ages, and she swears that she had to bribe someone to get a reservation at this new place in Santa Monica."

"Are you going to Surf's Up? It's supposed to be amazing. I'm so jealous."

"Are you?" My hopes for the lunch increase. Not that you can tell by the PB&J lunch, but Bree is both a foodie and a damn good cook. And if she says a restaurant is good, that means something. "In that case, I'll bring you back a full report. And I'll be home before Damien, I'm sure."

"No problem. But are you guys staying in tonight? Because I was thinking I might, you know, go out to a club or something with a friend tonight." A blush tints her cheeks.

I pause in the act of rummaging in my purse for my car keys. "For goodness sakes, are you really asking permission to go out after dinner on a Friday night. You know you're free unless we've specifically wrangled you into babysitting."

"I know. It's just..." She trails off with a shrug. "I guess I'm feeling guilty. I mean, since I'm leaving so soon," she adds hurriedly.

I shake my head firmly. "No guilt allowed for following your dream." She's been accepted into journalism school, and she's hoping to start a career reviewing restaurants and covering all things food-related. "You know how proud Damien and I are of you."

Her face tightens, and her shoulders rise and fall as she twists her hands together.

I frown, the hairs on the back of my neck starting to prickle with concern. "Bree?"

Her already huge eyes widen. "Sorry. It's just that I'm going to miss you all so much."

"Us, too," I say honestly. "But New York is only a short

flight away, and the good news is that you know someone who happens to own a plane."

As I hoped, she smiles. "I may have to take someone up on that."

I stand, and the girls scamper over to the toys as I cross to the stage that Bree's marked out. "So about this friend? Do I get a hint?" I recall the way she'd blushed earlier. "It's not Kari you're going out with tonight, is it?"

"Not Kari," she admits, referring to her best friend, one of the managers at Upper Crust, my favorite Malibu bakery, where I'm headed now for my interview. "But she introduced me to him," she adds with a sideways grin. "Rory Claymore. Isn't that the best name?"

"Sounds like something out of a Scottish romance novel."

Her grin widens. "So far I'll say that's accurate."

"Brianna Bernstein. I'm shocked."

"No, you're not," she counters, and we both laugh as I pick up Anne—who's come back to cling to the hem of my make-shift sarong. "How long have you two been going out?"

"Not long. This will only be our third date. But we've been texting. You know."

I think about all of the delicious, naughty texts that Damien sends me and bite back a knowing smile. "How does Kari know him? What's he do?" I force back a groan, realizing I've slid into full-on mommy mode.

"He's an account manager for one of the financial companies downtown. I can't remember which one. And he's a regular. Been coming to Upper Crust for a while, and they got to chatting. You know how it is."

"And so she fixed you up?"

"After he dropped a dozen or so hints. According to Kari,

he had his eye on me for a while before he finally hit her up for an introduction."

"Well, I couldn't be happier for you."

Her smile turns shy. "It's still new between us. But I'm hoping." A cloud crosses her face. "I'm not sure why, though. I'm about to move halfway across the country."

"Bree—"

"I know," she interrupts. "I'll worry about that when we get to it. And right now," she adds, scooping up Anne as she scurries by, "I know two little girls who have a show to rehearse. And you need to change and get to Upper Crust."

I glance at the clock. "Yes, I do." The interview is with a local reporter, Mary Lee, whose editor called my office a few weeks ago. Apparently, she wants to interview me for a magazine about Southern California moms who are also business owners.

"Be good for Miss Bree." I kneel and hold out my arms for Lara.

"Be good, Mommy!" she says, then gives me a sloppy kiss.

I hug her tight, then scoop up Anne, who Bree has just released, and dance butterfly kisses over her cheeks before turning her loose in the playroom.

I know I need to hurry, but I stand slowly, soaking in the joy that fills this cluttered playroom that's one of the hearts of this extraordinary house. I smile as my girls, still sticky-faced with smears of chocolate, look up at me, the love in their eyes making my heart swell even as tears prick my eyes. Because I never had this. Never had a mother who looked at me with genuine affection. Who did anything other than try to use me for her own gain, her perfect little trophy daughter who elevated Elizabeth Fairchild's status with each victory crown and pageant win.

Never.

The word cuts through me, dark and brutal, but I push the anger back, forcing myself back to center.

My mother's been out of our lives since before we left for China to get Lara. She's never seen her grandchildren, and I have no regrets. For the most part, I never even think of her, and that's a huge relief.

But ever since this interview was scheduled, Elizabeth Fairchild has crept into my thoughts. I look at Anne's blonde curls and see myself at that age, forced at two to learn to walk with a book on my head, my playtime filled with toddler pageants and every lesson imaginable so that my "talent" could be discovered. Had to get ahead of the competition, after all.

I'm certain that Ms. Lee is going to ask about my children and my mother. But while she can ask, I don't have to tell, and I've already decided I won't. I'm not going to spew neutral platitudes about my childhood or lie and say that it was sunny and bright.

And I'm certainly not going to tell the truth. There's a limit on my willingness to be open with the press.

If she wants to cover my relationship with my mother, she can seek it out on her own. The paparazzi have picked at bits and pieces of that in the past, and I have no way to erase those articles and social media blasts. But I'm certainly not hand-feeding her a story.

Damien and I decided a long time ago that where our kids are concerned, we're starting fresh. No Jeremiah Stark. No Elizabeth Fairchild. We're washing away their manipulation. Banning their games.

There's me and Damien and the girls. We're a unit. A family.

And the only direction we're moving is forward.

3

W hile our house is truly spectacular, I think the best thing about living in Malibu is the proximity to Upper Crust, a beachfront bakery and coffee shop that ranks pretty close to heaven as far as I'm concerned.

A converted house, the bakery sits on a rock outcropping just off the Pacific Coast Highway. I turn into the parking lot and have to remind myself not to steer Coop, my cherry-red convertible Mini Cooper, over to the drive-through window for a coffee and a muffin. Instead, I grab one of the coveted parking places, slide out of the car, and head for the door.

The bell tingles as I push inside, and I pause on the threshold, breathing in the scent of yeast and coffee. The Upper Crust is known for its variety of baked-daily bread and muffins as well as its proprietary blend of aromatic coffees.

Like I said—*heaven.*

Because I'm not the only one who thinks so, the line is seven people deep, and I scroll through my emails as I wait my turn. I'm ten minutes early for the interview, and as I'm

about to text Ms. Lee and ask what I can get for her, I realize
that I haven't actually communicated with her directly. Her
editor has always been a go-between.

Frowning, I scope out the line, wondering if one of my
fellow customers is the reporter. But nobody's carrying a
tiny tape recorder or a narrow, spiral-bound reporter's note-
book. More to the point, no one is looking around as if
they're trying to find me.

And surely she knows what I look like.

She still hasn't made contact when I reach the counter,
so I take a chance and order two nonfat lattes and two blue-
berry muffins. Worst case, I end up doubly caffeinated and
have a bonus muffin to go.

I wait my turn with the rest of the flock, then take the
drinks and muffins out the back door to the wooden patio.
Built on the same rocks that secure the bakery, the patio
extends out over the beach, with a wooden staircase leading
down to the dry, loose sand, and, further on, to the wet,
packed beach being rubbed smooth by a steady, relentless
surf.

Maybe it's because I grew up landlocked in Dallas, but I
never tire of watching the waves or the surfers who flock to
Malibu to ride them. Now, I'm watching as a kid who looks
about sixteen paddles out, then rises expertly onto the
board. I hold my breath, always fearful they'll fall, then
exhale with a yelp when someone pulls out the seat next
to me.

"Mrs. Stark?"

The speaker is a slender woman, probably five years
older than me, with a bland expression, equally dull gray
eyes and a smile that's so tight I'm certain she practiced it in
the mirror for hours.

Nerves, I decide. Then wonder why someone who

doesn't like chatting with strangers would possibly go into journalism.

Not a question I can answer, though, so I simply concentrate on keeping my own smile cheery and welcoming as I gesture to the chair opposite me. "Please call me Nikki. And you must be Mary. It's so nice to meet you."

She sits, looking a little more comfortable, then even grateful when I point out the coffee and muffin I grabbed for her.

"How long have you been a reporter?"

It's the right question. She tells me about how it had always been her dream. How she'd worked on all her school newspapers up until college. "But I didn't pursue it then. And later, when I realized how much I regretted it, I started trying to sell freelance articles." She lifts a shoulder in a modest little shrug. "Now I get regular assignments."

"That's so great." I mean it, too. I'm genuinely impressed by anyone who works hard for their dream.

"Hmm." She twists in her seat, looking behind her and up the coast. "I thought we might be able to see your house from here, but it's blocked by the hills."

"It's a bit of a drive with the twisty roads, but it's only a short walk down the beach. Damien and I walk here with the girls sometimes on the weekends."

"I didn't realize your house was so close. I'd love to see it. For the article, of course."

"Oh." I consider that. "We prefer not to have the press in the house. But we can walk to the bungalow. It's been my office for the past two years, and there's plenty of kid paraphernalia strewn everywhere to prove that I'm a working mom."

Since she thinks that sounds like a great plan, we leave

the ceramic mugs and plates on the table along with a tip,
then head toward the stairs.

We take off our shoes and carry them by our fingertips
as we slog through the thick sand, then walk easier once we
reach the surf. I've changed into a wrap-style skirt, and I'm
glad I didn't wear slacks, as the cuffs would be soaked from
the waves that keep crashing around my ankles, repeatedly
trying to topple me into the surf.

Even walking leisurely, it still only takes ten minutes to
reach the bungalow. It's bordered on the south by a narrow
concrete access road that the city utilizes for the bungalow's
trash pickup and also as emergency beach access. The road
runs from the beach to the main road on which the house
sits, and it's bordered by an iron fence that's repainted
monthly to keep the rust at bay.

Though the bungalow originally had no parking, when I
started using it for work, we removed a section of the fence
and expanded it inward in the form of an open-ended
rectangle, creating a fenced parking area just off the road
that's big enough to hold four cars. Access to the house
requires the gate code, after which it's a short jaunt down
the sidewalk to the front door. Either that, or the visitor can
walk down to the beach, hook a right, then shuffle through
the sand to the wooden steps that lead up to the second
floor, which is the bungalow's main level.

That's the entrance to which Mary and I go. It's fully
accessible from the beach, though the multitude of security
cameras makes it certain that no one is climbing those stairs
without being seen. As for actually entering the bungalow...
well, that's an even trickier proposition, requiring an entry
code and a separate code to disengage the yowling security
alarms that would otherwise begin to blare in less than sixty
seconds.

As soon as I hit the final button to disarm the system, the heavy metal shutters that block all the windows recede into their recessed pockets, allowing light to flood the combination living and dining space.

"Oh, my. This is lovely." Mary steps in behind me. "So homey and bright."

"It's one of my favorite places," I admit. "Let me give you the grand tour, and then we can talk on the rooftop patio."

I lead her through the place, letting her snap pictures with her smart phone of the kitchen and the bedroom that doubles as a play area for the girls.

"And your office?"

"There are filing cabinets hidden inside the kitchen island's woodwork", I tell her. "And I use the kitchen table as a workspace when my team comes in. Right now, it's a team of four, so we fit easily around it. Have a seat while I make us some coffee to take upstairs." I start to turn toward the coffee maker, then dive for the squeaky toy that is revealed when she pulls one of the chairs out to sit. "Like I said—working mom."

I flash her a bemused smile and am grateful when she smiles back. The setup works perfectly for me, but seeing it through her eyes, I can see that it might be unexpected for the wife of a billionaire—or for a woman running a company with close to a million annually in net receipts.

"I mostly work on a laptop," I explain, then wonder why I'm self-conscious. The point of this interview is to explore the fact that I'm both a business owner and a mom. And the scattered toys definitely add a touch of authenticity to the experience.

"So how did you get started?"

For a moment, the question lingers between us. Then she releases a nervous laugh. "I mean, how did you decide to get into the business. I don't think there's any point in going into the story about the painting." Her lips curve into a smile that's probably meant to be sweet but only makes me cringe. "I mean, *everybody* knows about that."

"Yes," I say, vividly recalling the day I was accosted by reporters all shouting invasive, tacky, horrible questions about Damien paying me a million dollars to pose nude. "Yes, they do."

"Do you ever regret that decision?"

"I really don't," I admit. I draw a breath and turn away from her, ostensibly rinsing out the coffee carafe, but really giving myself a chance to think. "It was an arms-length transaction," I say as I turn back around, then pour water into the machine. "And the actual portrait is very tasteful. At the end of the day, I was able to properly launch Fairchild Development years before I would have been able to if I hadn't posed."

She nods slowly, considering. "What if you hadn't ended up married to Mr. Stark? Do you think you would have regretted that painting then?"

It's such an odd question that I almost decline to answer, but she seems so earnest, and I think she's simply fallen into conversation rather than focusing on her pre-planned inter-view questions.

Besides, it's not as if my answer is any different. "No," I say. "Still no regrets. Like I said, the painting is tasteful and our negotiation was clear. And at the time I had absolutely no reason to believe I'd ever be Mrs. Damien Stark."

"Well, you definitely had a unique path," she says airily. "But I'm here for the rest of the story," she says. "How you grew your business. How you honed your skills. And," she adds as she pushes her chair back and stands, "I'd really love to hear why you think that paying for a child from China and giving birth to a baby you hand off to a nanny qualifies you to sell an app that's supposed to help mothers. *Mommy's Helper?* Please. What the hell do you know about being a mother?"

My mouth has gone completely dry, and my heart is pounding so hard in my chest that I'm afraid I'll crack a rib. Surely she can hear the pounding. I can barely think for the pounding.

Determined, I force myself to keep my expression calm. I focus on that. On hiding my emotions. On keeping my face perfectly blank, just as my mother always taught me. Because God forbid anyone should see your pain, because they'll surely kick you when you're down.

"It's time for you to leave." I can hear the tremor in my voice, and my legs feel like noodles. "Now," I add as I slide my finger under the quartz countertop and press the panic button Damien insisted we install.

"Oh, is our time already up?" She smirks, then pushes her lips together in an exaggerated pout. "I guess I got everything I need. And don't you worry. I'll be sure to send you a copy of my article. Hot off the presses."

I stay behind the island, my muscles tense and ready to flee if she comes toward me. She doesn't. Instead she puts her hand on the door and pushes it open. She steps out onto the wooden deck as the guard's cart squeals to a halt on the concrete service road.

"Stay right there," I hear him bellow, and though I can't see him from my position inside the kitchen, I'm certain he has a weapon trained firmly on her. "Mrs. Stark. Do you need assistance?"

"I'm fine," I call as her eyes cut toward me through the open door. "Please escort Ms. Lee off the property."

"Nice to have a little entourage at your beck and call. Just like all the average moms out there."

"Who are you?" Anger is rising in me, beating back the fear, and I walk toward her and onto the patio as she responds.

"The most dangerous person on the planet," she says. "A reporter with an agenda."

"What agenda?"

Her eyes widen. "Why, Mrs. Stark. Isn't it obvious? *You*."

And then she trots down the steps and wiggles her fingers at the guard. "No need for the ride, handsome. I can walk."

The guard—Peter—looks at me, and I nod in silent acquiescence as I hug myself and try to stop the quaking inside me. She can walk back the way she came, and good riddance to her. After all, it's a public beach, and she didn't actually do anything to me. She made no overt threats, didn't even hint at violence.

That's what I tell myself, anyway.

Bottom line, she was simply rude. But she pushed buttons that I thought would no longer affect me.

And that's what scares me most of all.

4

"I so sorry, Nikki." Rachel flashes me a sympathetic smile from behind the polished oak desk in the fifty-seventh floor reception area of Stark Tower. "He's not here."

I squeeze the bridge of my nose in frustration as I glance toward the closed double doors that lead to Damien's penthouse office. I managed to pull myself together in the time it took to drive from Malibu to downtown, but I'm still shaky. I'd been counting on the feel of Damien's arms around me, his body pressed close to mine. I wanted his kisses to bring me back to myself, and now that my plans have been foiled, I'm at loose ends.

With forced nonchalance, I lift a shoulder and sigh. "I wanted to surprise him."

"Honestly, I'm surprised to see you." She tilts her head, the ends of her neat ponytail brushing her shoulder as her chestnut-colored eyes nail me. "Didn't you have an interview today? You can't possibly be done."

"Oh, I'm very done. Believe me."

Rachel's brow furrows, and I backtrack, realizing suddenly that I don't want to get into it. Not with her. Maybe not even with Damien. A reporter was bitchy to me. Bitchy with a side of evil, true, but the sum total of it was attitude. And, honestly, if I can't handle obnoxious reporters after all this time, then I have no business being married to a man like Damien.

"It was just one of those interviews," I say with a casual wave of my hand. "A clunky reporter with a list of questions she doesn't deviate from. Painful because you can't ever get a conversation going." Not that I would have wanted one with Mary Lee, but it's a little white lie that keeps me from having to reveal what's truly upset me.

"Since it finished early, I have extra time before I meet Jamie for lunch, so I thought I'd come by and lay eyes on my husband. It's been so long, I've started to forget what he looks like."

"Like anyone could forget that man. Sorry." She holds up a hand. "I know he's your husband and my boss, but seriously. We both know I'm right."

"We do," I say, happy that she's coaxed a laugh out of me.

"You were looking to surprise him, which totally sucks because unless your lunch is downtown, that's a hefty detour."

"Santa Monica," I admit, confirming her assumption.

She sighs, as if I've placed a heavy weight on her shoulders. "Honestly, Nikki. How many surprises have I helped you plan?"

"More than a few," I admit. Rachel is Damien's Executive Assistant, and over the years, she's become a good friend. More than that, she's been my co-conspirator on several surprise getaways, including a birthday party for Damien that turned out to be more than anybody involved bargained for.

"Exactly. You should have called me. I would have told you he was out."

"Last minute decision," I say. "When will he be back?" I try to keep my voice casual, but I'm afraid I sound a little desperate. I'm calmer now, but my desire to see Damien isn't any less.

"It'll be a while, I think. Trouble at The Domino."

That sobers me up. "That's not good." The Domino is a business complex that Damien and Jackson are working on together. Or, technically, that Stark Real Estate Development and Steele Development are working on together. The office complex will cover three city blocks in Santa Monica, with space available for both sale and lease. And although tenants won't be limited to the tech and entertainment industries, the news has been touting the complex as the most high-profile addition to Silicon Beach.

"What's happened?" I ask Rachel.

"Not sure. But it's a massive site, so it could be anything. Hopefully nothing so serious it pushes back the Phase One opening."

"No kidding." The first phase is supposed to be ready for occupancy within the next sixty days, and I make a mental note to ask Sylvia. As Jackson Steele's wife and a Project Manager with Stark Real Estate Development, she'll have the scoop.

I tilt my head, considering. Most likely, Syl is downstairs in her office. I could ask her to come up to the apartment. The Stark Tower penthouse is divided into two halves, with Damien's office on one side and a luxurious apartment on the other. Before the kids, we spent a lot of time in the apartment, and it really was a second home. Now, it's become a convenient place for Damien to grab a meal and a nap if he's working late. Something else he rarely does anymore since he's almost always home by the girls' bedtime, and if he has work to do, it comes home with him.

At the moment, I just want to use it as a place to have a casual coffee with my sister-in-law. A good plan, I think. After all, I haven't seen Syl in weeks, I'm dying to know what's going on at The Domino, and the conversation will distract me from my encounter with the bitch from hell.

"You look like you're scheming," Rachel says.

"Maybe a little. Could you call down and see if Sylvia's around?"

"I could, but I don't need to. She's on-site with Mr. Stark and Mr. Steele."

I make a face.

"You could wait a little while. They might not be too long," Rachel says, obviously trying to be helpful. "He assured me he'd be back before heading home. He's got a few things to take care of here that are time-sensitive."

The idea is tempting, but I don't want to blow off Jamie. And after our lunch, I have errands to run.

I cock my head toward Damien's office. "I'm going to leave him a note, then I'll get out of here and let you get back to work."

As Rachel turns her attention to an incoming phone call, I head into Damien's lair. The space is huge, but over the years, I've become so familiar with the layout that I barely notice. I pass the wet bar and the informal seating area, smiling at the girls' framed finger paintings on the walls and the photos of me and the kids that cover a chrome and glass table near the window, bathed in natural light.

I go immediately to his massive desk, and settle into the

supple leather of his desk chair. Then I stare at the desktop, uncertain of what I want to write. I'd come wanting to pour everything out to Damien, knowing that he'd fold me into his arms and make me feel better.

But now I'm not even sure if I should tell him what happened. Not in a note, anyway. Yes, Mary Lee's rant disturbed me, but that's all it was. A rant. Pour my heart out now to Damien in a note, and I'll only worry him.

I roll the chair back and open his middle drawer, thinking I'll just scribble *love you, sorry I missed you* on a sticky note. But when I see the stack of notecards embossed with D.J.S., inspiration strikes.

I've left my purse on the floor beside the chair, and now I reach down, retrieving my lipstick. I brush color on my lips, pick up the card, and plant a lipstick kiss right in the middle.

I push back the chair and stand up, then position the card exactly in the middle of the blotter that tops Damien's desk. Not that he could miss it. The space is neat and clutter free, and the kiss from me definitely stands out.

It's not, however, enough. Not to underscore why I was compelled to drive here today. How much I craved his understanding and his touch. His strength and his kisses.

For a moment, I just stand there, thinking. Then it hits me. A deliciously wicked idea that will both cheer me up and, I hope, put a smile on Damien's face after whatever crisis has had him running all over town. I hurry across the room to the credenza, hoping that what I need is still there. I bend down, pull open the doors, and exhale with relief at the sight of the small brown paper shopping bag.

I take the bag back to his desk, then take out a folded bundle of white tissue paper and a spool of red ribbon. I need scissors, too, but Damien has a pair in his drawer.

The tissue and ribbon are from February, when I'd popped in while he was at a meeting and left a picture of me and the kids as a Valentine's Day surprise. I'd grabbed the supplies in the lobby gift store before heading up, and since it doesn't take much to wrap a small, silver frame, I'd tucked the leftover into the credenza, figuring it might come in handy someday. Guess I was right.

I take a sheet of his stationery, then write a quick note:

Sorry I missed you. I can't stop thinking about you.
Then again, I can't ever seem to stop thinking about you.
XOXO
Your wife

I fold the note into a square, then lift my skirt and wriggle out of my panties, white and silk with a delicate lace band. I place them neatly on top of the note. Next, I wrap the small bundle in several layers of white tissue paper and tie the whole thing with red ribbon, underneath which I tuck the lipstick kiss notecard.

I stand back and examine my work, feeling so much better. And, yes, feeling both devious and frustratingly turned on. But then again, that's part of the point. *Anticipation.*

I start to leave, then realize that Damien will have a million things on his mind when he returns. Odds are that he'll bring Rachel into the office, and he might open the present while they're talking. I doubt it ... but I could be wrong.

I backtrack to the desk, pick up his fountain pen, and add a neatly printed note to the bottom of the lipstick card: *Personal & Confidential.*

Satisfied, I hitch my purse onto my shoulder, put away the wrapping paraphernalia, and head out. Rachel's speaking to someone on the headset, but she mouths, *All good?*

I give her a thumbs-up and head to the elevator. I may not have seen Damien, but as I imagine his reaction when he finds that package, I can't deny that everything is good indeed.

5

I slide into the line for Java B's, the lobby coffee shop, figuring I'll grab a latte for the road. I have my head down as I wait, my eyes on my phone as I check my emails. I've missed a phone call, but I don't recognize the 917 number. That's New York, and I don't have any active clients there, nor is it Ollie's number. And since the caller didn't leave a voicemail, I chalk it up to a wrong number or a robocall and move on to my emails.

There's nothing urgent there, either, but as I'm skimming subject lines, a text from Abby pops up, saying she and Travis are running forty-five minutes late. Not a problem, except that we were supposed to meet early so that we can pull together a punch list for Luis Garza, the project supervisor. Now I have a gap to fill, and while I could go early to the new offices, there's no furniture yet, and I don't really want to camp out on the floor while I wait for my team.

Then again, this is LA, and since I'm already heading to Love Bites next, a high-end bakery in Beverly Hills, I probably shouldn't worry about how to fill less than an hour. Odds are, traffic will take care of that for me, and this way I don't have to worry about rushing out of the bakery if Sally wants to spend some time talking about the details of the girls' birthday cakes for next weekend's party.

I've reached the counter, so I stop worrying about it and order, then step to the side as I wait for my latte. I'm about to occupy myself by reviewing more emails when something catches my eye. I'm not even sure what, but I find myself looking across the lobby and out through the glass walls that reveal the pavilion.

There's nothing out there of any particular note, and I don't see anybody who looks familiar. Even so, I can't shake the unpleasant sensation that someone is watching me. And when the hairs on the back of my neck start to prickle, I almost abandon my coffee and head for the elevator to the parking garage.

You're being foolish.

The voice in my head is not only firm, it's right. I push aside my paranoia, even as I wonder what on earth triggered it. By the time the barista hands me my latte, I'm over it.

Or I am until I hit the midpoint of the lobby. The part with the broadest view of the pavilion. And now I know what caught my eye. A lean body. Short blond hair. Broad shoulders.

Eric?

I cock my head, wondering why my former client development manager would be here. The answer, of course, is that he wouldn't. And since I don't see him again on a second glance, I tell myself I'm imagining things. Which of course I am. Which sort of makes sense because I need to hire a new person to fill that slot, and so far I've been unimpressed by all the resumes that have crossed my desk.

Eric was great at his job, and both Abby and I had been blindsided when he'd accepted an offer from a company in

New York. Granted, there was amazing potential for a serious upside, so I understand why he did it. But I was still devastated. Not to mention irritated since his departure left Abby and me in a lurch during a key project.

I know from industry gossip that the potential didn't pan out. The opposite, in fact, and Eric ended up leaving and going to Austin, another tech hub like Silicon Valley near San Francisco and Silicon Beach, right here in Southern California.

All of which is to say that Eric isn't in LA, and I push thoughts of him out of my mind as I take the elevator down to the parking level. The garage is divided into sections, with several levels for employees of the various Stark divisions housed in the Tower. With the exception of the executives, there's no assigned parking. Damien, of course, has dedicated parking near the elevator. And although I told him it was ridiculous and wasteful since I don't work in the Tower, he insisted that I have a space, too. I argued, but ultimately conceded the point, especially when he pointed out that the Tower Apartment is one of my homes.

That's where I head to now, my slot tucked in next to Damien's. His prototype Tesla is there, his most recent new toy. I'd seen it as I pulled in and assumed he was in the office. Foolish, since I know that just because his car is on-site doesn't mean that Damien is, too. He habitually has Edward drive him to meetings so that he can review files on the way.

Now, I pass behind the Tesla, trailing my fingertips over the sleek, space-gray chassis as I approach Coop. I have the keys out, and I click the button to unlock the driver's side door. I pull it open, then toss my purse into the passenger seat as I slide in behind the wheel. As soon as I'm settled I see a folded piece of paper under my windshield wiper. I bite back a curse—no solicitation is allowed in the parking lot—and lean out of the car far enough so that I can reach around and grab the paper.

Since I'm certain it's an advertisement for a new fast food delivery service or a nearby carwash, I almost toss it into the backseat without even reading it. But as my fingers tighten to crumple it, I notice that the printing has bled through. Thick, black magic marker in what appears to be block letters.

Curious, I open it, then lean back in my seat, my heart pounding.

SPOILED

LITTLE

RICH

GIRL

A stare at it. One beat, then another. Then I realize that I've been holding my breath and suck in a gallon of air. Now I really do crumple up the note and toss it in the back, then I clutch the steering wheel and breathe. In and out, in and out. Again and again until I'm calm.

Mary Lee?

Could this note possibly have been left by Mary Lee?

I try to consider that rationally, and once my brain starts functioning again, I decide it's not her. I'd lingered before leaving. I'd had one of the security guards drive me back to Upper Crust. I'd paid attention to my surroundings once I got into my car and drove away. And I hadn't noticed anyone following me.

She'd have no reason to think I was coming to see Damien, so she wouldn't have beat me here.

So, no, surely it's not Mary Lee.

Which means the note was left by an unknown person. Still creepy. Still unpleasant. Still worthy of my sweaty palms.

But whoever left this note wasn't in my home.

Instead, it's an anonymous, jealous sender. And while I don't like feeling singled out, the note doesn't rock my world. After all, Damien has enough money to buy and sell the universe several times over, and I'm the woman he married. That makes some people curious. It makes others envious. Some, it makes downright mean.

This isn't the first time I've been vilified for marrying into money. But just because I'm not quaking in terror doesn't mean that I'm not affected, and I automatically reach for my phone, my fingers ready to call Damien.

I stop myself. There's no point. It's a mean note, left by someone sad and pathetic. But I've already reasoned that there's no more to it than that.

Still, I need to at least report it, and so even though I'm already in a hurry, I shove the note into my purse, climb out of the car, and head upstairs to the lobby.

"Mrs. Stark," Joe says, his basset-hound face lighting up with his smile. "I thought you'd left."

"I found this on my car," I say, handing him the note. "It's not a threat, but security should be aware."

He unfolds the paper, his expression going hard as he reads it. "I'm terribly sorry, Mrs. Stark," he says, his anger obvious even under the professional veneer. "I'll see to it."

"Thank you," I say, feeling remarkably lighter as I head back to the car. As if passing off the note has also passed off the weight of the writer's jealousy.

"AND YOU'RE sure the note didn't have anything to do with that bitch?" my best friend, Jamie Archer Hunter, asks.

"I'm sure." I've told her the whole story, of course. "At least as sure as I can be."

"Well, that's something. But still. What a bitch. What a total, fucking bitch. Mary Lee. Never heard of her. Probably some newbie trash magazine reporter who thinks scandal and bullshit gossip is the way to break in." Jamie leans forward, her dark eyes narrowed over the rim of her wine glass. "What can I do? Do you want me to find out about her? I could talk to some people. Make sure she never sells another story."

I'm tempted, but in the end, I shake my head. "Just let it go. I might call her editor and complain, but I'm going to wait a day and calm down more."

"Who's the editor?"

I check my phone again. "Ellen Anderson. *SoCal Working Mom Weekly*."

Jamie lifts a shoulder. "I don't know her, but I've heard of the magazine. One of those tiny things that's mostly supported by advertising, but it's legit." She wrinkles her nose. "But not very if they hire freaks like Mary Lee. I mean, seriously? What is wrong with people? You let her into your house. You granted her an interview."

She flashes me a wicked grin. "Hell, you haven't even given me an interview. It would be so easy. A quick run through the house, and then we could sit by the pool, and I could interrogate you about all your secrets."

"And that, James, is exactly the problem," I say, using my old nickname for her. "You know which rocks to turn over." I punctuate my words with a laugh, because the whole point of this conversation is to cheer me up, but her words set loose a herd of flustered moths in my stomach.

Jamie's not only my best friend, but also an entertainment reporter, and in all these years, it's never even occurred to me to offer her that kind of an in-depth lifestyle interview. Which makes me a crappy friend.

More to the current point, if I'd already done a Mom-In-Business interview with my best friend, I probably would have said no to the editor who sent Mary Lee.

"Don't."

I draw in a breath and meet Jamie's eyes. "Don't what?"

"Don't dwell on it. You're a celebrity now, Nicholas. Whether you want to be or not. That means you're like honey to an ant. Or a cockroach." She wrinkles her nose. "Do cockroaches go after honey?"

I don't even bother answering. "I love you, James."

"Well, duh. Why wouldn't you?"

She makes a good point, and I grin as I dig my toes into the warm sand beneath our table, feeling better already. Surf's Up is the hottest new restaurant in Santa Monica, or so Jamie tells me. I believe her. The small interior dining room's ambiance is bright and welcoming, but it's the outdoor section that really makes the place pop.

Even though Jamie told me that the place was on the beach, I hadn't taken her literally, and immediately upon arriving, I regretted my choice of heels. The hostess, however, suggested that I either leave them in a cubby by the back door and continue barefoot or switch to one of the complimentary spa-style sandals they provide for guests.

I'd opted for barefoot, and I'd followed her across the open-air dining room, the perimeter of which is marked by an insubstantial, whitewashed fence. The flooring is nothing more than the natural sand, raked flat beneath each of the well-placed tables, all of which are topped with tied-down white cloths and pale blue umbrellas. Just a few yards away, the Pacific crashes onto the beach, the roar of the waves and the brush of the salty wind adding both whimsy and character to the place.

All in all, the comfortable, fun atmosphere ensures that locals will flock to the place. But the stellar menu is what really puts it on the map.

"You picked the perfect place," I tell her.

"I haven't seen you in forever," she says. "I figured we should go for the gusto."

Forever is a bit of an exaggeration, but it's true that she's been so busy that almost two months have passed since we last got together. First, she flew to London to meet her husband, Ryan, when he decided to take a few days off before flying back to the states after a work gig. Then she went on tour for three weeks with Pink Chameleon, a Grammy Award winning band that she's been covering. We talked on the phone, and I caught a few of her interviews with the band and fans, but it really wasn't the same. I've missed my best friend. And now, with this stupid Mary Lee interview, I feel like I've totally taken her for granted.

"What?' Jamie demands, then takes a sip of the crisp Pinot Grigio she ordered before I arrived.

"Huh?" I look up, startled. "Nothing," I lie, then reach for my own wine and draw my finger through the beads of condensation that sparkle on the outside of the glass.

She pushes her dark, wavy hair back from her face as she shakes her head. "Oh my God. Don't even go there."

"Where?"

"Oh, please. You're feeling all guilty about not giving me an interview. Don't even try to deny it."

"Well, I guess that proves you're my best friend. You just read my mind."

"You don't owe me anything, you loon."

"I know I don't. But do you want one? A camera crew, open access? The full-meal deal. It honestly never occurred to me before, but I'm sure Damien would agree. And if we did a normal family theme—"

She bursts out laughing, but I just arch a brow and soldier on.

"—like showing the house and the kids and Damien cooking pancakes, then how bad could that be?"

"No way," Jamie says. "You know you'd hate it. But if we did, Lacey Dunlop would turn positively green. I mean, talk about a high-profile coup."

Lacey Dunlop is tall, lithe, eight years younger than Jamie, and the newest on-air reporter for the entertainment network where Jamie works. She's not nearly as pretty—but she's blonde, personable, and bubbly. In other words, the camera and viewers love her. She also has family in the business, which gives her access to loads of celebrities. And every time she's crossed paths with Jamie, she's been—in Jamie's words—"as cold as a dead Alaskan salmon."

"So, let's do it."

She tosses her hair. "Hell no. I love you way more than I want to show up Lacey Dunlop, even if she is stealing some of my plum assignments. Seriously, you're sweet to offer, but no."

I nod. That's the thing about me and Jamie—I know she means it. So, I lift my glass in a silent toast and make a mental note to mention the interview to Damien.

She tilts her head to the side and looks at me thoughtfully for so long I start to squirm under the inspection.

"What?"

"What, what? *Oh*." She shakes her head as if to clear it. "Nothing."

I raise my brows and stare her down until I see her shoulders sag in defeat.

"Fine. You got me thinking about you and interviews. And that got me thinking about you and reporters. And—well, look. I know I kind of pushed you into it. So, if you want to pull out, I totally get it."

She's talking about tomorrow, and the moths in my stomach that had fallen asleep burst back into action.

"It's fine," I'd lifted may glass to take a sip of wine, but now I put it back down, untouched. "I wouldn't have agreed to do it if it wasn't fine."

Tomorrow, I'm going to announce that I'm the newest Stark Children's Foundation Youth Advocate. Right after I give the keynote speech at the bi-annual fundraising brunch.

Damien set up the Children's Foundation years ago, the purpose of which is to help abused and neglected children in the Los Angeles area. It's grown over the years, and now has chapters all over the world.

The SCF has always relied on celebrities to help spread the word and act as a face of the organization, but the Youth Advocate role is relatively new. It was created by our friend, Hollywood A-Lister Lyle Tarpin. A hugely successful actor, he served as the celebrity liaison for the foundation until some of his dark secrets were outed during one of his public appearances.

While Damien had Lyle's back, the board insisted he step down as the celebrity sponsor. He did, but then later came up with the idea for the youth advocate program, wherein celebrities with issues—especially issues they battled in their childhood and teen years—go public so that troubled kids realize that they aren't alone.

That suggestion was enthusiastically received, and Lyle

became a great first Youth Advocate. As a bonus, he's also gotten his shit together, is happily married, and is a good friend.

Jamie and Ryan are both big supporters of the Foundation. And when the Youth Advocate program was created, Jamie volunteered to be on the committee that invites celebrities into the role.

I may not be an entertainment celebrity, but my marriage to Damien shoved me into the spotlight. And my history of cutting—and all the reasons behind it—makes me a prime candidate for the role of a SYA. I haven't cut for years, but it's still what I am, because I know the potential is always there. And when Jamie asked me to consider the position, I decided to do it.

Jamie runs her finger idly over the rim of her wine glass, but doesn't take a sip. "It's just that I'd understand if you want to back out. I mean, Damien's always been a little leery, and now ... I don't know. I guess I am, too."

"Because of Mary Lee," I say, and she shrugs.

I sigh, wishing I could just snap my fingers and erase her worry. Damien's, too. But I know that I can't. They understand better than anyone what I'm doing. What I'm revealing. And though they both repeatedly tell me that I'm strong, they also both know that I'm not shatterproof. And, yes, there were some definite cracks showing after my encounter with that bitch today.

So I understand her worry. Hell, I agree with it. Because even with Damien's love and the strength it's given me, this speech tomorrow has the potential to break me.

I'm better now, though. I know I am. First, Jamie and Ollie had my back. And then, with Damien in my life, I truly found the strength to fight back that need. That compulsion.

Even the therapist I saw before adopting Lara confirmed how far I've come.

Most important, I haven't gotten complacent. I know that the need is still inside me.

And going public—sharing my story with kids who have similar issues—is my way to keep on fighting.

Tomorrow, I guess, I'll be fighting Mary Lee as much as myself.

It's scary, sure, but I'm confident. And I guess I'll know tomorrow if I'm doing the right thing, or if I'm making a horrible decision.

"You know it's time for me to do this," I tell Jamie now.

She shrugs. "I don't, actually. All I can do is trust that you know it. And you know I trust you. Always. I just worry. BFF privilege."

I nod, tears pricking my eyes. "I love you, James."

"Back at you, Nicholas."

Our eyes meet, and we're both a little sniffily. Then she shakes her head, like a dog ridding itself of fleas. "Moving on to the important stuff," she says firmly, tapping her menu. "Are we doing appetizers?"

"What do you think?"

"I think I need to go to the gym," she says with a frown.

I cock a brow, because Jamie looks amazing as always. I love her, true, but it's not love or loyalty talking when I say that Jamie is drop-dead, camera-ready, Hollywood starlet gorgeous. For a while, she played the role of starving actress with her eye on the Hollywood dream. But she abandoned that dream when on-camera reporting fell into her lap. And when she got an entertainment gig, she found her own personal heaven. Or so she tells everyone.

I know her well enough to be certain that while she loves reporting on Hollywood, a small part of her still wants

to be in the game. But Jamie is both a dreamer and a prag-
matist. She has a good thing going right now, and she knows
it. But even though she hasn't told me as much, I'm certain
that if she was offered a film or television role, she'd snatch
it up so fast, the heads of everyone in Southern California
would spin round in unison.

"I'm serious," she says, obviously recognizing my expression. "And don't give me grief. This business is ridiculously
competitive, and I haven't been working out lately. It's
starting to show. Especially when I'm standing side-by-side
with the Lacey bitch."

"No way does she get to muscle you off the red carpet," I
say. "You're much better with talent than she is. Honestly,
James, you need your own show."

She wrinkles her nose. "Right now, I just want to lose
five pounds, tighten my ass, and keep my job."

There's a lighthearted flair to her voice, but her words
give me a chill. Surely, she's only joking. Surely, she'd tell me
if her job was really in jeopardy.

"Work out with me," I say, forcing myself not to interrogate her. "I've been wanting to change up my routine. We
could go biking together." I've been enjoying my mid-
morning rides in Malibu, despite the bitch of a hill that we
live on. "Or we could do a Barre class together. Or hire a
trainer?"

Back in my pageant days, my mother forced me to work
out—yoga, dance, cardio, weights—anything and everything to keep me thin and lithe and curvy. The trouble was, I
hated it. Once I finally escaped the pageant world, I bailed
on the exercise and went from ridiculously tiny to a normal
size eight. And that was fine by me.

After Anne was born, though, my body and my clothes
decided to mutiny. Parts of my body that had once been

comfortable and familiar shifted overnight, and nothing quite fit anymore. Damien never seemed to notice, but I did, and the post-baby weight prompted me to dive back into the once-despised routine of regular exercise.

What started as a chore turned into a habit. And now—miracle of miracles—it's a pleasure. Without my mother breathing down my neck with her tape measure and starvation plan, I'm enjoying putting my body through its paces. There's exhilaration and empowerment in knowing that I'm making myself stronger. A feeling of control. And God knows, I've been chasing control my entire life. And that need for control is part of the reason why I agreed to be a SCF Youth Advocate. Because then I'm owning the thing that I've been most ashamed of for years.

"I could go for a private training," Jamie admits. "But don't you work out with Damien?"

I laugh at the prospect. "He's way too intense for me." A former professional tennis player, Damien takes his workouts seriously.

"I get that. But I figured you shared gym time. After all, you have that sweet set-up."

"Yeah, well, you know…" The gym on our first floor is about as good as it gets. But the times we've worked out together have ended up with us hot and sweaty on the mat in a much different way. Not that I object to that kind of workout, but it's really not the kind of cardio I'm looking for.

"Naughty girl," Jamie says, clearly wearing her psychic best friend hat. "Then again, that kind of workout burns calories, too."

I'm saved from having to retort by the arrival of the waiter with the ceviche Jamie ordered before I arrived. We order salads for lunch, and as we dig into the appetizer, Jamie tells me about her time in London with Ryan, who also happens to be the Security Chief at Stark International and Damien's best friend.

"We rode the London Eye," she says, referring to the giant Ferris wheel that overlooks the city and sits on the River Thames. "Can I just say that I fully approve of incredibly big Ferris wheels that move very, very slowly."

"I hope y'all weren't sharing a cabin."

"Nope. Ryan bought the thing out. Privacy, privacy, privacy." She leans back as the waiter refills our water glasses. "I would have brought you some pictures of the view, but I was too distracted to take any."

"Oh, really." I stab a chunk of tuna with my fork. "Maybe Damien and I need to go visit the London office, too."

"Oh, definitely. I mean, surely you need to tweak some of the coding. They drive on the wrong side of the road over there, you know. Their information superhighway must be a mess."

I laugh, almost spitting the ceviche I've just put in my mouth. "Somehow, I don't think that'll be the winning argument."

"I never claimed to understand tech."

"I'm glad you had fun. You two haven't taken a vacation together in a while."

"We definitely made up for lost time." A wicked grin dances over her lips. "Then again, we still are," she adds, her cheeks blooming pink. Since I've never known Jamie to blush at anything, my interest is immediately piqued.

"Spill," I demand, and when she leans eagerly forward, I know that was just the invitation she was waiting for.

"Have you ever heard of a private club called Masque?"

I shake my head slowly as I sift back through my memory. "I don't think so. Maybe? I'm not sure."

"Well, that's incredibly vague."

"Best I can do. It sounds familiar, but I can't place it. Then again, maybe I heard about its scandalous nature in some gossip column."

"You don't read gossip columns," she reminds me. "And what makes you think it's scandalous."

Sadly, she's wrong about the gossip. I used to be completely ignorant of any and all gossip surrounding the rich and famous. Then I met Damien, and my circle of friends expanded to include those the paparazzi keeps in their sights. I wouldn't say that I actually *follow* the various gossip sites now, but I do check in regularly. I like to think of it as self-preservation for myself, my family, and my friends.

As for scandalous, I can only laugh. "James, anything that can make you blush has to be off the charts."

"True story," she says, without a bit of shame.

"I'm guessing it's a sex club?" After all, I doubt she's blushing about her utter inability to do math in her head.

"It is," she says, "and it's incredibly decadent. Everything is top of the line. The venue. The alcohol. The hors d'oeuvres."

"You've been to those kinds of clubs before. Why is this one such a rush?" Because obviously it is. She's as excited as a kid on Christmas morning. And the flush of pink has returned, only this time it's creeping up her neck, too.

"It's different," she says. "For one thing, everyone wears a mask. Completely anonymous. It's formal, too. Or at least it starts out that way. I'm not sure naked *can* be formal. But after going there a few times, I'm one-hundred-percent certain that bras and garter belts can be."

"James!"

"Just telling it like it is." Her lips twitch with amusement. "And it was pretty spectacular."

"Okay, fine." I lean forward, unable to pretend I'm not interested. "Spill. Every. Single. Thing."

"Well, it's a party. A very elegant, well-hosted party. With sex. Lots of sex. Right in front of everybody."

I feel my eyes go wide. "Jamie! You didn't!"

She nods, her lips pressed tight together. "It was so freaking hot. And honestly, I'm not sure I would have done anything if it wasn't anonymous, but it really is. I mean, there were a few people there I might guess at, but for the most part..."

"And Ryan was okay with this?" I couldn't believe that Ryan—who patiently fought the good fight to win Jamie's hand—would be okay with watching his wife sleep with another man, anonymous or not.

"No, no!" Jamie hurries to correct. "This was me and Ryan. I mean, some folks come as singles and some swap partners. But you don't have to. It's just—I don't know. There's a rush being out in the open like that. In watching and being watched, but knowing that no one knows it's you. Not really, anyway."

"But haven't you and Ryan already..." I trail off, feeling my own cheeks heat. "I mean, it's not like you've never been to a sex club." I know Jamie and Ryan have gone to BDSM clubs a couple of times. According to Jamie, they're not in the lifestyle, but they occasionally slide into pretty serious play. And from what I know about those kind of clubs, stuff happens in the open.

"We have," she says, her tone completely nonchalant. "But we've only mingled in the public areas. Anything more, and we go into a private room. Masque was an entirely new experience. And a much more glam vibe, too. Nothing dungeon-y, you know?"

"Wow," I say, trying to figure out how I feel about this

peek into my best friend's sex life. And trying more to figure why the thought of going someplace like Masque with Damien makes my skin heat and tingle in all sorts of exciting—an unexpected—ways.

Jamie tilts her head to the side, and from the way the corner of her mouth twitches, I know she's seen what I'd rather hide. "You should go."

I shake my head, but don't answer as the waiter steps up to deliver our entrees. He lays our plates and clears the ceviche, and all the while I'm trying to stop the X-rated Technicolor movie that is playing in my head.

"I'm serious," she says. "You and Damien should check it out. I swear it'll light a fire in your sex life."

I raise a brow. "I'm not sure ours could get much hotter."

Jamie waves a hand, dismissing my words. "I'm talking inside of the sun hot. Big Bang hot."

I grin. "So am I."

Jamie rolls her eyes. "Show off."

"Besides, it sounds like more of a y'all thing than an us thing." True enough. There are very few parameters on my sex life with Damien, but I know perfectly well that public sex isn't his thing. Which is fine, since it's not mine either.

At least, I don't think it is.

"You're intrigued." Jamie's brows rise, as if underscoring the statement.

"I'm intrigued by skydiving, but I'm never going to do it."

Jamie jabs her fork into her salad, then points a speared slice of avocado at me.

"Give it a rest," I order, before she has a chance to speak. "Keep bugging me about it, and I'll just lie and tell you we went. If it's anonymous, you'll never know the difference."

She scowls, then pops the avocado into her mouth.

"Fine. Subject dropped. All I'll say is that you have no idea what you're missing out on."

"That's okay, because I don't want to." My words are firm. Definitive. Strong.

And I can't help but fear that they're also a big, fat lie.

6

"Just one more bite, and then I need to run," Jamie says an hour later, her fork sliding into the cheesecake she talked me into sharing. Because, as she pointed out, calories consumed with a friend only count by half. "I have to get all the way to Redlands."

I snap my attention to her, ignoring my own forkful of dessert. "I haven't been to Redlands since the time Damien treated you and me to that overnighter at The Desert Ranch Spa." Jamie had stayed two full nights, but I'd left with Damien after only one. "It's an adorable town. We stopped there for dinner during the drive back," I explain.

"Just dinner?" Jamie says with a tease in her voice.

"It was a *very* good restaurant," I assure her. "With a damn nice alley behind it, too," I add with a cat-and-the-canary smile.

"Naughty girl," she says, then uses two fingers to pluck my cheesecake off my fork.

"Hey!"

"Don't even. I totally deserve this cheesecake. You get a sexy encounter in a dark alley, and I get to cover a high

school student film festival." As if in punctuation, she pops
the cheesecake in her mouth.

I laugh, conceding the point. "But you'll have a
great time."

"Yeah," she admits. "I will. I covered it last year, too, and
it was such fun watching the kids' films. They're not jaded at
all. Yet. That'll come in a few years when they graduate and
actually move the sixty miles to LaLa Land."

Since she's probably right about that, I refrain from
commenting.

"What about you?" she asks. "Back to work?"

"Eventually. But errands first. I've got to run by the space
to meet with the contractor. We're moving in on Wednesday.
But first I'm going to check on the cake for the girls' birthday
party. It's coming up fast." A week from tomorrow, actually,
and there's still so much to do.

Technically, the party doesn't fall on either of the girls'
birthdays. Anne turns two the following Wednesday, and
Lara's assigned birthday is the day before the party. She'll be
four this year, and it's hard to believe that not that long ago,
she was found in a wooden wagon near the gate of a
Chinese orphanage. Since there was no easy way to tell
exactly when she was born, the orphanage assigned her
Finding Day as her birthday, and neither Damien nor I see
any reason to change that.

"Speaking of," Jamie says. "I finally figured out what to
get them, but you'll have to wait until Saturday to see. Kids
are not easy to shop for," she adds, in the kind of tone that
suggests I personally erected a barrier between her and all
appropriate present ideas.

"I'm sure they'll love whatever you bring. You're Aunt
Jamie. You can't possibly go wrong." I mean what I say, but
that's because Jamie's calmed down a lot in the last few

years. There was a time when I'd have been slightly terrified at the idea of her picking out a present for anyone under the age of twenty-one. Fortunately, she has Ryan now, and I know he won't let her go too crazy.

Then I think about the parties at Masque, and I have to wonder if maybe Ryan isn't as calming an influence as I'd thought.

Those thoughts naturally lead to Damien. Which makes my skin tingle and my blood heat.

I take a sip of my wine and try to banish the thoughts as Jamie lifts a brow. "Did I lose you?"

"Sorry," I say. "You got me thinking about everything I need to get done today."

"Go," she says, waving vaguely inland. "I can deal with the check."

"You're sure?"

She gives me a look that is so Jamie it makes me laugh, and I stand up. "Love you, James."

"Back at you. Oh! Wait. I talked to Ollie this morning. He said he'll be in town for the girls' party."

"Seriously?" I pause with my hand on the back of my chair. "That's fabulous." Ollie is the third leg of our BFF trifecta, although it's not been as stable since Damien entered my life. They've warmed to each other—hell, they even respect each other—but they're never going to be tight.

Ollie's a lawyer, and for a couple of years now, he's been spending more time in New York than he has in LA, where he's technically based. Some big corporate litigation. But now Jamie says that things are slowing down and he's coming back to the LA office for good.

"That's so great. I feel like the girls barely know him."

"True that," she says, but hurries on so quickly that it's obvious that Ollie's relationship with my daughters is way down her priority list. "But do me a favor and don't ask him about his house, okay?"

I frown, cocking my head a bit as if that will make the words more cogent. It doesn't work. "Huh?"

"He's selling it."

"What? Are you serious? He hasn't even started the renovations." He'd bought a dilapidated two bedroom, one bath in the hills with a huge lot, a stunning view of Universal Studios, and tons of renovation potential. But then the firm shipped him back to New York, so he postponed the renovation and turned it into a rental. Not terribly snazzy, but livable. "What happened to all his plans? I thought he was going to ask Jackson to help with the remodel." Sylvia's husband is a world-renowned architect. He's also Damien's half-brother and a genuinely nice guy. And he'd offered to do the work for Ollie at a discounted rate.

I pull my chair back and start to sit down again, but Jamie waves her hand dismissively.

"Go do your thing," she says. "Because now you know all that I do. And maybe I misunderstood. But I don't think so. Honestly, I think he's having money problems."

A wave of guilt crashes over me as I realize how much I've lost touch with one of my best friends. He'd told me he was looking to buy an investment property, and at the time I'd offered him dinner and the chance to interrogate Damien, who's a whiz at all things financial. Ollie had brushed it off, though, telling me that one of his clients was advising him, and that he knew what he was doing. And since I was exhausted with a baby and a toddler, I didn't press the point.

Now, I'm wishing I'd insisted. Not that Damien's advice would have necessarily saved him, but at least then I'd know I did everything I could to help my friend.

"Don't worry about it," Jamie says, her dark eyes studying me. "He's a big boy."

True, but half an hour later, as I aim my cherry-red Mini Cooper toward Beverly Hills and my party related errands, I'm still thinking about Ollie.

Ollie *and* Damien. Because my friend's financial situation has underscored how lucky I am. God knows I'd love Damien even if he were a pauper, but there's no denying that his wealth is a blessing.

There are downsides, of course. Mary Lee underscored that pretty damn well this morning.

And, yes, we've suffered through more than our fair share of scandal and drama, stalkers and paparazzi. Incidents ranging from so mundane they're almost laughable to so deeply disturbing and horrific that absent Damien, I'm certain I couldn't have coped without the sharp edge of a blade to release the pressure.

With Damien, I'm strong. Even when I'm not in his arms, like earlier at the bungalow, his love flows in my blood, anchoring me to him.

And right now, I'm counting the minutes until tonight, when I can fold myself in his arms and let the rest of this day fade away.

I DON'T FORGET about Ollie and Mary Lee immediately, but as I navigate traffic, I forcibly push all that drama aside in order to focus on more important things. Like colorful candy sprinkles, plastic tablecloths, and toddler friendly games that will satisfy a houseful of little kids.

Fortunately, both Bree and Gregory—Damien's valet/butler/general-house-guy—are helping out with planning and prep for the party. Even with their help, though, I'm overwhelmed, a not unfamiliar state these days. Damien keeps telling me I need to hire a personal assistant to help me with whatever comes up either in business or at home, since Bree's duties really don't extend beyond the kids.

I've told him I'll think about it, but so far, I've avoided the issue. I know that Damien has a slew of personal assistants, all overseen by Rachel, but I can't wrap my head around having someone similar for me. After all, there's already staff for the house. On top of Bree and Gregory, we have a housekeeper who comes in daily, a groundskeeper and his staff, a rotating team of security guards, and a part-time chef. Not to mention the drivers who technically work for the company, but are at Damien's beck and call.

As much as having a helper at my elbow might be useful, I don't think I need to add to the crowd. I've been managing fine so far. Busy, but fine.

The bottom line is that I'm not Damien. My company is relatively small, my responsibilities much less vast. I don't need a full staff to keep my daily life running smoothly.

And that's one hundred percent okay with me.

Besides, if I had an assistant, odds are good she'd be the one visiting Love Bites instead of me. Which means she'd get to taste the cake samples and talk about decorations. And that would be a damn shame, I think, as I pull up in front of a valet stand. I slip out of the car, hand the valet my keys, and start walking the few blocks up Rodeo Drive and then over to Beverly Boulevard.

A shiver runs through me as I head to the corner. *Like someone walking over my grave.* My grandfather's voice fills my head, flooding my memory with his Southern sayings and superstitions.

Or maybe not superstitions...

I turn quickly, expecting to see someone staring at me from across the street. But when I look around, I see nothing out of the ordinary. Just tourists and shoppers, laughing and smiling and enjoying the gorgeous day.

I cross the street, then pause again, but the sensation of being watched has faded, and I chalk it up to heightened paranoia because of the day I've had. By the time I reach Love Bites, I've pushed it firmly from my mind.

"Nikki!" Sally Love spreads her arms as I push through the glass door and breathe in the rich, enticing aroma of freshly baked cakes and cookies. Her smile blooms bright and her cheeks flush pink as she hurries toward me and envelops me in a hug. A celebrity chef, Sally hosted her own cooking show for years before leaving television to focus on a countrywide chain of high-end bakeries, Love Bites, with the shop in Beverly Hills being her flagship location.

"It's so great to see you." My words are genuine. I've used Sally for a number of different events, and while I truly love her confections, I also adore her as a person. Only a few years older than me, she has a maternal personality, as warm and comforting as freshly baked chocolate cake.

"I've been thinking about the girls," she says, leading me past the display cases and into the private tasting area set up to resemble a homey kitchen with countertops and cabinets lining two walls, along with a refrigerator, stove, and cook-top. It's a new feature she added when she expanded the bakery into the space next door, and she gestures for me to take a seat at one of the stools surrounding the quartz-topped kitchen island that dominates the center of the room.

She stands beside me, her hip brushing the stool as if she's thinking of sitting as well, but can't quite commit to the action. "At the risk of it looking like I have no imagination at all, I think we might want to go with cupcake displays again. Only this time with a little bit of a twist."

"A twist?" For our wedding, Sally had designed cupcake towers. The finished product had been stunning, and the guests were able to pick whatever flavor they wanted from the five tiers of beautifully decorated, fondant-iced cupcakes. My mother had been mortified by the idea, but I'd been thrilled.

Sally nods, then bends down to open one of the cabinets under the island. When she stands, she's holding a huge platter with a two-layer round cake, perfectly iced with a thick chocolate frosting so enticing I want to drag my fingers through one of the ridges and taste the gooey sweetness.

"Something like this for the center," Sally explains. "But I'll build out and up for the kids."

Once more, she reaches into her cabinet of goodies. This time, she pulls out a mountain of cupcakes. The center, as she described, is the double-layer of chocolate cake. But that base is ringed by two concentric circles of cupcakes, one frosted with what looks and smells like butter cream, the other with chocolate.

Four spikes extend upward from the main round cakes and act as support for the first layer of a tower that is topped with a collection of cupcakes. Another four spikes extend up from that, and this layer is smaller in diameter and hosts fewer cupcakes. The top layer has one over-sized cupcake.

"For the birthday girls," Sally says, pointing to the top cupcake. "Obviously, we'll have two towers, one for Anne and one for Lara. Each with birthday candles, of course. And I can frost in their favorite colors if you want."

"I love this," I say, genuinely delighted.

"I'm not done yet." This time she doesn't reach below the island, but goes to the shelf above the sink upon which sits a collection of her published books along with a few three-ring binders.

She pulls down one—a pale blue binder, lightly dusted in a layer of white flour. Inside are pages of photos protected in clear plastic sleeves. She flips quickly through, then shows me a photo of the tiered cupcake tower surrounded by a decorating station with plain silver bowls filled with colorful sprinkles, candies, and other cupcake toppings.

"It will be messy," she says. "But I promise the kids will have fun. And when we set it up, we'll put down a protective flooring that looks and feels like regular carpeting. We can even bring toddler tables if you need."

"I've got that covered," I tell her, then look up quizzically. "I didn't realize you did such a booming business for the under five set."

She laughs. "I catered my nephew's party, then figured what the hell. Now I'm able to offer full-service toddler parties." She winks. "I love my work, but there's a special reward in watching a little kid grin at me with a mouth covered in frosting."

"Can't argue with that. I hope you'll be able to attend yourself?" Sally often sends one of her employees to her catered events, but she's known Damien for years, and we've asked her to join us as a guest after the cupcake station is set up.

"I can't wait. It's been far too long since I've seen your girls. Or you and Damien, for that matter."

"We've all been busy," I say. "Anything new in your life?"

"With everything I've got going in this business? Who has time for new?" She smiles as she speaks, but under her words, I think I hear a hint of regret. I start to ask, but stop myself. It's not my place. More than that, it could very well be my imagination.

We wrap up the details for the party, making the final frosting and decorating choices right as Sally's next appointment walks in the front door, a tall, young woman whose face is glowing in such a way that I'm certain she's there to talk about wedding cakes.

All in all, I spend about half an hour in Love Bites, then I walk leisurely back to the car. Unless there's been a wreck on Santa Monica Boulevard, I should arrive at my new office space in plenty of time to meet Luis and my team.

Love Bites is on Beverly Boulevard, and my car is parked a few blocks away on Dayton Way at Two Rodeo Drive, one of the many upscale shopping destinations in the area. I'd been hurrying after I dropped the car off, focusing entirely on my destination. Now, I walk back more leisurely, letting my gaze wander to the storefronts.

The perfectly cut flirty dresses displayed on headless mannequins. The elegant evening gowns that cost more than most people's cars, and will be worn down the red carpet, then zipped into a garment bag and tucked into the back of a closet or donated to charity. The meticulously constructed handbags. The stunning jewelry that glitters and sparkles under the hidden lighting, designed to display every piece to its best advantage.

I generally don't pay much attention to labels, but I can't deny that there is a world of beauty and opulence tucked into the blocks surrounding the famous Rodeo Drive. The prices are out of reach for so many, and yet the well-known shopping district is a draw for tourists and wealthy locals, both craving the glitz and the glamour. The attention to luxury and comfort and detail that acts like a balm against a world that can be harsh and brutal.

As I walk along, I soak in the colors and the patterns, then stop short in front of a window filled entirely with black and white images of nude women in undeniably erotic poses, modest only because of the contrast of shadow and light.

I know these pictures—they're the work of Wyatt Royce, a rising star in the world of photography. His real name is Wyatt Segel, but since his family is Hollywood royalty, he changed it for work, wanting success on his own terms, without trading on his family name.

He's also a good friend, and though I don't really expect him to be inside the gallery that is hosting his art, I step inside anyway. Photography has been my hobby since my sister gave me a Nikon when I was in high school, and I crave a closer look at Wyatt's beautiful compositions and stunning imagery.

I'm drawn first to a photograph of his wife, Kelsey, who was his model when he finally broke out in a big way. Her face isn't identifiable in this photo, but she'd told me about the shoot, and I'm certain it's her. Taken in her dance studio, she stands at the barre, one foot flat on the ground, the other flexed on the wooden rail. She's bent over, touching her toe, wearing only her ballet shoes and a tutu. No tights, no leotard. Her long hair loose around her face, as if it's that neglect—and not the lack of clothes—that is the affront to ballet.

She has a dancer's lithe body, the lines of muscle revealed. And because he shot the image at an angle that captures three of the four walls of mirrors, it seems that there are an infinite number of Kelsey's. The photo is both sensual and sweet, and though it seems tame at first glance, the more I look at it, the more I think that it will be the one that stays with me after I walk out of this gallery.

"Good afternoon. Can I help you?"

A tall, slim woman with short silver hair that accents

sharp cheekbones steps toward me. I guess that she's in her mid-sixties, probably more than twice my age, and I hope that I look as amazing when I'm that old.

She offers me a welcoming smile, and I notice that she wears a small, neatly engraved nametag identifying her as *Emily*. "Are you looking for something in particular?"

"To be honest, I was heading back to my car. I saw Wyatt's work and had to pop in."

"You're familiar with Mr. Royce?"

"I'm both a fan and a friend. Nikki Stark," I add, extending my hand.

"Ms. Stark, it's a pleasure. I feel almost like I know you."

I tense, and she laughs, a little awkwardly, as if hiding embarrassment.

"I'm sorry. That came out wrong. I meant that Mr. Royce has spoken highly of you and your sister-in-law. Ms. Steele? I understand you've both studied under him."

Immediately, I relax, understanding that her perception of me wasn't fed by the tabloid's fascination with my marriage, the infamous painting, or Damien's money.

"I'm not sure I'd call it studying," I tell her. "Syl and I are both amateurs. But I do love photography, and I know good work when I see it. Wyatt's work is outstanding."

"That it is." She waves an arm, indicating the free-standing display wall on which much of Wyatt's work is displayed. "I don't know if you're interested in other mediums, but the gallery is currently exhibiting *Sins of the Flesh*, a curated exhibit of erotic art for sale in a number of mediums by a number of different artists."

I can't help the smile that tugs at my lips. "Love the title."

"In that case, I'll take credit for it. I confess I was inspired by *The Rocky Horror Picture Show*. It was a guilty pleasure of mine back in my youth, and I've always loved the music."

"I wondered," I admit. "My sister snuck out to see the movie when she was in high school, then bought the soundtrack. She played it over and over. Originally to irritate our mother. But then the songs started to grow on us. It was completely inappropriate for me, of course, but it was our sisterly secret." I smile wistfully. I'd forgotten those memories until this moment, and now I blink rapidly, trying to forestall tears.

"Why don't you take a look around," Emily says, and I nod in gratitude, certain that she's seen my distress and is giving me an easy out.

"I will. You've got me curious now." That's the truth, and though I'll have to hurry to my meeting, I can spare a little time.

I walk along the wall, taking in Wyatt's prints, a couple of which I saw at his studio the last time I was there. Then I reach the end of the freestanding wall, round the edge, and stop short. *I know these paintings.*

Not *these* paintings, but ones so similar that my legs feel weak simply from the memory of it. Because these are Blaine's paintings, so like the ones that hung at Evelyn's house the very night that I met Damien in LA. The night that started it all.

I take a step forward, realizing that I've wrapped my arms around myself. Not in protection, but in an act of pure selfishness. I want to hold these images close with my memories. As if the taste and texture of those past moments could be lost if I don't hold tight to them.

Never. Those moments are burned into me. Seared on my heart. And I want nothing more than to have Damien beside me right now.

Since that's not possible, I let myself slide into the desire that these paintings have sparked. Memories of those moments with Damien, before we were together, but when our attraction burned like wildfire—hot, dangerous, and out of control.

The painting in front of me reflects a different type of desire. While Blaine's earlier work focused on reds to accent the often black and gray images, this canvas is dominated by bold strokes of stormy blue—ribbons tied fast around the nude woman's ankles and wrists, binding her tight to a chair. She is arched back, her torso shadowed by the lines of her ribs. Her face is tilted up toward the ceiling. Her long hair falls backwards, a few strands trailing over her shoulder and curling over one bare breast.

Her sex is hidden in shadows, the brush strokes subtle, and with her face raised, there is no way to see her facial expression. Is she aroused, waiting for a trusted lover? Nervous, playing sex games with a man she hardly knows? Is she there of her own volition, or is this an image of fear and violation?

I tremble at the thought, then jump when I feel the pressure of a man's hands cupping my waist as he steps close behind me. My body tenses, a fight or flight reaction that I can't control in the split second it takes for my mind to send the message to relax. Because there's nothing at all to fear.

Damien.

I start to turn, but he increases the pressure, keeping me firmly in place.

"D—"

"Shhh." I feel his breath on my hair. "Stay just where you are, baby, and don't turn around."

7

His name dies on my lips, but I hear it all the same in my head. *Damien.* My voice breathy. Full of need.

He eases me back so that my body is flush against his, and I close my eyes, losing myself in the way his touch makes me feel even while fighting the urge to step away. To tell him to stop. That we're in public, and we can't do this.

But I don't. I stay, and as I close my eyes in acceptance of my own desires, I hear his low, soft moan of satisfaction and feel the swell of his erection against my lower back, his arousal growing with my acquiescence.

Mine, too.

Because while I may not want to be the kind of woman who gets turned on by her lover's touch in a public gallery, I can't deny the heat building between my thighs any more than I can deny the basic truth that where Damien is concerned, there are no limits. Not because I have none, but because he knows how to take me right to the edge. To make me breathless and needy and desperate. But never to push too far.

I'd changed before meeting Jamie for lunch, and now I'm wearing a knit tank that hugs my body and a wrap style skirt that fastens with a single button at my hip. His hands are pressed against the curve of my waist, the heat of contact burning through the black knit of my top. I make a small move as if to turn around, but he tightens his grip, his utterance of *no* so soft that I may have only imagined it.

But I know I'm not imagining the motion of his hands as he slowly eases them up my body, making my heart beat faster with each millimeter of progress higher and higher. My breath is shallow, and I whisper his name, "Damien," not certain if I'm acknowledging the moment, pleading with him to stop, or begging him to continue.

His hands curve under my breasts, his palms lifting them as he presses his thumbs down until my nipples are pinched tight between his thumbs and forefingers. He increases the pressure, and I suck in air, squeezing my legs together, my clit throbbing as I bite my lower lip and fight the urge to surrender to the heat that is building inside me.

"You're wondering if it's pleasure she's feeling," he says, and my mind has traveled so far from these walls that it takes me a moment to realize that he's referring to the woman in Blaine's painting. "Pleasure or embarrassment," he adds as his right hand eases lower, his fingers finding the flap of material where the ends of the skirt overlap.

He slips his hand in, his palm sliding over the brushed cotton, his fingers slowly tugging the interior layer toward him. It bunches within his hand, and I bite back a gasp when his fingertips graze the bare skin of my thigh. "Was she turned on by the knowledge that so many would see her portrait?"

His fingers slowly ease higher, closer and closer to my bare sex. I bite my lower lip and close my eyes, my entire body aching with need, craving his touch. I can imagine his hand cupping my sex, his fingers sliding inside as his lips brush my ear while he whispers to me, his sensual words making my imagination soar as my body quivers and tightens and explodes around him, and I taste blood from biting down so hard to keep from crying out.

I imagine all of that. Craving it. Desperate for it.

And at the same time terrified of it.

"Not here," I murmur, resting my hand over my skirt. Over his hand. "Not now."

His fingers still, but he inches closer, his heat burning into my body, the beat of his heart reverberating through me.

"I got your note. And your present." His whisper rumbles through me, his words making me even more aware that I'm bare beneath this skirt. "I missed you by just ten minutes."

"How did you find me?"

"I have my ways. And I'm willing to use all my resources to get what I want."

There's a tease in his voice, and I smile in realization and amusement. Because it didn't take too many resources. Just the app that's installed on both our phones as well as our cars—and Bree's, of course, in case we need to find her and the kids.

He would have checked his phone, seen that I'd parked in Beverly Hills, and remembered that I was going to check on the girls' cakes today. Presumably he was following my route and saw me step in here.

"Do you really think I need a tracking device to find you?" he counters, after I tell him all that. "Don't you know that you're always in my heart, and how can I lose track of that?"

I smile and sigh happily, his words delighting me. And, who knows? Maybe it's true. My husband is a remarkable man.

"I wanted to see you." There's a tone of finality in his voice. As if the details simply don't matter. As if his will alone is enough to find me.

Maybe it is.

"To touch you." The fingers of his hand that still cup my breast tighten on my nipple, sending a new shock of desire running down to my core.

"I wanted to know if you're still bare, or if you've put on a fresh pair of panties." His hand stays perfectly still, but, damn me, I relax the pressure of my own hand that's been keeping his in check.

"We can't." It's a public gallery. Anyone could come in. But even as I think that, my eyes scan the room. The section we're in has no windows. And the gallery is empty and echoey, with a bell over the door. We're alone, except for Emily. And if she comes this way, her heels will undoubtedly click on the floor, giving us plenty of warning.

The thought—the fantasy—makes my body tighten. "We can't," I repeat, as much to underscore the point as to remind myself of that very basic truth.

"No?" His mouth brushes my ear, his breath disturbing my hair and sending shivers down my spine. "What if I told you that Emily was busy at her computer. That she's locked the door for lunch. That I'm certain we won't be seen."

I swallow and say nothing, afraid that if I speak, my desire will betray my common sense.

"She won't want to disturb us. Not when we might be contemplating a purchase. Destroy the moment, and she could lose a sale. She knows that. Knows that a client needs to get lost in the art. In the moment."

His thumb has been making small circles on my breast, and my heart is beating so hard now that I'm surprised Emily can't hear its echo on the far side of the gallery. On my legs, his fingers move subtly. Not rising, but neither are they still. Instead, his fingertips brush my bare flesh in sensual movements designed to entice and tease.

"What do you want, Nikki?" His words are as tender against my flesh as his fingers. "Do you want me to move higher, millimeter by millimeter, up your wet thighs as you hold your breath in anticipation? Would you cry out if I stroked your clit, unable to hold back the explosion?

"Or maybe I shouldn't stroke you there at all. Maybe I should slide my fingers deep inside you. Feel how slick you are, the way your body will clench around me, drawing me in as I use my thumb to tease around your clit. Never quite touching, but drawing you up and up, until you can't take it anymore."

I can't take it right now, and I'm certain he knows it. I want to tell him to stop—except I don't want him to stop.

And so all I do is whisper his name. A plea. A prayer.

"*Damien.*"

"That's right, baby." I hear heat in his low, melodic voice, a passion now equal to my own. "Would you scream my name when you explode? Or would you be so quiet as you tremble in my arms, that I'd be the only one who knows the force of your orgasm rocking through you?"

I'm trembling now, so close to the explosion he's describing that my skin seems to sizzle. The thin whisper of air from the ducts above does nothing to cool my heated flesh. I want the release, crave it, and yet I can't quite let myself go. Not here. Not like this.

Damien knows that, of course. His real purpose isn't to make me come—it's to take me to the precipice. Pleasure,

yes, but underscored by frustration. By need. And, ultimately by anticipation.

"Tonight," I whisper, then boldly—and a little regret-
fully—ease his hand off my thigh.

"I look forward to it, Mrs. Stark."

He takes a step backward, releasing me entirely. I
draw a breath, mourning the loss of contact. And,
maybe, perhaps, regretting that this encounter didn't go
further.

"It was both, by the way," he adds.

He is still behind me—just as he's been since he first
approached me in the gallery. Now, I turn, but only enough
so that I can see the shape of him in my peripheral vision.
"What was?"

"The model. Pleasure, yes, but tinged with a hint of
embarrassment. Not because she's on display—that isn't
what embarrasses her."

He falls silent, the obvious question going both
unspoken and unanswered.

"Then what is?" I ask, when the quiet becomes
too much.

He bends toward me, his breath tickling the back of my
ear. "That she likes it."

The words shoot through me, and I tremble from the
force of that simple sentence.

"I'll see you at home," he says, taking another step back,
and this time I don't mourn the distance. On the contrary, I
need it. Distance and time if I'm going to pull myself
together by the time I get to Santa Monica.

I turn, taking his hands as I look into his face. It's the
first time I've looked straight at him in days, and I revel in
his beauty. The raven-dark hair. His dual-colored eyes, one
black and one amber. That lean, muscled body that seems

to have been designed for a tailored suit, but looks damn perfect without one.

But it's not his looks that make him so compelling. It's his bearing. His confidence. As if there's nothing in the world that he wants that he can't have. Including me.

The thought makes me smile, and as always, I'm struck as much by the beauty of this man as by the love for me reflected in his eyes. "I'm glad you came."

"But I didn't," he says, managing to keep a straight face.

I bite back a laugh, then flash him a stern look. "Mind out of the gutter. You know what I mean."

"I do," he says. "And we'll take care of my interpretation later."

I flash a coy smile. "Is that a promise?"

He hooks a finger under my chin, his eyes locked on mine. "Baby, it's a demand."

"IT's A WONDERFUL GALLERY," Damien says to Emily as we walk back into the reception area.

"I'm so pleased you enjoyed the exhibit. Is there anything that called to you in particular?"

"The Blaine piece with the woman in the chair. I believe it's called *Woman and Blue*." He releases my hand so that he can take a slim wallet from the interior pocket of his suit jacket. He pulls out an American Express Black Card and hands it to her. "Please ask Blaine to call me to arrange a time for delivery and installation. He has my number."

She doesn't even bat an eye at his request that doubles as an order. Or at the fact that he didn't even ask the price. "Certainly, Mr. Stark."

They finish the transaction at record speed, and after

Emily and I say goodbye, I step through the door with Damien and blink in the sunlight.

"Where do you plan to put it?" I ask. "It's not very kid friendly."

"That's true," he says, with a slight downward curve to his mouth that tells me he hadn't thought of that. He simply wanted the painting, and so he bought it.

His smile fades, and his expression grows serious. "You do like it?"

"The painting? Of course." That's the truth, but I hope he doesn't see the rest of the answer in my eyes. Because there's more to it than that. The power of money. The wish fulfillment. And the messages that we send to our kids. But that's a different conversation. A harder one. And definitely not a conversation we need to have on a Beverly Hills sidewalk.

"Good." He tilts his head, looking back toward the gallery, presumably picturing the painting and imagining it inside our home. Maybe he's thinking about the Blaine portrait that hangs on the third floor, affixed to a stone wall at the top of the stairs. A nude of a woman standing, her wrists bound, her face turned away. It's me, of course, and that simple fact makes it difficult for me to look at it objectively.

Difficult, but not impossible, and the truth is that while there is an element of eroticism in the image, it is not an erotic painting. That wasn't what he'd commissioned. Instead, the portrait is a life study of nude woman, her face hidden. It's beautiful and tasteful.

And the girls, of course, don't yet know that the model is their mother.

In contrast, *Woman and Blue* is one of Blaine's overtly

sexual images, especially so since the woman is facing the viewer, her legs spread, her body bound.

"We'll find a place," he says. "Maybe our bedroom. We can install a recessed frame with automatic shutters. When the girls are in the room, we'll have a remote that can hide the painting."

I can't help myself. I laugh, then slide into his arms. "You have an answer for everything, Mr. Stark. And I think you just increased the cost of that painting—including installation—by several thousand dollars."

"A small price to pay for the memory of this afternoon." He releases my waist, then cups my cheek. "I want to see it and remember the package on my desk, then finding you here with your gaze locked on that painting while you remembered that first night at Evelyn's when we saw the painting of the woman bound in red. And I want to look at the woman in blue and think about the way I held you today. Touched you. I want to hold the memory of the things I said close, along with the knowledge that if I'd taken it further, you would have gone there with me." I see the movement of his irises as he studies me. "Wouldn't you?"

"You know I would."

A smile touches his lips, conveying both gratitude and a hint of melancholy. "And that's my final reason. I want to stand in front of it and recall the satisfaction of knowing the depth of your trust today. Do you know how much that means to me?"

"Of course, I do." I search is face, and for a moment I think I see a flicker in his eyes, as if there's something troubling him. "Damien?"

He reaches out, then slides a strand of my hair through his fingers. "You should have called me." I have no idea what he's talking about, and it must show on my face, because he continues. "The reporter. The security buzzer. Nikki, dammit, why the hell didn't you call?"

His voice has gone from soft to urgent, and my stomach twists as I understand his fear. Of course, he receives alerts when our security system goes off. That hadn't even occurred to me.

"It was nothing," I say. "You must have called the guard-house. You know I was fine. It was no big deal."

He searches my eyes, but says nothing.

"I'm fine, Damien," I assure him. "But, yes, I was a little shaken. That's why I went to the office. Just leaving you that note calmed me down." I rise up and brush a kiss over his lips. "I'm fine," I repeat. "Truly."

He draws me to him and wraps his arms around me, one hand cupping my head as I press my cheek against his chest. I hear the steady beat of his heart and close my eyes, wishing I could reassure him even more.

Except it's not my reassurance he needs. He already knows I was fine. Knows that I would have called him first thing if I weren't. This is about something else entirely.

I ease away, then tilt my head up to look at him, my expression like a question mark. He answers with a kiss, hard and deep and so deliciously intimate that I moan and move closer, ignoring the passersby on the sidewalk. Ignoring everything, even the certain knowledge that I'll see a picture of this moment if I log onto social media later today.

But I don't care. He needs this. Needs to touch me. To hold me. Our moments in the gallery were for play, a follow-up to the present I'd left on his desk. This is for him. For reassurance that all is well. That I'm here. That I'm his.

I don't know why he needs that now, but it doesn't matter. I'll always give Damien what he needs.

My knees are weak when he finally releases me, and as I step back, I notice the gawkers nearby. I focus entirely on my husband as they pass on, realizing that the show is over. "Careful, Mr. Stark," I say, lacing my voice with a tease. "I have to get to Santa Monica to meet my team. We don't have time to rush over to the Beverly Wilshire for a quickie."

The corners of his mouth tug into an amused smile, but a shadow remains. Something dark and impenetrable. Something I'm certain has nothing to do with me.

Something I don't understand.

Not yet.

But I will. Because I'm going to make it a point to find out.

8

My phone rings as I'm turning onto Wilshire Boulevard, a few miles from my new office space. I hit the button to connect the call, then hear my sister-in-law's voice over Coop's speaker system.

"Where are you?" Sylvia asks.

"Santa Monica," I say. "What's up?"

"You're heading to the walk-through and final punch list, right? Do you want me to come?"

Since I'm not leasing space in a Stark building, Sylvia wasn't involved in finding the office or finalizing the deal. But real estate's her business, and she's family, so I know she's sincere in the offer. Even so, I decline. "I appreciate it, but I think we're in good shape."

"Fair enough, but if you hit any snags, just text me. I'm all done at The Domino, so I can be there in fifteen minutes, tops."

"What happened there? Rachel said there was some big crisis."

"She got that right. Hang on." I can make out voices, some shuffling, then I hear her swallow. "Sorry," she says when she comes back. "I'm trying to cut down on caffeine, but this is one of those days."

I imagine that she's sipping a coffee at The Domino Cafe, a kiosk with outdoor seating that's already opened on site. It's a breezy, sunny day, and she's probably settled into one of the colorful plastic chairs. She'll be wearing sunglasses that hide her whiskey-colored eyes, and the ends of her short brown hair will be fluttering in the breeze, giving her an elegant, but carefree look.

"I'm having a day, too," I say. "Tell me yours and make me feel better. Plus, I want the Stark office gossip."

As I'd hoped, she laughs.

"Today was supposed to be no big deal. I had a few onsite meetings about the new phase, and that was all. But then all of a sudden Richard Breckenridge was there, and he's shouting at me and telling me that he's getting an injunction to block construction and freeze occupancy and that he's going to destroy The Domino and Damien and me and anybody else who stands in his way."

"Shit," I say, which really doesn't sum up the situation. Breckenridge is a local businessman with international holdings, and he was one of the original investors in The Domino. He seemed perfectly nice when I met him for a business dinner with Damien one night. A little self-involved, but easy enough to talk to.

Not that long ago, however, he got caught up in a #metoo scandal that had all the signs of being not only legitimate, but pretty damn nasty. And rather than stay in business with the man, Damien—or rather the company—utilized an escape clause in the deal to buy out Breckenridge's investment, cutting him out entirely. Good for Stark International, but Breckenridge was royally pissed.

"Damien and Jackson came right over, of course, and

security had to escort Breckenridge off the property. Honestly, I thought our guys were going to have to call the cops. And I didn't hear what Breckenridge said to Damien when they were talking, but if Damien's face was any indication, it wasn't good."

"No," I say thoughtfully, as I recall his shadowed expression, "I don't think it was."

"It's over now, though. Damien and Jackson headed back downtown ages ago. I've been here playing catch-up on other stuff. So, like I said, I can meet you if you need me. But if you really don't, I'm going to head home early and cuddle my kids. It's been a day."

"I hear you," I say, thinking that as soon as I'm done at the office, I'm going to do the exact same thing. "We're still set for tomorrow, right?"

"Totally. Ronnie's beside herself," she says, referring to her precocious daughter. "She's already rearranged the playroom. She says they're going to play school. I think she's mostly giddy for an opportunity to boss around her brother and cousins."

"Well, the girls won't mind. They idolize her." Jackson's daughter was three when he and Sylvia met, and after they married, Sylvia adopted little Veronica Steele. Now Syl and Jackson have a son as well, and the four cousins are best friends despite the staggered ages. We've all been so busy that it's been a while since the kids got together, though. So tomorrow, since all the adults are going to the Foundation brunch, the kids are staying in the Palisades at Jackson and Sylvia's house.

"Who'd you end up getting to watch them?" I ask as I slow down for a right turn. I'd originally intended to ask Bree to watch all the kids, but when she asked if she could come to the brunch to hear me speak, I had to revise that plan.

"Moira's on deck," Sylvia says, referring to Ryan's little sister. She might be my best friend's sister-in-law, but since she's in grad school at UCLA, I don't see her that often. But she's responsible and sweet, and she's babysat for both me and Sylvia before, so I know she can handle the kids.

"She's not coming to the brunch?" While I'm fine with not having all my friends and family watch as I share my deepest secrets with the world, I am surprised that she's not coming. After all, both Jamie and Ryan are deeply involved in the organization, serving on several committees and sponsoring two kids.

"She wants to, but she's got something due to her advisor on Monday. She said she'd bring her laptop and work while she watches the kids."

"So Ronnie's school day theme is on-point."

Syl laughs. "I guess so."

"I just got here, so I'm going to let you go." I slide into a sweet parking place in front of the building, not bothering to head into the parking structure. "I'll see you tomorrow."

"Sounds good. Fingers crossed you don't hit a snag on the property."

I second that, then kill the ignition. I'm leaning over to grab my purse when I shiver, a sudden sensation of being watched rolling over me. I jerk up in time to see the glass doors into the lobby swing shut. Someone's just stepped inside, and once again a familiar glimpse of short blond hair jerks me to attention. A man, I think, and I lean forward, trying to focus. But the reflection on the doors prevents me from seeing through the glass. And though I hurry out of the car and into the building, there's no one in the lobby when I get there.

The eight-story building is half a block off Wilshire in a mixed-use area of Santa Monica with offices, storefronts, and plenty of restaurants. Fairchild & Partners Development now occupies the northwestern corner of the top floor. I enter, expecting to see the mystery man, but there's no one in the lobby. Just four chairs surrounding a low coffee table to form a waiting area.

I glance toward the elevator bank and look up, but there's no display to show me which floor either of the two cars are on. The button, however, is not lit. Presumably the man has already reached his floor. Either that, or he left through the delivery entrance in the rear.

A directory on the wall between the two elevator banks lists the tenants, and though I scan it, I have no clue who could have preceded me in. And since there's no security desk, there's not even a guard on staff to tell me if I'm imagining things.

Which, of course, I am. Because Mary Lee threw me for a loop this morning, and I've been on edge ever since.

I shake my head in frustration, like a dog drying himself after a dip in the lake. Then I push thoughts of Mary Lee and the mystery man from my head even as I push the button to call the elevator.

There's no security guard in the lobby, but a keycard or punch code is required to access the first floor stairwell or the elevator. I slip my card into the slot, watch the doors slide closed, and lean against the back wall as the elevator ascends.

The elevator bank on the eighth floor opens onto a central area with a hallway leading off to the left and the right, and a set of glass doors between them. And right there on the doors, in gold lettering, is the name Fairchild & Partners Development. I smile, realizing in this moment how much I've missed having an actual office. I step out of the elevator, cross the open area to my office, then pull open the doors.

They're not locked, which makes sense, as Abby, Travis, or Luis probably got here before I did. "Hello!" I call, expecting an answer. But none comes.

That's not too concerning, as the space consists of a reception area with a view of the ocean, then offices that follow the wall and continue down around the north and south corners. My office is in the northwest corner, and two smaller offices have northern facing views, with only a sliver of ocean off to the left.

In other words, we took space designed for growth, so there's a significant amount of square footage. Plus, the offices—along with the interior break room, conference room, and file room—all have heavy doors to block out sound and other distractions. So I'm not surprised no one heard me.

I'm about to step further into the office when my phone rings. I don't recognize the number, so I almost don't answer it. But then I realize it could be one of the many contractors dealing with getting the office up and running. "This is Nikki Stark."

"Ms. Stark. I'm glad I caught you." The voice is clipped and business-like, and I don't recognize it at all.

"Who is this?"

"Richard Breckenridge."

I remember everything Sylvia told me. "What do you want, Mr. Breckenridge?"

"I want to know how you can live with a man like your husband. He cut *me* out because of my indiscretions? Fuck that. Hasn't your husband ever heard of clean hands?"

Anger bubbles through me. "I'm hanging up now."

"Do you think I don't know what he and that little slut Sofia did?" The sentence comes hard and fast and so loud I hear it even as I'm pulling the phone away from my ear.

"Bet that got your attention," he says. "The incredible Damien Stark and the coach's daughter? So what if he told the world? It still reeks. And he thinks he's better than me? Do you think I don't know what he paid you to do? That painting. That money? He paid you like a whore, little girl, and then he married you to make you both feel better about it."

"You're wrong," I say, then end the call, because I do *not* have to listen to this asshole, whose only purpose is to harass me and malign Damien. *Fuck.* No wonder Damien was in a mood at the gallery after dealing with this jerk. Hell, maybe he's the one who left the note on my car, although I'm not sure how he would have managed that if he was at The Domino with Damien, Jackson, and Sylvia.

I shove my phone in my purse, telling myself I'm shoving the creep out of my mind. Then I step further into the office and call out, "Abby!" Her office is next to mine, and if she's in there with the door closed, soaking in her view, she probably can't hear me. Surely she would have stepped out if she overheard the conversation I just had.

I'm about to head that direction, when I hear the ding of the elevator behind me. I turn, and through the glass, I see the second elevator's doors sliding open, revealing Abby, her shoulder-length blond curls framing her downturned face, and Travis beside her, his Paul Newman blue eyes looking right at her.

Our contractor, Luis, stands behind them. A short, dark man with a genial face and a belly that protrudes over his belt, he's flipping pages on a clipboard, oblivious to the tension that surely fills that small box.

I frown, as they step off the elevator. Not because of the budding office drama between my two co-workers, but because the door was unlocked. I step through the glass doors and meet them in the open area in front of the elevator bank. "Did you guys walk through already?"

Abby's brow furrows, then she shakes her head. "We just got here."

I glance back inside. "Marge, maybe."

"She's on her way up," Travis says. "She left her phone in her car and went back for it."

I exhale in frustration as my eyes meet Luis's. "It's not that big a deal while the place is empty, but I've got furniture and computer deliveries on Monday, files and other paperwork on Tuesday, and we'll all have our personal stuff in here by Wednesday. So long as your team is working here, make sure everyone locks the door when they leave. Lunch break and the end of the day."

I point to the short hallways on either side of the elevators that I know lead to other leased space. "There are two other tenants in those corner offices, and an access code for the elevator doesn't keep the place secure."

"Of course, Mrs. Stark," he says, looking embarrassed. I don't blame him. I hired him because of his stellar reputation, and I expect someone on his team is going to get a stern lecture later today. "I will speak to my team personally. They all know better than this."

I nod, satisfied, then lead the others in after propping open one of the double doors. "Go check out your offices. I'm going to work my way down to mine while I wait for Marge and make sure there's nothing left for Luis's guys to do in the break room and the file room. Then I'll go over reception with Marge when she gets here. Just give Luis your notes."

They both nod, and as they move together toward the hall that leads off toward the right, I see Travis raise his hand as if he's going to rest it on Abby's lower back, then quickly pull it down and shove his hand into the front pocket of his jeans.

The aborted gesture is intimate enough to make me think that something went on between the two of them more serious than office flirting. And his swift recall of the motion makes me certain that it didn't end well.

I bite back a frown. In theory, I don't have a problem with co-workers dating. But if there's tension between them…

I shake my head, frustrated by my own wandering thoughts. As far as I can tell, they're both being professional. As long as that stays the case, I don't need to worry.

I'm saved from further musings by the ding of the elevator and then Marge's hurried footsteps as she calls, "So sorry. My phone slipped between the console and the seat." She arrives breathless, her pale skin ruddy with exertion and beads of sweat dotting her forehead where her short cap of silver-gray hair frames her face.

After assuring her it's no problem, she and I go over all the public and group areas that make up her domain as the office manager. We spend some time discussing the cabinetry in the file room and the placement of furniture in the break room and reception area. Then we head to Travis and Abby's offices, too. Marge is going to be onsite for all the deliveries next week, so she's taking copious notes about where everything can go. We pop into Travis's office first, then move down to Abby's.

It's next to mine, so while Abby describes how she wants her credenza in relation to her desk, I wander the few feet to my door, then push down on the handle and give the door a gentle shove. The lights are off and the blinds are down, so I reach to my right and flip the switch—and that's when I see it. The wild X's and streaks of red splattered across the walls and blinds. And the vile, horrible word painted huge across the wall.

BITCH

I hear a strangled cry and realize that it's coming from me.

"Nikki?"

I turn, only then noticing that I'm pressed against the far side of the hallway wall. Somehow, I backed out of the office and crossed the hall without even noticing. My hand is over my mouth and my heart is pounding so loud I can barely hear Abby, who's standing in front of me now, her hazel eyes wide, concern painted all over her pretty face.

I suck in air, determined to get myself together. "I'm okay," I say. "It's just—"

What? What can I say? It's just another shitty brick in a day stacking high with the stinking things? Is it Mary Lee? Breckenridge? Someone else entirely? Someone determined to gaslight me?

Or is it just a stupid prank by someone who managed to wheedle their way into our personal space?

All true, but no words make it to my lips. Instead, I point. By that time, though, I don't need to. Travis has reached my office, Luis fast on his heels.

I hear Luis curse, but Travis reacts more smoothly. He comes up beside me and hooks an arm around my shoulder. "Let's get you out of here." He's tall, with a firm chest and well-muscled arms, and though it's Damien I want, I appreciate his strength.

"Thanks," I say as we reach the reception area. I slide away from him and draw in a deep breath. "It's just that this is getting to be a little too much for one day."

Abby's brow furrows, and I see Travis catch her eye. Neither understands, obviously, and I'm not in the mood to explain.

"What is it? What's going on?" Marge hurries in from the other direction, and I assume she was checking out the storage closet at the southernmost end of our space.

"Go see," Abby says, pointing. "It's awful."

"Who did this?" Luis demands at the same time, his complexion flush with anger. "Not one of my men. Mrs. Stark, you know this—"

"Of course, I know that. But someone got in here, and—" *Ding!*

Marge stops in mid-step, and we all turn and look out through the propped-open door. We're staring straight at the brushed steel elevator doors, and my pulse picks up tempo as the reception area grows quiet and we hear the whirring of the cables and gears grinding to a halt.

The doors slide open, revealing a flash of blond hair. I gasp, everything falling into place. The figure I saw at the Tower pavilion. The feeling that I was being watched. And most of all, the short blond hair and familiar beard stubble on a face and body I know only too well.

"Eric?" I whisper, as someone even more familiar steps into view, my husband's reassuring smile wide as he looks into my eyes.

"Look who I found getting off the elevator in the lobby." Damien leads Eric out of the elevator and into the open area as I stay frozen in place, my gaze firm on the young man who used to work for me but then moved to New York. And undoubtedly has a 917 area code now.

"Nikki?" Damien takes one step toward me as Eric takes a step back. "Baby, what is it?"

"Why the hell did you do that to my office?" I'm staring right at Eric, fury and hurt bubbling inside me.

"No," Eric says. "That wasn't—"

But he doesn't finish the thought. Damien's realized that something's happened and that Eric's at the center of it. And before I have time to process what's happening, he has Eric backed against the far wall, his forearm tight against my former employee's neck.

"All right, Eric," Damien says, his voice more dangerous than I've ever heard it. "I think we need to have a talk."

9

"Tell me what happened," Damien demands. I've moved out the reception area and into the open area outside the elevators. Damien's eyes are locked on Eric's, but I know the question is for me.

"My office," I say, pointing vaguely in that direction. "There's red spray paint everywhere. And the word *bitch*. We got here. The place was empty, but the door was unlocked."

I look at Damien as I speak, but I can see Eric, too. There's fear in his eyes, and he's shaking his head in small, frantic jerks, as if he fears that any larger movement will prompt Damien to lean harder against his throat.

My stomach curdles. He was my friend. A trusted colleague. And I don't understand any of this. Not what's happened today. Not now. Not why he would do something like that or why he'd want to hurt me.

Damien's expression never wavers. It's cold. It's ice. And as much as Eric sickens me at the moment, I hope he stays perfectly still. Because right now, I think that Damien is capable of anything. And God knows he has the strength in his arms to kill a man.

I hear movement behind me, then Abby appears in my periphery. Travis is behind her, his hand on her shoulder, as if he's holding her back from launching an attack. And I think that it's a mark of just how confused and angry she is that she doesn't shake it off.

"Why?" The word snaps out of her, hard and fast and brutal. "Why the hell did you do this?"

Eric's eyes are wide, and he's still shaking his head. Now, though, his lips are moving, too. "I didn't." I can barely hear his words. "It wasn't me."

"You all came up together?" Damien asks, his attention on me.

"I came up." I take in a breath, determined to stay calm. "Then Abby and Travis with Luis. Then Marge."

"He must have been here before we arrived. Then gone down when we all went inside." Abby nods toward the corridor that leads to the eastern facing offices that are leased by another tenant. "He could have been waiting around the corner until." She looks at Damien. "You said he was getting off the elevator in the lobby, right?"

"He was," Damien says. "What floor were you coming from?"

"Here, of course," I say, then take a step toward Eric. "You've been following me all day. What the hell, Eric? Why would you—"

"I didn't do this. I swear. And yes, I've seen you. I called. And I wanted to talk to you at Stark Tower, but I chickened out. And then I called Rachel, and she gave me this address. And so I came here."

"And tagged her office?" Abby snaps.

"No!" Eric's eyes plead with me. "You know me, Nikki. You know I wouldn't do this. Come on, Mr. Stark. Let go of me."

Damien looks at me, his brow rising in question. I draw a breath, then nod, trying to calm myself.

One beat, then another. Then Damien steps back, releasing the pressure on Eric's neck. He slides down the wall, then just sits there looking up at us.

"It really might not be him," I tell Damien. "Believe me when I say I've got suspects."

"The reporter," Damien says.

I nod. "And Richard Breckenridge." I make a face. "He just called me. Said all sorts of nasty things, mostly about you. You're not on his favorite person list today."

Damien almost smiles. "No, I'm not. And while I wouldn't put graffiti past him, I'm not sure he's had the time."

"Maybe not. But I don't think Eric did it either." I turn my attention to my former employee, still on the ground and looking miserable. "I'll agree that vandalism really isn't your style. But why have you been following me?"

"Are you sure he was?" Travis asks me, his brow furrowed as if this whole situation is a line of code he's trying to figure out.

I start to nod, but then doubt overtakes me and I stay silent.

"I was," Eric says, and I see Damien's fingers curl into a tight fist. I step to his side, and gently cup his wrist. "I wanted to talk to you about a job," Eric continues.

I blink. "You have a job. I saw the announcement when you moved to Austin."

"Yeah, well, that didn't work out. And I missed California, and, oh hell, Nikki, I realized what a good thing I had with you. I should have called you, but I wanted to talk in person, without setting an appointment and having all sorts of preconceived ideas running through your head before we talked."

He presses his fingertips to his temples and rubs. "I went to Stark Tower to get your new office address. Then I came here since Rachel said you were coming by today. I didn't even realize the elevator needed a keycard. I got in with some guy going to five, and I just pushed eight. I was going to wait in reception, but you have no furniture. So I walked the offices, thinking you might have moved in your desk. And that's when I saw the graffiti."

"And you just bolted?" Damien asks.

He shrugs. "I guess I figured that under the circumstances, today might not be the best time to talk about a job. And it's not like I knew who did it." He looks miserably at all of us. "It was stupid. I should have called and told you. Or called Rachel. But dammit I just … fuck, Nikki, I left with such big plans, and then everything crashed under me. And I just didn't want to deal with this, too."

"The paint's dry," Travis says, stepping back into the open area where we're all still gathered. I hadn't even realized he'd gone back inside, much less down the hall to my office, but now he walks to Eric. "Hold out your hands."

Eric's brow furrows, but he does as ordered, and both Travis and Damien look down at his fingers.

"Hard to use spray paint without leaving any residue on your fingers," Damien says.

"He could have been wearing gloves." Marge takes a step forward speaking for the first time. "But I don't believe it. This is our Eric. He wouldn't do this."

"Even if he was wearing gloves, the paint on the walls would still be tacky." Damien looks over his shoulder at Travis. "I'm guessing it's bone dry?"

Travis nods. For a moment, nobody moves. Then Damien extends a hand down to Eric. He hesitates, then takes it, letting Damien help him to his feet.

"I'm truly sorry," Damien says. "I hope you understand how the situation looked."

"I do." He rakes his fingers through his hair. "Believe me." He meets my eyes, his a little sad. "I'm really sorry. Doubly sorry at the state this leaves you in."

It takes me a second to interpret his meaning. Then I realize that if the tagger wasn't Eric, we have no idea who did that to my office.

Damien is way ahead of me. He's already on the phone telling someone he needs them here right away. "No," he adds. "Not a social call. I'll explain when you get here, but we have a security issue. Ryan," he adds to me, after he slides his phone back into his inside suit pocket. "Show me your office."

I nod, then turn my attention back to Eric. "I can't talk about work now. But we'll be moved in by Wednesday, and we have interviews scheduled for Thursday, including a few candidates for your old position. Do you want a slot?"

"Yeah," he says. "I do."

I see Abby nod. "I'll check the schedule and email you with a time. In the meantime, email us a current resume."

"Appreciate it." His chest rises and falls as he looks at all of us in turn. "I'm really sorry about the confusion."

"Back at you," Damien says. "And sorry about the throat."

"Remind me not to piss you off for real," Eric says wryly, then adds, "Then again, you'd have to be an idiot to piss of Damien Stark."

Damien glances into the office space, and I know that

he's imagining my walls, covered in blood red paint. "Some-one's an idiot," he says softly. "And someone's definitely going to pay."

10

"I'll get with the building management and pull the security feed from the lobby and the elevators." Ryan Hunter, Jamie's husband and the Security Chief for Stark International, looks around my office. He's lean and strong, with chestnut hair and piercing blue eyes. And right now, his jaw is tight, his body tense. In that regard, he looks much like Damien. Two men with blood in their eyes, and no idea who to lash out against. "We'll find out who did this," he says. "I promise."

"I know you will," Damien says. "Make it sooner rather than later."

"You got it." Ryan pulls out his phone and starts tapping, presumably rattling off instructions to his men. The rest of my team has already gone, and it's just me, Ryan, and Damien in the empty, echoey offices.

After a moment, Ryan looks up from his phone. "I'll have the building feed within an hour. I'll let you know what I find."

Damien nods, then holds out his hand, palm up toward me. "Car keys."

I pass them to him. And he tosses them to Ryan. "Get one of your men to get Nikki's car back to the house. You're riding home with me," he adds, and I simply nod. That's perfectly all right by me.

His free hand is resting lightly on my back, where it's been for the last fifteen minutes as we've talked with Ryan, giving him the rundown of everything that's happened all day, including the interview with the reporter and the note I found on my car.

Ryan holds up Mary Lee's business card. Damien's already seen it. In fact, he snapped a picture of it. "I think it's a legitimate publication," Ryan says, "but I'll double-check. A lot of these small local presses have similar names."

"Even if it is legit, it doesn't mean that the reporter is."

"I know," I say, because Damien's right. "But the office number is the one I called to confirm. I spoke with her editor." Then I shrug as I meet Ryan's eyes and lean closer against Damien. "Or, at least, I thought I was speaking to her editor."

"Don't beat yourself up," Ryan says. "Like I said, she may be legit. And if she's not … well, it was a pretty smooth scam."

"This bitch reporter was in the bungalow with you," Damien says. "It could have been a hell of a lot worse."

I nod. He's not telling me anything I haven't already thought of. Beside me, his body is tense, anger and worry bubbling through him. I ease away, forcing his hand off my back so that I can take it in my own. *I'm fine,* I want to tell him. *I'm really and truly fine.*

"I'll get the note from Joe," Ryan says, "then I'll pull the feed from the parking garage, too."

"You really think that's connected?" I ask.

"I do. And it's better if it is. I'd rather there be one person out there harassing you than several. Don't you think?"

And since I can't argue with that, I don't.

"Why'd you come by, anyway?" I ask Damien a half hour later, once we're tucked into his black Ferrari and speeding toward the Coast Highway.

"My schedule changed, so I thought I'd see how your space was progressing." He glances sideways at me. "Not well, I'd say."

I make a face. "I'm not moving offices."

His expression a little too bland. "Did I suggest that?"

"You're thinking really loud."

"Was I?" Now he looks amused. I consider that a good thing.

"You were thinking I should have taken office space at The Domino, like you'd suggested months ago. But it wasn't ready then. And you know why I don't think it's a good idea to be in a Stark property. It's all about perception."

"If it's a question of perception versus your safety, then fuck perception," he says, then continues before I have the chance to speak. "But I'm having second thoughts about wanting you at The Domino." He stops at a red light and turns his attention to me. "I have half a floor available at Stark Tower. I can have it remodeled and furniture in there by Monday."

He could, too. And I can't deny that it would be nice to be that close to him. To the apartment. The kids have a room there and so does Bree. If I were in a crunch time, it would be so easy. Almost like the arrangement we have now with the bungalow.

"No," I say. Despite all the pluses, taking Stark space is just a flat-out no. "I'm willing to take your advice. I'm willing to accept your referrals. And I'm more than willing to license my products to any Stark company. But I have to have professional autonomy."

"At the risk of your personal safety?"

I cock my head. "And if it was you? Would you suddenly start working from home?"

"Nikki."

I cross my arms and settle back into my seat. "I'm just saying."

He takes my hand, then immediately releases it to shift gears. "I drove the wrong damn car today," he says, and I have to laugh. "You should have told me about the note," he adds, and this time there's no humor in his voice.

"I would have, once I got home. At the gallery, though..."

"What?"

"Well, that would have been a buzz kill, right? And later, when you asked me about the reporter at the house, I honestly didn't connect the two. I'm still not sure they're related."

"Two could be a coincidence. Three makes a connection."

"Maybe." I shrug. "I don't know." Mostly, I just want it all to go away. I don't say that, though. I don't need to. Damien knows me too well.

He reaches over and brushes my cheek, and I sigh and lean into him, like a cat soaking up affection. "I don't like seeing you hurt or scared or worried." His voice is low but intense, and I have no doubt that today has thrown him almost as much as it has me.

"I know." I reach up and take his hand, then kiss his fingers. "But you're the reason I can handle being hurt or scared or worried. Because I know you'll always be there to help me through it."

"Always," he says, his voice heavy with promise.

We drive in silence for a while, and Damien takes back his hand as we maneuver the twisting Malibu streets that lead to our property. "I have an idea," he says as we soar down the canyon road. "Let's cut Bree loose for the rest of the afternoon, then take the kids down to the bungalow. We can grill burgers on the deck and make sand castles on the beach."

"Yeah?" I shift in my seat so that I'm facing him, my smile so wide I feel the tug of skin across my cheekbones. "I like the sound of that. A lot."

He reaches over, and rests his hand lightly on my thigh. "Give Bree a call. Tell her to get the girls' things together."

I'm already pulling my phone out of my purse and hitting speed dial. Three rings, then Bree's cheery voice asking me to leave a message. I do, then call her right back. That's one of our strictest rules—*always* answer calls from me or Damien.

Again, the call goes to voice mail.

"Damien."

"It's fine," he says, his voice tense. "You're just nervous because of today."

Possibly true. But the fact that he even said that tells me that he's nervous, too. "You try. Maybe my calls aren't ringing through for some reason."

He presses the button on the steering wheel, says, "Call Bree," and I listen to the crackle of the ringtone, frowning because the lack of clarity means we're getting close to the dead zone that covers a two mile stretch of road leading to the house.

Again, we get her message.

"I don't care if it's paranoid," I say. "Call the guardhouse."

"Already on it," he says, and does just that. But the call doesn't ring through. Instead, there's just dead air.

"Fuck. You call."

I already have my phone out, shaking my head when I see the No Service message in the upper left corner of the screen. "Damien." I hear panic in my voice.

"I know," he says. And he floors it.

11

D amien sails onto our property through the
underground garage, the fastest route since it
avoids the long driveway that leads to the upper-
most section of the property, providing guests with a
majestic view of the house, grounds, and ocean beyond. The
Ferrari practically flies through the cavernous space,
emerging into the light right in front of the house, the tires
skidding on the crushed stone drive.

I have the door open before we're even at a full stop, and
I stumble out of the car, then sprint to the front door,
punching in the key code faster than I ever have in my life.
It's maybe seven seconds from the time I leave the car to the
moment the lock releases, but it feels like eternity.

I throw open the door, burst inside, then stop dead at the
sight of a strange man standing on the threshold between
the sliding glass panels that mark the far end of the room
and the flagstone pool deck that abuts the first level of
our home.

A huge bag of Ruffles potato chips is tucked under an

arm that's also curled in front of his body, cradling a shrink-wrapped twelve-pack of apple juice boxes. In his other hand, he holds two plastic bottles of sparkling water.

He's wearing swim trunks and flip-flops and nothing else, and the sight of him is so contrary to the scenario of murder and mayhem and home invasions that had been racing through my head that I simply stand there staring at him. He stares right back, and I realize in that moment that I probably look like a crazy person—eyes wild, body tense, the terror that had been clinging to me morphing into some sort of confused miasma of emotions.

Damien is right behind me, and as I hear his low exhale of relief, I downshift even more. Whatever is going on, chips and juice don't add up to murder and mayhem.

Then Lara's high-pitched shriek cuts through the silence. My blood turns to ice, and Damien springs past me, only to stop cold when Lara scurries into view, racing across the flagstones and then into the house, ending the journey with a loud cry of "Baba!" as she leaps into his arms, her name for Damien that she alternates now with cries of *Daddy*, too.

"Who the he—who are you?" Damien's tone is harsh, his words tempered only because of the little girl in his arms. In front of him, the stranger looks terrified, and I don't blame him.

I may know Damien well enough to understand that his tone and his posture and the fury on his face are all the remnants of fear. I understand that we're past the moment of crisis, and whoever this guy is, he's not currently at risk of Damien beating him to a bloody pulp.

This stranger, however, only knows what he sees—and I hurry to Damien's side and put a calming hand on his arm as I flash a quick smile at Lara, who's thankfully oblivious to the still-simmering drama.

"Where's Bree?" I ask the guy.

"Outside with Anne," he says. "I went for snacks."

The statement is so ridiculously normal that I almost laugh. Instead I say, "We called. Several times."

"I—" He shakes his head. "She has her phone. It didn't ring." He holds up the hand with the juice boxes. "Swear."

"Who are you?" Damien demands again.

"Rory," he says, and I relax more, understanding. "Rory Claymore."

"Mr. Stark?" Bree hurries across the flagstones, then pauses on the threshold, Anne in her arms. "Nikki?"

She looks between me, Damien, and Rory, her expression at first confused and then slowly shifting to understanding. "We're having outdoor time," she says. "Rory called to see if I could go out, and I told him I couldn't. But I asked if he wanted to come." She meets my eyes. "You always say that it's okay if I want to have a friend over every once in a while, and I figured it's even better having two adults if we're playing in the pool."

"It's fine," I say, moving to her side, and taking Anne, who squeals, "Momma!" and wraps her arms and legs around me like a little monkey. I dance kisses over her cheek, then close my eyes as the last bit of terror drains from me, only now realizing how far I'd let my imagination run.

"We called," Damien says, his voice razor sharp. "Of course, you can have a friend over, but that doesn't excuse you not answering the phone."

She swallows, her face pale. "I didn't hear the house phone. And my cell didn't ring. Not once. I'll show you." She races outside before either Damien or I have a chance to speak.

"It really didn't," Rory says. "It was sitting on that little table by the pool the whole time. One of us would have heard it."

Damien's head is cocked slightly, his eyes narrowed like he's studying the guy. I take the opportunity to do the same, since my first impression was skewed by fear. Rory's tall and lanky, with rich brown hair that looks stylishly messy, a few locks falling onto his forehead and brushing his wire-framed glasses. He has an attractive, intelligent face, with round features, giving him a somewhat soft appearance that's counterbalanced by the intensity of his dark, deep-set eyes.

"We've met," Damien says, and Rory takes a step toward him, as if leading into an answer, but his words are cut off by Bree's return, her phone clutched tight in her hand.

"I'm so sorry," she says. "It's dead. It was on the charger all day until we came outside, so I have no idea why. It's just dead." She thrusts it into my hand. "I didn't mean to scare you."

I glance at the phone, and she's right. It's completely non-responsive. I look up and catch her mortified expression, and the last sliver of icy fear shatters. "It's okay. I'm just glad everyone's safe."

I glance at Damien while I'm talking, and though he's still holding Lara tight, his eyes are on Rory. His words come back to me. *We've met.*

"Rory was one of the Stark Education Foundation recipients," Bree says proudly. "I just found out today."

Rory ducks his head modestly. His shoulders rise and fall in a self-deprecating shrug as he meets Damien's eyes. "I was one of the early ones. I met you in the interview, and then my picture was in the newsletter. The SEF counselors helped me find scholarships and work-study, and they

closed the gap with a grant. Couldn't have done it without
you, man. So thanks."

"No thanks necessary," Damien says. "That's exactly how
it's supposed to work." He extends his hand, and Rory takes
it. "It's a pleasure to meet you again. Sorry about the
dramatic circumstances. It's been a hell of a day."

"That reporter?" Bree asks me.

"And more," I say, then wave off her follow-up question.
"Later. No point bringing a downer to the pool party."

Since the girls are already dressed for swimming—and
equally excited by the promise of potato chips—they head
back out with Bree and Rory while Damien and I go change.
The revised plan is to spend an hour at the house, then walk
down to the bungalow, leaving Rory and Bree to their
evening. A plan that lights up Bree's face when I outline it
for her.

Forty-five minutes later, she and I are stretched out on
lounge chairs, drying in the sun, while Damien and Rory
entertain our two little bundles of energy in the pool.

"I'm so sorry," Bree says for the fortieth or fiftieth time
since I gave her the full rundown of my day. "To not be able
to get in touch with me after all that drama. Honestly, I'm
so sorry."

"No more apologies. It's all fine. Really." I sit up, turning
slightly so that I can see her. "How come you didn't tell me
that Rory was a grant recipient?"

"I didn't have a clue until today. He called to ask if I
wanted to go out tomorrow night, and I told him I wasn't
sure if I could because I was going to a Stark Foundation
brunch, and I didn't know how long it would go or if you'd
need me to work afterwards. And then he asked me why I
was going, and I realized I hadn't ever told him who I
work for."

She reaches for the sunscreen and squirts a liberal amount into her palms. "I never do," she adds, as she starts to rub the lotion on her legs. "I mean, once I know someone, sure. But not at first. I told you that when I interviewed."

"You did, and I'm glad to hear you've been diligent about that. It was one of the things that impressed me from the beginning."

"I appreciate you letting me have friends over to the house. It's hard since I live on the property. Juggling my life and my work, you know?"

"I do," I say. And I mean it. Even so, I'm glad she doesn't take advantage. And I'm also glad that Rory is a Stark grant recipient. At the very least that means the Foundation checked him out. I know that Bree trusts him, obviously, but I also know they haven't been dating long. And at the end of the day, I care about my kids' safety a hell of a lot more than Bree's social life.

From the pool, I hear Lara squeal as Damien lifts her up and tosses her into the deep end from where he stands waist-deep in the water. I peer over the rim of my sunglasses at the descending sun, then raise my hand to signal Damien. We changed our timeline so we could hang with Rory and Bree, but the plan is still to take the girls down to the beach. A walk in the surf to look for shells, then dinner on the patio followed by the original *101 Dalmatians*. Or, as Anne calls it, *Puppies!*

After a day of sun and water, I doubt she'll make it all the way through, but that's okay. I can't think of a nicer way to spend my evening than leaning against Damien on the couch with my youngest in my arms and our oldest sprawled out with her head resting on her daddy's leg.

"About ready?" I call to Damien.

He nods and starts herding the kids out of the pool.

"Anything you need from me?" Bree asks. "I'm so sorry for the crazy day."

I shake my head and smile. "It's all fine now," I say.

And I hope like hell I'm not tempting fate.

12

"And this is the moat," Lara says. "See, Anne? It goes around the castle."

"Moat!" Anne says, then splashes her hand into the seawater-filled trench. "More water!"

"No, no, no." Lara wags an imperious finger. "Croca-dolls live there."

Croca-dolls? Damien mouths.

I shrug, wishing I'd thought to videotape this entire exchange.

"Croca-dolls?" Anne repeats, frowning at the water. "Where the crocs-dolls?" She bends closer, then splashes again before frowning at her sister. "Nah-uh."

Lara looks me straight on, then rolls her eyes so dramatically, I have to clench my teeth together so as not to laugh.

"What's in the middle?" Damien asks, deftly deflecting what would otherwise devolve into a serious discussion about the lack of crocodiles on California beaches. He crouches beside the sandcastle. "Who lives here?" He points to the bucket-shaped pile of sand that sits on the little island inside the moat.

"Daddy!" Anne yells.

"The king!" Lara corrects.

Anne points to Damien. "King Daddy!"

"That's right," Damien says, grabbing both girls around the waist as he rises, then spinning slowly so that they squeal as they fly. "King Daddy says it's time to go in."

"Nooooooo!" Lara's protest rings out across the beach.

"Oh, yes," I say as Damien deposits them both on their feet. "Unless you want to skip the movie tonight and go straight to bed?"

Lara looks like she'd willingly agree, but Anne looks frantically from me to Damien and then back to me again. "No puppies?"

"Yes, puppies," I say. "So long as two little girls scoot on into the house. Take your toys," I add, pointing at the mesh bag that holds their collection of plastic buckets and shovels.

While they gather toys, Damien and I scoop up the towels, then follow as the girls race to the door. Despite her earlier protests, Lara seems to be completely down with the puppy plan, and by the time Damien and I reach the outdoor shower at the base of the stairs, Lara's already rinsed off the sand and is racing up to the deck.

We follow quickly with Anne, and soon everyone is clean and dry and settled on the sofa in pajamas. At first the kids are calm between us, but Anne is in constant motion, and when we see Cruella driving her car, Anne has somehow managed to get herself completely upside down on the couch.

She's asleep—still upside down—before the movie's over. And although Lara makes it all the way to the end, her eyes droop all through her protests that she's not sleepy at all.

"Well, that's good," I say, as Anne blinks her eyes and yawns as we settle her into bed. "That means you're awake enough to read *Pajama Time* to your little sister."

She looks up at me with big, brown eyes. "What about *Goodnight, Sleep Tight, Little Bunnies?*"

It's her favorite story, and unfortunately the book is in the main house. But when I tell her that, she just smiles. "That's okay. I know the words."

She does, too, and as Damien and I sit on the edge of the bed, she "reads" her favorite book to her little sister. "That was awesome," I tell her as Damien carries her from Anne's toddler bed to her twin on the other side of their room in the bungalow.

I bend down to kiss Anne, who's already out again, her little fingers curled around the satin edge of her favorite blanket. Then I move to Lara and kiss her goodnight as her eyes flutter and she loses the battle with sleep.

We pause in the doorway, and I tilt my head for a kiss from Damien before looking back at the kids, their faces softly lit in the glow of their nightlight. I press my back against Damien, and as his arms encircle my waist a shudder runs through me, like a cold chill coming off the ocean.

"Hey," Damien says, pressing a kiss to the top of my head. "What is it?"

I just shake my head and lead him into the kitchen, then pass him a bottle of wine to open. He does, then pours two glasses. "Tell me," he says, as he passes me one, then leads me back onto the porch, the baby monitor clipped onto the waistband of the sweatpants he pulled on after the beach.

"I don't know," I admit. "It's just—" I shake my head, cutting off my words as I try to gather my thoughts. "I never thought we'd have kids. Not at first. I didn't think..." I raise

my shoulders in a small shrug as I take a sip of my wine.
"Well, you know."

He nods, his expression serious. There were other
reasons, of course, but mostly I feared that my history of
cutting would mean I'd never be a good mom. Or, worse,
that the stress of parenting would feed that urge I'd worked
so hard to suppress.

Damien knows all that, of course. Just as he knows that I
got past it. Or, rather, that we got past it together.

"Now I can't imagine life without them. And standing
there, watching them tonight…"

"Nikki."

I put down my wine and hug myself, and my voice is
hoarse as I whisper. "I can't imagine losing them. I don't
think I could survive."

"Oh, baby." He has me in his arms within a second. I'm
not crying, but I feel dried out and hollow, as if I've shed a
thousand tears, and have a thousand more left. "You've had
a hell of a day."

I nod. He's right, of course. This isn't about the kids. It's
about everything that's happened today. "Have you heard
from Ryan about the office?"

Damien's face goes hard. "The lobby security camera
shows a teen with a plastic shopping bag going in. And he
had a security card. Probably stolen. Probably hired by
someone to get in and tag your office. I'm still guessing this
Mary Lee person. Ryan didn't have anything more on her
when we talked," he adds, anticipating my question.

I nod. "Well, that's more than enough for today. Tomorrow's going to be a doozy, too."

He nods in acknowledgement. "You haven't mentioned
your speech at all today."

I raise a shoulder, then slide out of his arms so that I can reach for my wine. He takes my free hand as we head back inside to our bedroom. "I've been in denial," I admit, making him laugh. "A speech. What the hell was I thinking?"

"That the foundation means something to you, and you want to share that with the guests."

He's right. That's why I agreed to give the keynote speech tomorrow. "That's not the part that has my stomach in knots," I tell him. "Public speaking isn't one of my fears." I don't have much for which I thank my mother, but at least her obsession with entering me into every pageant imaginable eventually made speaking on a stage to large groups of people seem as natural as breathing.

But it's one thing to give a speech that welcomes the guests and tells them about the mission of the Stark Education Foundation. It's something entirely different to publicly share my battle with cutting. To reveal such a private part of myself, even if it was my idea, and for an exceptionally good reason like bonding with the kids that make up the heart of that organization.

"I know." His voice is soft, and he gently cups my chin then meets my eyes. "Have I told you how proud I am of you?"

"More times than I can count." I squeeze his hand that's holding mine. "I'm nervous, though."

"Why wouldn't you be?"

I can't help but smile at that.

He shifts on the bed so that he's facing me more directly. "I know how hard it can be to reveal something so personal," he says, and I nod in understanding, my heart squeezing as I remember what he went through when he talked about everything he and Sofia went through with his tennis coach, Merle Richter. Secrets that he released so they couldn't be held over his head, holding him hostage to a dark past. Instead, he embraced that darkness. He sacrificed privacy, and in doing so called on a strength beyond what he knew that he had.

"You were my anchor through all of that," he tells me. "Tomorrow, I'm yours."

"Tomorrow?" The corners of my mouth tug up into a smile. "You're always mine."

"Oh, yes," he says, then pulls me close for a gentle kiss. "If I'm not mistaken, I believe I promised that I'd make love to my wife tonight."

"You did," I agree, my breath coming faster as his hand moves down over my T-shirt until he reaches the bare skin exposed between the shirt and the waistband of my baggy sleep shorts. "And my husband is a man who always keeps his promises."

"Definitely." His lips brush mine, softly at first and then with more intensity. The scruff of his afternoon beard rubs enticingly against my chin, and I shift on the bed, opening my mouth to deepen the kiss.

With one hand, he cups my head, his tongue working magic on my mouth, teasing and tasting as his fingers find their way under my waistband, then slip down, lower and lower over my bare skin.

I gasp as his fingers form a V, so that he's stroking me, dancing around my core, but not yet touching me the way I crave. I shift my hips, and Damien chuckles. "Problem, Mrs. Stark?"

"Never," I say as I spread my legs, silently demanding more before I slide my fingers through his hair and pull him even closer, deepening the kiss, our tongues clashing as my body burns hotter, desire pouring through me.

His fingers continue their tease, stroking me intimately,

but never enough. My clit is throbbing, desperate for a touch that doesn't come, and I whimper, then close my legs, trapping his hand. "Please," I beg, my body screaming for release. For Damien.

He pulls back, his dark eyes searching mine. Then he pulls his hand free, the sound of my protest lost in a gasp when he roughly tugs me down the bed so that I'm flat on the mattress. He straddles me, his hands sliding up my body under my thin shirt to cup my bare breasts, his thumbs and forefingers tight on my nipples.

The sensation is exquisite, and I gasp, arching up as he bends over, his lips dancing over mine before moving slowly down along my jawline, then my neck. He replaces the hand on my left breast with his mouth, but keeps a tight grip on my right nipple, twisting and teasing.

At first, his tongue dances lightly over my areola. But soon he's flicking my hard, sensitive nipple. As he teases me, his fingers slide down under my shorts again, only this time, it's a different kind of tease. Light brushes over my clit, then a finger sliding inside me.

I'm wet, and with every intimate touch—with every long suck on my breast—I become more and more aroused. It's as if a hot wire of pleasure runs from my breast to my core.

My body is throbbing. Longing for him. And though I don't want these wild, glorious sensations to end, I also want more. *Need* more.

"Please," I beg.

He lifts his mouth off my breast, and the sensation of air against my damp nipple makes me shiver. "Tell me what you want."

"You," I beg. "Inside me."

"Like this?" he asks, making me gasp as he thrusts his fingers deep into me. I close my eyes and arch back, my hips moving of their own volition as my body craves more and more and more.

"Yes." My voice is breathy. "Yes, but more. Damien, please."

"Please, what?"

"Fuck me. Please, Damien. Take me now."

Our eyes meet, and the heat I see reflected back almost melts me.

He slides down my body, then lifts my hips as he pulls off my sleep shorts, leaving them in a crumpled heap on the bed. I expect him to tug off his sweats, but instead he spreads my legs wider, then kisses the inside of my thigh.

I moan with pleasure, then cry out when he moves higher until his tongue is stroking my clit and his fingers are thrusting into me. I curse, begging him to fuck me, but at the same time lost in these glorious sensations. I want more —I want him inside me, filling me—but I don't want this to end. This growing, consuming pleasure.

Shamelessly, I grind against him, surrendering completely as my body tenses with my approaching release. I'm close—so damn close—and I crave the explosion. Right now, I need it more than I need air. I'm trembling on the edge, Damien's mouth sucking my clit, his fingers sliding in and out in a glorious rhythm until finally, *finally,* the world falls away, and my body breaks into a million pieces, an entire universe of pleasure spread out before me—

—and then hurtling me back down to reality when I hear that one little word.

Mommy?

I crash back to earth, see that the door is moving slowly open, then catch Damien's eye before we both start laughing.

"Well, her timing could be worse," I say, scrambling to put my shorts back on.

His eyes narrow with mock reproach. "I believe you owe me."

"Definitely," I say, then nod toward the door and the little girl creeping into the room. "But later."

"Somebody's supposed to be asleep," Damien says to Lara.

She blinks big, watery eyes. "I had a bad dream." Her lower lip protrudes, quivering a little. "Croca-dolls."

"Oh, no." Damien smooths back her hair and kisses her forward. "Well, it's safe here with Mommy and me, okay?"

She nods, then wraps her arms around his neck as she snuggles close. He brings her to the bed and she shifts her snuggles to me.

From the monitor, Anne's sleepy voice calls for her sister. I catch Damien's eye and grin. "Well, we did come down to the bungalow for family time."

His mouth quirks up on one side. "I'll go get her," he says, then returns quickly, adding a second sleepy girl between us.

I'm sleepy myself, and as I close my eyes, I reach across the girls to find Damien's hand. Our fingers twine, and I open my heavy lids long enough to see him watching me. I sigh, content, then let sleep pull me under.

Or I try to at least, because the next thing I'm aware of is a soft punch to the chin. My eyes fly open, and I realize that some time must have passed, because Anne's upside down, and her foot is in my face. How such a little person can manage to take up so much of the bed is beyond me, but every time she shares our bed, she manages to get completely twisted around.

On top of that, she's a light sleeper, and whenever I try to adjust her in bed, I inevitably wake her. Since Damien is much better at rearranging our youngest without disturbing her sleep, I yawn and stretch toward his side of the bed, intending to shake him gently awake.

Except he's not there.

I collapse again on my pillow, a tiny bare foot under my chin. My brain's not awake yet, but I think that it must be morning. I reach for my phone to check the time, and see that it's only one-fifteen.

So maybe he's in the bathroom?

I call quietly for him, but get no response, and even though I know I'm over-reacting, tiny frissons of panic spread through me. I carefully extricate myself from the bed, then move quietly through the house, looking for him.

When I don't find him, those fingers of panic tighten their grip, and I hurry to the patio, wondering if perhaps he'd stepped outside to look at the stars. He's not there, and I'm about to go back inside to find my phone and text him, when I see movement on the beach. Just a shadowy flicker, but when I look closer I can see that it's a man. *Damien*. Even from this distance on an almost moonless night, I recognize him, and I exhale with relief, then take a step toward the stairs, intending to go join him.

Except, of course, I can't. The girls are in our room, so there's no monitor in there, and I'm not about to leave them alone.

I stand there, the door to the house open behind me, hoping that he turns and sees me. Something must be on his mind to send him wandering in the night, and I hope that he's not worried about me and tomorrow's speech.

He moves, a dark figure shifting on the beach, illuminated only by the dim light from the sliver of a crescent moon. I see him take a step toward the house, then see something white fluttering near him. I bend forward, as if an extra three inches is somehow going to magically make everything clear.

It doesn't. Because even though I'm hit with a sudden understanding of what the fluttering thing is, I have no idea what woman Damien could be talking with on the beach in the middle of the night.

Because that is definitely a skirt. Now that it's clicked in my mind, I can see that there is a second shadowy figure by Damien. A woman. There's no question in my mind.

But who is she? And what are they talking about?

I run back inside and take the monitor from the girl's room, then put it on the dresser in the master bedroom.

Then I grab a bathrobe to cover my tank and sleep shorts. I shove my arms through the sleeves and tie the belt around my waist as I step out onto the patio again. I have the receiving end of the monitor in the robe pocket, and I start down the steps, only to realize that the woman is gone and Damien's on the path back to the bungalow.

"Nikki?"

I conjure a smile. "Hey, I woke up and came out here for some air."

"Me, too," he says, hurrying up the steps to my side. "Girls?"

I hold up the receiver.

He searches my face. "How long have you been out here?"

"Oh." I shrug. "Not that long. I saw you on the beach with someone." My voice sounds strange to my ears, and I want to kick myself. I'm not sure what he was doing, but I know he wasn't doing anything nefarious. Certainly he's not cheating on me. That's not something I'd ever believe.

But keeping secrets...

Well, I'm not so sure about that.

"Jenny," he says. If he's noticed that strangeness in my tone, it's not reflected in his voice. "That dog of hers again..."

"Seriously?" Jenny and Phil Neeley own the property next to ours, and their house is about a half-mile down the beach from ours. "Did she find him?"

"He was having a grand time racing up and down the beach in the surf." He holds out his arms and folds me into his embrace. "God, you feel good. It's been a hell of a day."

I nod silently and tighten my arms around him, holding him tight.

After a moment, we both relax, then pull away just enough to look into each other's eyes. "Do you know how much I love you?" he asks.

"Yeah," I say, shocked by how much of a weight seems lifted from my shoulders. "I do."

13

I 'm walking the path by the tennis courts that take up a good chunk of the Foundation's property when I hear a familiar male voice call my name. I turn to find my brother-in-law, Jackson Steele, striding toward me, his hand up in a wave. Like Damien, he's dark and magnificent, a corporate god standing at the helm of an empire.

"Hey," I say, smiling into his Arctic blue eyes as he pulls me into a hug. "I thought I'd see you this morning when we dropped off the kids."

"I thought so, too. But duty called."

I nod. When Damien and I arrived with the girls at Jackson and Sylvia's house, Jackson was already gone. "The Domino?"

He shakes his head. "Thankfully, no. This was just a high maintenance, but very high-profile, client." He lifts a shoulder. "I could have sent someone else, but he's one of my favorite directors and she starred in some of my favorite movies as a kid."

I bite back a laugh. In the world of architecture, Jackson Steele is about as famous as they come. So it's pretty adorable to see him playing fanboy. "Did you get an auto-graph?" I tease.

"Hell, yes," he says, and we both laugh. "And I didn't stop you just to say hi," he adds, pulling out his phone. "I wanted to show you this text from Moira. Hang on." He taps the screen, then passes me the phone, now displaying an adorable video of my girls waving wildly, along with their cousins, Ronnie and Jeffery. "Looks like they're having a great time."

"They always do when they're together," I say. "You guys still off to Europe tomorrow?"

"The whole lot of us," he says. "I'm trading on family and using one of my brother's jets."

"No better way to travel," I say with a grin. Jackson already knows that, of course. His company owns several private jets, too, but none set up for trans-Atlantic flights. "Is Ronnie taking her camera?" I gave Ronnie a camera last Christmas, and Sylvia and I have since taken her out for photography sessions several times. She's got quite a good little eye.

"Oh, yes. All packed and ready."

"Excellent. Tell her I can't wait to see her pictures. Oh, and tell Syl to find me later, would you? Right now, I need to check in and find out if there's anything else I'm supposed to do before my keynote."

I also want to find Damien. But since that's pretty much my constant state of mind, I don't bother saying as much.

He promises to relay the message, then continues down the path, calling out a greeting to someone I'm pretty sure I once met at a cocktail party, but can't recall at the moment.

The Beverly Hills property is huge, and Damien and I walked the perimeter upon arriving, since we both like to interact as much as possible with the kids that the two main

Stark foundations support. The original foundation—which Damien started before I met him—was the Stark Education Foundation, with its mission to identify and help underprivileged kids with an aptitude for math or science.

Then, after the dirty truth about Damien's childhood came out in the context of his murder trial, he funded the Stark Children's Foundation, the primary mission of which is to help abused kids recover through play and sports therapy.

Stark International supports numerous other charities, both social and educational, but those are the two that are closest to Damien's heart. And to mine. And while both are independent organizations, there is some overlap in the kids the foundations serve, especially when a particularly bright child comes from an abusive background.

Today's event celebrates that overlap, and kids from both organizations are being honored, funds are being raised for both foundations, and after my keynote, I'll be announcing myself as a new Stark Youth Advocate, a position that's formally affiliated with the SCF.

The brunch isn't being served for another hour, and we're ninety minutes away from me taking the podium, so I'm walking leisurely back toward the main building, waving and chatting as I meander the path past the stables where several kids are taking turns riding the gentle horses around the arena. I see Lyle Tarpin—a Hollywood A-lister and the original Stark Youth Advocate—leading a white horse on which sits a blonde haired little pixie of a girl.

He catches my eye and grins, then flashes a thumbs-up at the little princess, who responds in kind, her smile so bright you'd think it was Christmas.

I'm so busy waving that I almost walk right into Evelyn Dodge, who takes me by the shoulders and steers me to the side of the path. "Texas! I was hoping I'd get the chance to talk to you. I haven't seen you in weeks."

I give her a huge, heart-felt hug. I may technically have a mother, but it's Evelyn I asked to stand with me at my wedding. That was before I met my father, of course, but even if I'd known Frank back then, I still would have wanted this woman by my side. She's brash and opinionated and her sense of humor leans toward raunchy, but she's also brilliant and loyal and kind.

Plus, she's one of the few people other than me who Damien trusts wholeheartedly, and I know she'd protect him—and his kids—with her life.

And that's more than enough for me.

"You're coming to the house next weekend, right? Lara will be despondent if you're not at their birthday party."

"Miss my girls' party? Never happen. Frank and I will be there with bells on."

My father's a travel photographer who's currently in either Sweden or Switzerland—I honestly can't remember. But I know that he's supposed to return next week. And considering the amount of time he spends with Evelyn when he's in town, I'm not surprised they're coming together.

She hooks her arm with mine, and we continue walking toward the main building. "I bumped into your boy a few minutes ago," she says, and I smirk at her reference to Damien as my *boy*. "He says you and he will be adding a new Blaine original to your collection."

"We will," I say, keeping my eyes straight ahead even though I'm dying to look sideways so that I can read her expression. "We stumbled onto a gallery in Beverly Hills and found a piece that called to both of us. I got the impression that he's doing really well."

"That's what I hear." There's a deliberate lightness in her tone that is very un-Evelyn-like.

I frown, trying to read her, but not having a clue. "Do you guys stay in touch?" When I first met Evelyn, she and Blaine were hot and heavy despite a more than fifteen-year age difference. She was his biggest champion and supported his career, sponsoring showings, getting him into galleries, and generally playing the role of patron.

"A bit. He's supposed to be in LA soon, so I'll probably see him. Or not." Her tone is light and airy, as if suggesting it doesn't matter one way or the other.

But I know Evelyn, and as she gives me a hug and hurries ahead to catch up with a client she's just seen, I can't help but think it matters. In fact, I think it matters a lot.

"You're frowning."

I blink, then realize that I've been so focused on watching Evelyn disappear down the path that I hadn't even noticed Jamie's arrival. She looks amazing, as always, but with a heavier layer of makeup than the occasion calls for, which to me translates as a very bad sign. "Tell me you're not covering my speech."

She bites her lower lip. "Sorry. You're news and the Foundation's news. And when someone like Lyle is involved in the organization that makes it entertainment news. So it was either me or Lacey." She raises both shoulders almost up to her ears. "I figured you'd rather it was me. Or am I wrong?"

I roll my eyes. "Not wrong. Be kind."

"Oh, please. You'll be fabulous. When have you ever choked on a stage?"

She's right about that. In fact, my stage presence was probably my biggest downfall. I kept winning pageants, and my mother kept entering me in them, one after the other after the other, until the only way I could escape from that nightmare of a life—from her hellish grip and sick, restrictive rules—was to take control in the only way that was left to me.

I'd already started cutting by then, needing to be in control of something, and finding satisfaction only by being in control of my own pain. But I'd been cutting in secret, my blade marring areas on my body that were hidden. Invisible to my mother's prying eyes. And when I couldn't take being paraded around like a pretty little paper princess, I let the blade I'd come to trust work a new kind of freedom for me.

So, yes. I can handle being on stage. But that doesn't mean I want to be in the spotlight.

"Nicholas," she says, lowering her voice and taking my hand as she steps closer. "I'll back off if you want me to, but you know it's going to be me or someone else. And considering what you're about to share with the class, I figured you'd rather it be me."

I nod and squeeze her hand. "You're right."

She studies my face. "So we're cool?"

"Totally," I assure her.

We fall into step together, and Jamie starts rattling off everyone else she's going to be interviewing during the course of the brunch. Lyle, of course. But she's also hoping to grab a minute with Damien and Jackson and a long list of actors, musicians, and other celebrities.

"Haven't heard of half of them," I tell her with a grin.

"You're such a liar," she chides, and I have to laugh. The truth is that I haven't heard of several of them, but most of them I've either met or have at least heard their name. Which is weird, because until I started dating Damien, I was clueless about any film star who graced the screen after, oh, Sean Connery's debut as James Bond.

Now, though, it's hard to avoid celebrity gossip. My best friend is an entertainment reporter and my husband ranks up there on the gossip radar. And, by default, so do I.

I don't love it, but I do love Damien. And that makes it all okay.

"Mrs. Stark! Mrs. Stark!" I turn around to see a broad-shouldered man hurrying toward me, a little boy of about six or seven in tow. There's something familiar about both of them, and it's not until they're almost in front of me that I realize that both the man and the boy bear a resemblance to Damien, with their dark hair and strong jaw. The boy's eyes are different, though. They're cool blue, not warm amber.

I'm certain I've never seen either before, but I pause and smile in anticipation of an introduction. "Daniel Bryson," the man says, extending his hand in greeting. "And my son, Nate."

"It's a pleasure to—oh!" I meet Mr. Bryson's eyes and see the spark of humor there. "I'm so sorry," I say. "It took me a moment to place the name."

"No apology necessary," he says. "I just spoke to your husband, and I wanted to find you and thank you personally as well. I know both you and Mr. Stark put up with a lot from Marianna. You had no obligation to help me or my boy. I just—I just want to say that your help meant the world to me."

"Mr. Bryson, you don't have to thank us at all. We're just happy that you and Nate are together."

He cups the back of the boy's head, then points to a small petting zoo set up on the other side of the path. "Looks like they're handing out feed for the goats. Why don't you go see if you can make a furry friend?"

The boy glances warily at me and Jamie, then at his dad, who nods. Then he flashes a tentative smile before scampering across the path toward the volunteer who is doling out feed to the kids.

"Got the ruling from the judge two weeks ago," Mr. Bryson says. "I now have full custody of Nate, and thank God for that. Marianna started spiraling down rapidly after Mr. Stark's people tracked me down. Ranting and raving and swearing that she'd destroy me." He casts a worried glance toward the boy. "I almost didn't come down today. But my mother lives here, and Nate wanted to see Grandma. And, obviously, we wanted to be here for the brunch. The grants from the foundation have helped more than you can imagine."

"I'm so glad you're both doing so well. Thank you for coming and for letting me know."

"Of course. And anything you ever need, Mrs. Stark. You or your husband. I don't know what I could ever do for you, but if there is anything, don't hesitate to ask."

I assure him that we won't, and he hurries over to the petting area to gather up his son.

"That's the little boy who's not Damien's, right?"

I shoot her a sidelong glance as we fall in step together and continue toward the main building.

"What? I'm right, aren't I? He's that nutcase bitch's son. From a few months back. The woman who tried to say that Damien was the father, even though she knew perfectly well that he wasn't."

I nod, conceding the point. Not that long ago, Marianna Kingsley had come out of the woodwork claiming that Damien was the father of her young son. "Thank goodness Quincy tracked down the real father. Mr. Bryson seems nice. And sane."

Damien had enlisted the help of Quincy Radcliffe, a ridiculously sexy but somewhat mysterious British intelli-

gence officer who moonlights for a vigilante group called
Deliverance that I'm supposed to know very little about.
Quincy, thankfully, had been able to track down the real
father, revealing in the process that Marianna had known
the truth all along, but had set her sights on Damien's bank
account, legitimate paternity be damned.

"What was he talking about with the grant?"

"Damien and I thought that the poor kid had been
through a lot, what with Marianna using him as a negotiating tool. So we arranged a scholarship fund for when he's
older. And it turns out the kid tests high, but with his dad
being a single school teacher in San Francisco, there's not a
lot of money for education or extracurriculars."

"Which means the kid would have probably gotten help
even without you and Damien pushing his name through."

"Assuming anyone thought to apply on his behalf," I say.

"And now he's living in the Bay area with his dad? Marianna was okay with that?"

"Bryson sued for custody," I remind her. "I told you
about it back then, remember? Damien had Charles help
him out," I add, referring to Charles Maynard, Damien's
attorney.

"Right, right. I'd forgotten." We've reached the entrance,
and she pulls open the door for me.

"You coming in?"

She shakes her head, then checks her watch. "I've got an
interview with Lyle in ten. Then I'm doing some one-on-
ones with the kids. But I'll be back in time for your speech."
She takes my hand and squeezes. "I'm really proud of you. I
know I already told you that, but it's true."

My stomach twists with nerves, but I nod, then give her
a hug. "See you soon," I say, then head inside. I wave to the
staff members I know, the ones who are supervising the

catering set up, then say hi to a group of teens—young grant recipients—who are helping to set up the last of the tables for the brunch.

"Getting ready for the farce?" The voice is cold and familiar, and I turn to find myself facing Mary Lee.

My entire body goes tense. "What the hell are you doing here?"

Her brows rise. "Maybe I have a press pass."

"We'll see about that." I glance around, looking for the foundation's press liaison. I know I saw him when I came in, and I raise my hand, planning to signal to one of the volunteers who can go track him down for me.

Before I manage that, Marianna continues. "Do you ever look at him and wonder what he sees in you?" Her low, dangerous voice freezes me in my tracks. "Someone weak," she continues. "Just a little pageant princess. Someone so disrespectful of herself that she'd take money so that some man could paint her and another could ogle her." She takes a step toward me, and my heart pounds against my ribs. "Weak, stupid, little bitch who has no business raising kids."

"Get away from me." Somehow, I keep my voice from shaking. "Just get the hell away from me."

"*Nikki.*"

I hear Damien in the same moment that his hand closes over my upper arm, and when I turn to look at him, I see pure rage on his face.

"What the hell are you doing here?" he demands of Mary Lee, stepping in front of me, his body a physical barrier between me and my tormentor.

"Wait." I turn away from her and focus entirely on Damien. "You know her?"

"Unfortunately, yes. Nikki, meet Marianna Kingsley," he says in a voice laced with rage. "Nate Bryson's mother."

14

"You can't make me leave," Marianna says after Damien tells her exactly that. "My son is a grant recipient. I have a right to be here."

"No," Damien says. "You don't."

He takes a single step toward her, and she backs up, upsetting one of the dessert tables and sending cookies and cake bites tumbling to the ground. "You keep your hands off me," she shrieks. "You can't manhandle me. You can't touch me."

"You're leaving, Marianna," Damien says, the deceptive calm of his voice hiding an ocean of anger. He lifts his left wrist and glances down at his watch, then taps the watch face. "You can leave civilly or you can leave with an escort. But either way, you're ending up outside those gates in less than five minutes."

"Fuck. You." She thrusts her chin out, then steps right in front of Damien, her eyes narrowed into slits. "You think you're above everything, don't you. Well, think again. You've crossed the wrong person, Damien Stark. I'll destroy you. You just wait and see if I don't."

The doors open to the left, and I see one of the wide-eyed volunteers hurry that direction, presumably to tell the new person that the hall isn't yet ready for guests. Except the person stepping into the hall is Ryan, and he makes a subtle hand motion that has the volunteer backing off. Then, with laser focus, he approaches Damien, acknowledging me with a quick nod and Marianna with a dismissive glance.

"Trouble, Mr. Stark?"

"Ms. Kingsley has become confused and can't remember the way out. Could you escort her off the premises?"

"Not a problem." He stares down Marianna, his expression cold enough to freeze ice in hell. "If you'd just come with me, please."

For a moment, I think she's going to argue. Then her gaze skims over Ryan, who stands there looking strong and dangerous. I see her swallow, then nod.

They get about two steps away when she turns back, her expression hard. "This isn't over, Stark."

"Noted," he says, then turns his back on her to take my hand and lead me to the far side of the room.

"Can she?" I ask.

His eyes narrow slightly. "Can she what?"

"Well, she said she'd destroy you, and I know she can't manage that. But can she make trouble?"

He strokes my cheek as he shakes his head. "Baby, she already tried that and we beat her. All she can do now is talk big. And we don't have to listen."

"Good." I brush a light kiss over his lips. "That's exactly what I hoped you'd say."

Outside, someone clangs the triangular bell that hangs in front of the dining hall, signaling to everyone that the food service has begun—and signaling to me that I'll soon be standing at that podium spilling my heart out to a room full of people.

"You okay?"

I look up, realizing that Damien is watching me intently. "Of course." I force a smile. "Mind wandering."

From his expression, I'm not sure he believes me, but the next moment he's called away by one of the foundation's board members. I kiss him on the cheek, then point to Jamie, who's just entered the hall alongside Ryan. "Find me later," I tell him, then scoot away before I catch another worried glimpse.

"What's up?" Jamie asks when I come up and hook my arm around her waist, then lean against my best friend for support.

"Nothing," I say, which is a lie that has her rolling her eyes.

"Ignore her," Ryan says, obviously referring to Marianna and not to Jamie. "She's no threat to Damien."

"Of course she's not," I say. "Doesn't mean I have to like it when she gets in his face."

All of which is true, but I can tell from Jamie's expression that she knows that's not the entire story. "Spill," she orders me after she tugs me to the side with the excuse that we're making a run for the dessert table before all the kids pick it clean.

"I guess this is moot now, but I called the magazine. That editor? Doesn't exist. And they've never used a reporter named Mary Lee, freelance or staffed. She was totally scamming you."

"Considering what just happened, I can't say I'm surprised."

"But you're okay?" Jamie's eyeing me intently.

"Absolutely."

She's silent for a beat, then she cocks her head to the side, crosses her arms, and stares me down. "Um, BFF here, remember? You want to try that answer again?"

I sigh loudly. "It's nothing. Really." I speak firmly, because I mean it. "She just got in my head."

Jamie wrinkles her nose. "Well, get her out. Ick."

I laugh, feeling better. Then better still after I snag a tiny cheesecake and follow Jamie toward a table in the back. We're about halfway across the room when Bree bounces up with Rory in tow.

"Having fun?" I ask unnecessarily. It's clear from her face —not to mention the way her arm is linked through Rory's —that she's having a great time.

"I just wanted to say thanks again for letting me have the day off. I really wanted to be here for your talk, and then when I found out that Rory was coming, too, well, you know." She lifts her shoulders in a happy shrug. "And, yeah, we're having a blast."

Her happiness is infectious, and I grin. "I'm really glad to hear it. And it's great to see you again, Rory."

"You, too, Mrs. Stark." He aims a finger at me. "Looking forward to your speech."

"Great," I say, as a fresh lump settles in my gut.

"Interesting fellow," Ryan says after Rory and Bree are out of earshot.

"You know him?" I frown as we settle at a table.

"I know *of* him," Ryan clarifies, then grabs a bite-sized chocolate cake off of Jamie's plate.

"Um, hello?" she says, then frowns. "Never mind. Go for it. I have to be on camera soon anyway. Save my teeth from flecks of chocolate and my hips from Lacey Dunlop."

"What do you mean, you know of him?" I press, ignoring

Jamie. "Oh, Ryan, you didn't," I continue, ignoring my own question.

He pops another little cake into his mouth. "It's what I do," he says after he swallows. "You don't really think Damien would have it any other way?"

I frown because I should have realized that Damien would have his people check out our nanny's new boyfriend. "All right. What did you learn?"

"Rough past. Abusive dad who skipped out, thank goodness. Mom with no education who struggled to feed him, then bounced. He ended up in foster care. Walked when he was fifteen. Lived on the street, supported himself by selling pot. Not a user, though. Or not much. Took the GRE. A ridiculously smart kid," he says. "Got lucky a cop saw potential and offered to pay for a few community college classes if he quit selling. Rory did, and the cop kept his word. Then got his name in front of the foundation way back in the early days. Now he works as a financial manager at one of the investment firms downtown."

I nod; Bree already told me that.

"He's good at his job, but he's Peter Pan." Ryan says this part with a smile, and Jamie rolls her eyes. I, however, frown at him, confused.

"He's been at four different firms in half as many years," Ryan explains. "Does well, but hasn't settled."

"He's saying Rory hasn't grown up," Jamie translates.

"That kind of childhood, might take him a while to find his place," I say.

Ryan nods. "And if the profile that his foundation scholarship was built from is any indication, he should be working in R&D. Not moving other people's money."

"Cut him a break," Jamie says. "Hell, I'm still not sure that I've figured out what I want to be when I grow up."

I meet Ryan's eyes and we share a grin. We both know that Jamie is doing exactly what she was born to do.

"All I care about is that he's right for Bree," I say firmly. "And so far, they seem giddy together."

Damien joins us, but waves off Jamie's invitation to sit. "Nikki and I are needed in the back. You ready?"

I want to say no—my stomach is in knots—but as soon as Damien takes my hand, I feel calmer. This is my choice, after all. I can do it. With Damien at my side, I can do anything.

As Annabelle Tate, the recently appointed Executive Director of the Foundation, steps up to the podium, Damien and I disappear toward the back. We pass Jackson and Sylvia's table, and they both mouth words of encouragement, as do Bree and Rory, who are sharing their table. I haven't seen Abby and Travis, but I'm sure they're around somewhere, and I know Jamie will invite them to join her and Ryan before Jamie goes off to meet her cameraman and do her reporter thing.

The podium is set up in front of the hall's far wall, a curtain behind it that leads to an open door. Damien and I are now behind the curtain in a staging area that leads to the kitchen. Servers and foundation personnel move with purpose all around us, but Damien doesn't pay them any attention at all. Instead, he is focused entirely on me.

"I'm fine."

"I know you are," he says, his eyes never leaving my face.

"Damien?" The corner of my mouth twitches. "What?"

"Just this," he says, then bends to claim my mouth with his. Not a soft kiss, appropriate for planting on your wife in front of your coworkers and employees. No, this kiss is pure sin. Wicked. Wild. And it sparks a raging fire inside me that roars white hot through my blood and my mind, burning away reason and etiquette until there's nothing left but raw, brutal need.

I hook my arms around his neck, only then realizing that he's pulled me close so that my breasts are crushed against his chest, our bodies melding into each other. I can feel every hard inch of him, and all I want in that moment is to surrender.

All I get, though is his kiss. Then his hands sliding down my arms. Then his fingers twined in mine as he lifts our joined hands and kisses my fingertips. "I love you," he says, and I feel my answering smile burst through every part of me.

"Break it up, you two."

I hold onto Damien, but turn my head to smile at Lyle, who's standing with Evelyn, both of them grinning right back at me. With his rugged good looks and hypnotic blue eyes, Lyle looks every bit like the bankable star he's become after starring in several blockbuster action films, then winning an Academy Award for a smaller family drama.

"Where's Sugar?" I ask, referring to the wife he met under circumstances that rival the nude portrait that was the catalyst to me getting together with Damien.

"You'll see her when you step to the podium," he says. "We'll both be at the front table, cheering you on." He glances toward Damien, then looks back at me, his expression serious. "Are you sure about this? You were there when all my secrets came out. It can be a rough gig."

I understand that he's giving me an easy out. The four of us standing here, plus Jamie and Ryan, are the only people who know that I'm about to announce myself as the newest Youth Advocate.

I say nothing. Just release Damien's hand, walk to Lyle's side, and kiss him on the cheek. Then I return to my husband, shrugging as he lifts a brow. "Showtime," he says, as Annabelle wraps up her speech by introducing Damien, and the audience bursts into applause.

He runs the pad of his thumb over my lower lip, then steps forward to move through the curtain to the podium. I listen as the crowd calms, then hear Damien's strong, confident voice as he greets the foundation's guests.

"He's in his element," Lyle says.

I shake my head. "No. Being in front of an audience is your element. His is in smaller groups. Making deals. Or sitting around a table thinking up crazy tech that sends his R&D folks off in nine hundred different directions.

"Fair enough," Lyle says. "And yours?"

He means it as a tease, but the question resonates. Am I in my element at work? With my kids? With Damien? And if the latter, what does that say about me? That I love my husband, yes. But what about *me*?

"Nikki?"

"Me?" I shrug my shoulders, a little sassy, a little flirty. "I'm an enigma. Or hadn't you heard?"

Outside, the audience applauds, one of those examples of perfect timing. Beside me, Evelyn hooks her arm around my shoulder. "You're going to do just fine, Texas," she says, and I can't help but wonder if she's talking about my speech or something else entirely.

"That's you," says Annabelle, who's now standing just inside the curtain listening to Damien sing the praises of the foundation and the kids it supports. She's pointing to Lyle, and he nods, ready to go out and introduce me as this year's keynote speaker. The Youth Advocate announcement will come solely from me, along with my story that tells the audience my particular pain that qualifies me for that role.

He takes a step toward the curtain, then pauses and

turns back. "I know it's nerve-wracking. Just remember that everyone who's gone before you up to that podium had a story to tell, too. And everyone felt a hundred pounds lighter afterwards."

Beside me, Evelyn snorts. "We'll need to tie you down before you start talking. Lose a hundred pounds, and someone will blow you away from just cooling down their coffee."

"Hysterical," I say.

Evelyn winks at me. "I do my best."

We stand side by side until Annabelle signals that it's my turn. Then I take a deep breath, step through the curtain, and take my place at the podium.

It's easier than I expected, mostly because I see Damien first thing. He's sitting at the VIP table with Lyle, representatives from local government, Damien's lawyer—Charles Maynard, who's also a major contributor to the foundation, and three of the kids who've come through the program and are about to graduate from college with honors.

Behind them, I see that Jackson and Sylvia have joined Bree and Rory at a table, and that Abby and Travis are with them as well, and Jamie and her camera operator are off to one side, talking in whispers. For that matter, everywhere I look I see friendly faces. People I know well. People I've met at various foundation functions. It's a warm group. A kind group. And I'm proud to be a part of it.

That, in fact, is the theme of my keynote, and although I have my notecards available, I know this talk. This message. And my speech comes from the heart.

The applause I receive when I finish wraps around me like a warm blanket of encouragement, and I hold up my hand to signal that I have more to say. This part I didn't write cards for, though. I thought about it—I rehearsed it in

my head and in the shower more times than I can count—
but it's different now with eyes on me, and it takes time for
me to find the words to get me started.

Time that passes as I scan the room, certain that the
friendly, supportive faces will push me forward.

And they do. Jamie. Sylvia. Lyle.

And Damien.

Always, Damien.

I meet his eyes, see his encouraging smile, then lean into
the mike. "I won't keep you much longer," I say, "but I do
have one more thing to add. Don't worry—it's more of an
announcement than another long-winded speech."

The crowd laughs as I'd hoped, and I let my gaze drift
over the faces, starting with Damien and then crossing the
room, my plan being to start speaking again when I'm
looking to that far side, which so often gets neglected by
speakers.

That's where the door is, and as my eyes land there, I see
a man step in. A man I've met before, and whose voice I
hear echoing in my mind.

*Do you think I don't know what he paid you to do? That
painting. That money? He paid you like a whore, little girl, and
then he married you to make you both feel better about it.*

It's not true. I know it's not. There's not a doubt in
my mind.

But it doesn't matter. The words are in my head, old
fears rising. Old doubts. That horrible night when the first
man I was serious about—the only man before Damien—
got drunk and told me how disgusting I was. How sick my
scars made him. How it was damn good that the rest of me
was pretty because otherwise he'd never get through it. And
my shame and fear when I first showed Damien my scars.

You're past that, dammit. I tell myself that. Hell, I shout it inside my head.

Right now, though, I don't believe it.

And as I face the room full of expectant faces, I do the only thing I can do. I tell the crowd that Damien and I are endowing a new scholarship fund that will allow the organization to help up to ten additional incoming freshmen annually.

In other words, I lie, knowing full well that the moment this brunch is over, Damien will make my story a reality.

He'll fix it, just like he always does.

But as much as I wish he could, the truth is that Damien can't fix me.

15

"I couldn't do it." We're in the back, and the brunch is over, and Damien is holding my shoulders, his eyes looking deep into mine. "I couldn't get the words out."

My voice sounds frantic. Panicked. I take a deep breath, trying to calm myself. Trying to ignore the servers who move around behind us, cleaning up after the brunch. I'm certain that they're watching me. Wondering about the strange woman who gave a speech and is now melting down. "I just couldn't do it," I repeat, as if he hadn't heard me the first time.

"Then you were right not to."

"Damien, no. I—"

He silences me with a finger to my lips. "Baby, this isn't a test. It's not a rite of passage. When you're ready—if you're ready—you will. And if that day never comes, then it's not the end of the world."

I make a scoffing noise. "All my big talk about being open and honest. About revealing myself and my weaknesses so that our girls and the kids we help understand strength. So that they get that nobody's perfect and everyone has flaws. So much for being a bright and shiny role model."

"You're an incredible mother. Making a speech won't change that any more than *not* making a speech. "

"I want to be strong for them. For me."

"Sharing your secrets doesn't make you strong. Living with the pain. Getting past it. That's strength. And that's you." He cups my face. "You planned your speech with good intentions. And you didn't fail anyone today."

"Except myself."

He shakes his head. "No. What would have been a mistake is pushing yourself to do something you're not ready to do."

I want to believe him. But...

I lift a shoulder in a shrug, which is the best I can manage.

He studies my face. "Do you trust me?"

My answer is automatic. "You know I do."

I see a flicker in his eyes, and I frown, remembering a similar reaction when we were outside the gallery. "You do know that I trust you, right? With my life. My heart. My everything."

"You? Of course, I do. I've never doubted it."

I nod slowly, trying to parse through what he's not saying. Because trust isn't a bond he has only with me. Trust is at the heart of the business he's built. It's the key to his reputation and the spark that fires his empire. My husband can be ruthless in business, but he doesn't play games. His word is his bond, and it always has been.

"Damien, what's happened?"

For a moment, he says nothing. Then he shakes his

head. "It's not important. Just something Breckenridge said when we were at The Domino."

My eyes widen. "Breckenridge? Well, isn't he the annoying prick these days?"

"Never mind," Damien says. "We should mingle. Then we're spending the afternoon with two little girls. And after that…"

He trails off and I raise my brows, intrigued. "After that?"

His smile is the kind that makes me weak in my knees. "You'll see."

THAT SMILE LINGERS in my mind for the rest of the brunch and on into the late afternoon when Damien and I are back home with our girls.

"Daddy! Daddy! Do you wanna see our show? Can we show you the show? Please, please, pretty please?"

"Pretty please!" Anne adds, as if Lara's plea needs additional help.

We're sitting around the table in the third floor dining area, and now Damien leans back in his chair. "Well, I don't know. Usually shows are reserved only for little girls who eat their vegetables."

"Okay!" Anne says, then picks up two green beans and shoves them in her mouth.

Lara just wrinkles her nose. "Do I gotta?"

"Have to," Damien says. "And I think you do. How about you, Mommy? Do you think she has to?"

"Afraid so, kiddo. I ate mine." Canned green beans aren't my favorite either, but they are kid friendly. And there are no more left on my plate.

Lara makes a show of sticking out her tongue, and

Damien and I do a valiant job of keeping a straight face when she complains, "Parents!"

"Eat!" Anne says to her sister, then jumps out of her chair and does a wobbly pirouette. "Eat! Eat!"

"Okay, okay." Lara stabs her fork onto her plate, comes up with three green beans, and shoves them into her mouth. She chews, swallows, and scowls. "Can we *go* now?"

"Dishes to the sink," I say. "Then off to the playroom."

"Come on, Anne," Lara orders, carrying both their plates. "You're coming?" she asks Damien and me.

"Right behind you."

They scamper to the elevator—Anne's not allowed on the marble stairs without an adult—and Damien and I quickly load the dishwasher and then follow.

The show is a delightful mess of little girls bouncing around to a child's version of Mozart on the makeshift stage that Bree taped off earlier. This goes on for over half an hour, and when it's over, Damien and I clap wildly, equally pleased that the show is over and delighted by the energy and imagination of our kids.

After the show, we settle down for a game of Memory, which Lara aces, and which leaves Anne mostly giggling, much to her sister's consternation.

When that's over, Damien announces that it's bedtime, which draws a string of sleepy protests from both girls. "Oh, no," he says. "Begging won't get you extra time, but if you're good, that might earn you a piggyback ride."

Both girls immediately make lip-zipping motions, and Damien hoists Lara, and I haul up Anne, and we all bundle into the elevator for the ride up to the third floor. We tuck them in, read them a story, then kiss both our babies goodnight.

By the time we slip quietly out of their room, our exhausted little girls are already asleep.

I pull their door shut, then slide into Damien's arms. "Bedtime," I say. "Sounds like a good idea to me."

"Always a good idea," he agrees. "But right now, I have a better one."

I bend back, my arms still around his waist. "Do you? What's that?"

He doesn't answer. Instead, he pulls his phone out of his pocket, then hits a button for speed dial. "We need you tonight" he says. "Unless you already have plans."

I frown, my head cocked. "Bree?"

Instead of answering, he says, "The sooner the better. We'll be staying the night in the Tower, so if you can handle the morning as well."

I release him and take a step back, holding out my hand for the phone. He grins, then complies.

"It's me," I say.

"You two do keep me on my toes," Bree says, sounding as amused as I feel.

"You're sure it's okay? You didn't have a date?"

"Yeah, I did. With Tom Cruise. I downloaded three *Mission Impossible* movies. But Tom and I will do just fine together in the big house. Trust me. It's really not a problem."

"And tomorrow morning? Anne has—"

"Lovely Littles, I know." It's a toddler art class that Anne absolutely loves. "I can take Lara, too, but—"

"She'll whine. I know. I'll ask Moira. I bet she can babysit in the morning."

"That'll work," Bree says. "Have fun."

I tilt my head to look at Damien. "I will."

"So we're heading to the Tower Apartment?" I settle into the Lincoln's passenger seat. "I approve of this plan." Actually, I approve wholeheartedly. Right now, we need each other. Need to burn away all the bullshit and fear and pain. My self-recrimination. My disappointment in myself.

I always need him. But right now, I need the passion that proves the words. I need him to make me feel strong again.

And Damien ... I don't know what's happened, but I do know that he needs to see my trust. To touch it as he touches me.

"Later," he says, surprising me. "We're going somewhere else first."

I shift in my seat, confused, but he's looking straight ahead, and I can't make anything from his expression. For the first time, however, I consider the car that we're in. Not the Tesla or the Bugatti or one of his Ferraris. Not a showy car that stands out. A plain, black Lincoln Town Car, just like hundreds—maybe thousands—of sedans in this city.

I sit back, considering. But I honestly have no clue.

We drive in silence for a while, but when he turns onto the 10, I can't hold back any longer. "Okay, I give up. Where are we going?"

"I talked to Ryan the other day," he says conversationally, as butterflies start to flutter in my belly. "He mentioned that Jamie had sung the praises of Masque to you."

"Oh." The butterflies morph into something harder. Heavier. Something that makes my thighs quiver and my breasts feel heavy. "Oh," I repeat.

Damien glances sideways and his gaze skims over me. Then he turns his attention back to the road, saying nothing.

I lick my lips. "You know about Masque?"

His smile is slow. "I know about Masque."

"Uh-huh." I cross my arms, then make a show of looking him up and down. "I assume you know about a club like that from your wild days. You know, the days before you met me."

"I'm glad you explained. I thought my wild days were the ones *with* you."

I press my lips together until I'm sure I won't laugh. "I'm talking about your lonely, wicked single days."

"Ah, those days. Actually, Masque hasn't been around that long."

I cock my head. "Don't even tease me. I know you're not sneaking off to sex clubs without me."

"It's Matthew's club," he says. "Of course, that isn't common knowledge."

"Matthew? Matthew Holt?" Our friend Matthew is a triple threat in this town, into movies, television, and music, with shelves and shelves of shiny awards for each. The man has serious pull. Apparently, he has secrets, too.

"He offered me an ownership interest a few years ago."

"Wait. You own part of a sex club?"

"California is community property, my love. If I own it, you own it."

"*We* own a sex club?"

"We don't, actually. I turned him down." We're at a light, just about to turn onto Beverly Glen and head up into the hills. For the first time, he looks straight at me, the heat in his voice matching the heat in his eyes. "I thought tonight we'd go see what we've missed out on."

"Oh."

"Unless you'd rather not..."

"I, um, I'm just surprised," I admit.

"But not uninterested?"

It's a loaded question, and I bite my lower lip, strangely shy. "Are *you* interested?" I ask, which is a stupid question considering he picked the destination.

He reaches over and takes my hand. "Yes."

I swallow, remembering the way I felt in the gallery when he touched me in such a public place. The tinge of jealousy when Jamie had described her adventure.

But all of that is simply prurient. A sexual rush. A physical craving.

There's more. A deeper need. *Trust.*

"Nikki?"

"Yes," I whisper.

"Yes, what?"

My cheeks burn as I whisper, "I'm interested."

He turns onto a quiet street, then reaches in front of me and opens the large glove box. He takes out a pair of three-quarter face masks, then hands one to me.

"You came prepared."

"They're the tickets for admission. I didn't know if we'd ever use them, but Matthew gave them to me when I sold him the house."

I blink. "You sold him the house? The house where we're going? Where Masque is located?"

He turns into a circular driveway in front of a stunning classical-style mansion that looks like it should be on a plantation in Georgia and not in Beverly Hills. "This house, actually."

"This used to be yours?"

"It was a rental. Matthew made an offer I didn't want to refuse."

A valet approaches the driver's side, and Damien holds

up a finger for the man to wait. "Are you sure? You can still say no."

I wipe my palms on my skirt and wonder if Damien can hear the echo of my heart. But that's just nerves. Underneath, I want this adventure. I want it with Damien.

"Not a chance," I say. "We're going inside."

16

D amien and I put on our masks before leaving the car. They're made of black cloth, both decorated with gold dust and gemstones. Faux, I assume. But then again, under the circumstances, who knows.

I check my reflection in the visor mirror. The mask covers my face almost completely, leaving only my lips free. My eyes, too, but my brows are covered, and I doubt anyone would recognize me like this. The thought relaxes me somewhat.

Then I look at Damien. At those famous, dual-colored eyes. And in that moment, I realize that he's not anonymous at all. For that matter, how could I have ever imagined that he could be? Damien is larger than life, and the thought that something as simple as a mask could erase him is absurd.

And if Damien isn't anonymous, then I'm not either. Because it's no secret that I'm the only woman who would ever be on his arm.

"Something wrong? The valets won't say a word," he continues, apparently thinking that's my concern. "Matthew assures me that they're paid extremely well for their discretion. Though some people don't even trust that. It's common to arrive already masked. But to be honest, that didn't even occur to me."

"I don't think it matters," I say. "Damien—"

"Do you want to leave?"

I don't know if it truly hasn't occurred to him, if this is a test for me, or if he actually wants to be recognized. But then I realize that it doesn't matter. Because I don't want to leave. And, honestly, the idea that everyone inside those doors will be unknown to each other is a fantasy. The point isn't actual anonymity. It's the idea of it. The freedom and the rush that comes with the concept of Masque. Not from the reality.

"Nikki?" I hear the concern in Damien's voice.

"What? Oh, no." I look at him. At the strong jaw extending from beneath the mask, as if he's a superhero. "No," I repeat. "I don't want to leave."

I know him well enough to read his expression even with a mask, and I'm certain that it's relief I see. He raps his knuckles on the driver's side window, and the valet magically reappears. Two, actually, as there's a man in livery at my side as well.

He opens my door, then helps me out. Damien picked out my outfit for the evening, and I emerge carefully, making sure that the black skirt's thigh-high slit doesn't reveal too much. Then I bend my head, hiding an ironic smile. If the night goes as I expect, I'll probably be revealing a lot more than too much thigh.

Damien circles the Lincoln, and I watch him move, theoretically anonymous in his mask and slate-gray suit. But he's not. Even without those eyes, how could anyone not know this was Damien simply from the way he carries himself, cool and confident, as if there's nowhere he doesn't belong, and no room he doesn't control.

"Milady," he says, grinning as he extends his arm for me. I take it, and we go to the entrance. Two more servants in livery and eye masks pull open the double doors. We step over the threshold and into a spacious entrance hall. Classical music plays from hidden speakers. The lighting is dim. Waiters move among the crowd holding trays of finger foods and glasses of wine and champagne. There are several bars set up for hard liquor, and I nod that direction, thinking that right now a whiskey is just the thing.

Because in addition to all the opulent normalcy, it's clear this isn't a normal party. The guests are masked, which is no surprise. For that matter, the sexual nature of the party shouldn't have surprised me either. But even so, I can't help but gawk at what I see. A nearby couple on a divan, the woman fully naked except for her mask, the man's face between her thighs as her fingers twined in his hair.

The two topless women near the back of the room, one leaning against a pillar as they lose themselves in a wild, deep kiss.

I see a threesome walking hand in hand up the stairs. And on the other side of the room a single man in a tux walks up to a fondling couple, taps the man on the shoulder, then gestures to the woman. The first man leaves, and the new arrival steps up, boldly sliding his hand up the woman's leg under her skirt.

"Did you see that?" I whisper to Damien, who nods and hands me a whiskey before tossing his own back and ordering a second.

I feel a bit as if we've gone down the rabbit hole and Wonderland turned out to be pornographic. But I've watched my share of porn, and most of it is raw and raunchy. This place has a beauty to it. An odd sort of class. An elegance.

I remember what Jamie said about it being formal, and she's absolutely right.

And while I'm a bit shocked by what I see, I can't deny that I'm also turned on.

Beside me, Damien takes my hand. "Well?" There's heat in his voice, but I hear the question loud and clear. *Do I still want to stay?*

I hand my empty drink to a passing waiter, then step closer to my husband. Boldly, I reach out, pressing the palm of my hand against his crotch. He's hard, and I keep my hand in place as I step closer, now hearing his tight, controlled breaths. "Yes," I say. "I want to stay." I meet his eyes. "So do you."

He inclines his head, just a hint of motion, but in clear acknowledgment.

"Turn around," he demands, and when I do, he slides his hand into my shirt. It's a backless silk tank, held in place only by a single tie at my neck and another at my waist. I'm not wearing a bra, and my nipples are hard against the material. Or they were. Now their hidden behind Damien's hands as he plays with my breasts while we both watch the crowd.

"Tell me why you like this," he demands.

"I don't know."

"Because there's something exciting in seeing someone else's arousal. In knowing that you're not alone in feeling such a deep desire. But it's more than that," he continues. "It's wanting to claim what's yours." His fingers tighten on my nipples as he speaks. "In showing the world what—who —you have. And who has you. What you value. What you're willing to claim."

I nod, his words almost a background noise for the pleasure that's stealing through me, so much more vibrant because of where we are.

He keeps one hand on my breast, but the other slides up the slit in my skirt. It's too clingy, and so I'm commando tonight, and I bite my lower lip when his fingers find my slick inner thighs and seriously wet core. "You do like it," he murmurs.

"Yes," I admit.

He pulls me closer, so that I can feel his erection against my ass. "Me, too," he says, sliding his fingers in and out of me in a wildly sensual rhythm that is setting my blood on fire.

His fingers are inside me like that, his other hand cupping my breast, when another couple walks over. The woman runs her tongue over her lips as she looks at Damien. "I like the way you touch her," she says, even as the man says, "Shall we swap?"

I tense, a tremor running through me as my body clenches around Damien's fingers. I hold my breath, certain that he'll say no, but nervous nonetheless.

"I don't share," Damien says.

The man runs a slow gaze up the length of my body. "Pity," he says, then turns and leads his partner away.

"The thought turned you on," Damien says, and I shake my head.

"No. I don't want that. Not ever."

"Oh?" There's a tease in his voice, but at the same time, I know how my body reacted and I fear that he doesn't believe me.

"What turned me on is knowing that you wouldn't ever do that. That I belong to you."

I feel the rise and fall of his chest as he draws breath. Then he steps back, his hands slipping from my clothes.

I turn to face him, afraid something is wrong, but the heat I see in his eyes soon dispels that fear. "With me," he says, then leads me to the far end of the room and up the staircase to the first landing.

"What—?"

But he cuts me off with a kiss, long and so deep a shudder runs through me, a tiny hint of the explosion that's to come.

"Look at them," he says, turning me around so that I'm looking down into the grand room, at the people touching and kissing and petting. I watch, my blood heating as I do, and my breath coming faster as Damien's hands stroke lightly over my back and then down to cup my ass.

He bends forward, and I feel his breath on my neck, then I gasp when I realize that he's used his teeth to tug the bow free. My blouse falls, attached only around my waist, my breasts now completely bare. "Mine," he says, then starts to tug up the back of my skirt.

"Damien..."

"Trust me," he says, as inch by inch more of me is revealed. Because of the slits, the front remains down, so I know my scars remain hidden, but soon enough I'm not only topless but my backside is bare except for Damien's palms cupping my ass cheeks.

A tremor cuts through me, and I close my eyes. He needs this, I realize. My trust. Tonight. But I want it, too. And what I'm feeling now is as much arousal as it is embarrassment.

"Touch your breasts," he says. "And spread your legs."

I hesitate, but do as he says, then moan as he slides a hand between my legs, finding me ridiculously wet. "Bend forward," he orders, "and don't close your eyes."

Once again, I comply, this time without hesitation, and as I watch the crowd below, I hear Damien's zipper, then feel the pressure of his rock hard erection against my core. I gasp as he enters me, my hips thrusting back in a silent demand for him to go deeper, to thrust harder.

He keeps up a slow, steady rhythm, and as he bends over me, fucking me on these stairs for all the guests to see, he cups my breast and tells me I'm beautiful. That I'm his. And that he wants to feel me come.

"Now, baby," he says, his fingers tight on my nipple and his cock thrusting hard into me. His other hand slides around, teasing my swollen clit. I'm incredibly wet, my body on full awareness, right on the cusp of exploding. "Come with me," he demands, the tension building in him. Both of us climbing higher and higher until—*oh, God*—I actually scream when my release comes in time with his, and a dozen faces below turn and look as I shatter in Damien's arms, my knees going weak as I sink to the ground with him beside me.

We cling to each other until sanity returns, then he finds the tie for my shirt and fastens it behind my neck.

We're both breathing hard, but he pulls me close and kisses my temple.

"Are you okay?" he whispers, his lips brushing my ear.

I nod, my heart still pounding. "Yes. I think so."

"Think so?" There's concern in his voice.

"I just mean that I liked this," I confess. "I liked it a hell of a lot more than I thought I would."

His eyes study mine, intent behind the mask. "I will never share you," he says, and I shake my head in a firm *no*. "But I liked it, too. A hell of a lot more than I thought I would," he adds, his words mirroring mine.

"Take me home," I say. I slide my hand around, cupping the back of his neck. "Take me home so that you can undress me and make love to me while you tell me about tonight. About what you liked the most. What turned you on. About what you want to do if we come back." I study his face then smile. "*When* we come back.

"Tell me all that, Damien, while you're deep inside me. Then do what you can't do here. And watch my face when I come."

17

I wake to the warmth of the sun on my face and the sound of the shower running in the attached bathroom in the Tower Apartment. I stretch, my body stiff and deliciously sore. And while I'm tempted to join Damien in the shower, the gurgle of the coffee maker and the aroma of freshly brewed coffee is too compelling. I slide out of bed, slip on my robe, and head toward the kitchen, planning on pouring us both a cup and then heading for the shower.

The Tower staff keeps the apartment's refrigerator stocked, so there is fresh cream for my coffee, and I pour in a nice dollop, feeling indulgent. I take my first sip and sigh with pleasure, then pick up both mugs. I'm heading toward the bathroom when I hear my phone ring, and I detour toward my side of the bed just in case it's Bree or Moira calling about the kids.

It's neither. The caller ID shows up as Jenny Neeley, our neighbor, and I frown in concern as I answer. "Jenny? Is everything okay?" We're casual acquaintances, not close friends, and the first thing that pops into my mind is that there's an issue with our adjoining properties.

"What? Oh, everything's fine. At least, I assume it is. I'm still at Martha's Vineyard."

"You're in Massachusetts?" Something about that strikes me as wrong, but I can't put my finger on it.

"That's why I'm calling. Our trip went longer than we planned, and I'm supposed to be hosting a lunch for a small group of volunteers just a few days after I get back. I thought I'd have plenty of time to get everything organized, but, well, you know how it goes."

"I—sure. What can I help you with?"

"Could you text me the contact info for the caterer you used when you and Damien hosted that lovely open house at the bungalow? The one last summer."

"Oh. Of course. Hang on." I switch the call to speaker so that I can continue the conversation while I look up the information, then press the button to text her the contact card.

"You're a doll. This is one less thing to worry about. We'll be back the day after tomorrow. I'm picking up Dover at ten. Thank goodness that dog thinks that going to the kennel is a vacation. He's been there four days longer than we'd planned."

I can practically feel my thoughts sliding into place. "So Dover wasn't loose on the beach recently?"

"God, I hope not or I'll be speaking harshly to someone at Happy Tails." There's a pause, then she asks, "Why?"

"I saw a dog on the beach," I lie. "Since Dover's an escape artist, I assumed it was him. But obviously it wasn't, not if he's kenneled."

"Maybe that means someone near us has a new dog. Dover could use a buddy. At any rate, I need to run. And thanks so much for the info."

I assure her it's no problem, then end the call. I sit on the edge of the bed and pick my coffee back up, frowning as I take a sip and consider everything she said.

There was no loose dog. Jenny isn't in Malibu.

I look up as Damien comes into the bedroom, his hair damp, a towel wrapped low around his hips. He looks magnificent, and all I feel is cold. All I can think about is last night. About how much I trust—trusted—this man.

"Who was she?" I ask, proud of how steady my voice is.

He cocks his head, his confusion obvious. "Who?"

"The woman on the beach who wasn't Jenny Neeley."

I watch his face, looking for a reaction, but there's nothing. That goddamn, famous control. Something I obviously don't have, because I'm on my feet now, coffee sloshing all over the sheets. I slam my mug down onto the side table, then clench my hands at my side. "Dammit, Damien, answer me. Who the fuck was she?"

"Sofia."

My knees go weak, and I sit back down, realizing that I knew it all along. Who else would he keep secret from me? I know he wouldn't cheat on me, and we're nowhere close to my birthday or our anniversary or any other event that would have him planning a surprise for me. Certainly not on the beach in the middle of the night.

Which means Sofia Richter, Damien's childhood friend. The woman he suffered through abuse with at the hand of her father, his tennis coach. Sofia, the woman who harassed me and gaslighted me, all with the intent of getting me to cut again. Or worse.

"I thought she was better," I say, my voice tight. For years, Damien has paid for her care. The best doctors at the best facility money could buy. And two years ago, her

doctors assured Damien that she was better. She went
through a twelve-step program and everything, apologizing
to me as part of that process. She even came to Lara's
welcome party when we brought her home from China and
was very sweet and sincerely apologetic about the past. Or
she seemed to be.

"She is better," he says.

A slow rage starts to bubble inside me. "Then why the
hell are you keeping secrets? Seriously, Damien, we've been
down this road before."

"Because she asked me to," he says. "She called and said
she was outside on the beach. That she needed to talk to me.
And she asked me to not say anything. She wanted my
opinion before I talked with you—before *she* talked
with you."

"With me?" I stand. "Sofia wants to talk with me?" I press
my fingertips to my temples. "Have you been paying attention? The note on my car? The vandalism in my office? And
oh, so coincidentally, there's Sofia sneaking around?"

"She had nothing to do with that." I hear the tight edge
in his voice and know that his temper is rising, too. Well,
that's too fucking bad.

"Oh, really?" I snap. "And how the hell do you know
that? What did she want? Why exactly did she come to
Malibu and creep around on the beach in the middle of
the night?"

His entire body seems to crumple, and he moves to sit
on the bed. I shove my hands in the pocket of my robe,
forcing myself not to go to him. To wait, and to learn.

"She had a miscarriage," he says, and I take a step back,
shocked and saddened by his words.

"I—I'm sorry."

He nods. "Me, too. It got under her skin. She told me

that she spent days crying, then days wrapped in relief because she's not ready to be a mother. Then she'd do nothing but sleep from the guilt of feeling even the slightest bit relieved at having lost the child."

"How far along?"

"Two months," he says. I just nod, remembering those horrible days after I miscarried. Then the euphoria when I finally got safely past the first trimester. The plans I made. The joy. But I'm not Sofia. Not by a long shot.

"She didn't want you to know."

"Why on earth not?" I ask.

"Don't you get it? She holds you up as a standard."

The words knock me backward, though I suppose I shouldn't be surprised. For so long, she wanted Damien. Maybe she still does. And I'm the woman who won his heart. Maybe that's all the standard she needs. "She shouldn't," I say softly. "She knows better than anyone how weak I am. Back then. Today." I think about the brunch and meet Damien's eyes. "Nothing has changed."

"Bullshit, Nikki. Everything has changed, and you know it. You've changed. And Sofia's changed, too."

He's right, of course. And I'm truly glad for Sofia's recovery and sorry for her loss. But that doesn't change the fact that whenever Sofia's name is mentioned, my composure goes to shit. I want to trust her—I know how much she means to Damien—but there are hard memories wrapped up with that woman, and I just can't manage.

"Nikki?"

I hold up a hand as I gather myself. Then I take a deep breath and look at my husband. "So you're telling me that she came to the beach in the middle of the night to tell you that she had a miscarriage? Did she go to a hospital?"

He shakes his head. Just one small movement. "The

miscarriage was a few months ago. She called me because she wanted my help. I don't know why she wanted to meet in the middle of the night—why she didn't come to the office or ask me to meet her somewhere during the day—all I know is what she asked."

I wait, saying nothing.

"She wanted a job, Nikki. She knew that Bree would be moving to New York, and she wanted to talk to me about being our nanny."

"Are you fucking kidding me?" The words explode out of me, and I realize that I'm in motion, pacing the bedroom with my eyes on Damien. "How the hell can her doctors say she's sane? That's the craziest thing I've ever heard. If you think I would let that woman near our kids like that, then—"

"I told her no." He's on his feet, his hands on my shoulders, his eyes hard on mine. "Of course, I told her no."

Relief washes over me, and I step back, breaking contact, then look around the room, my mind whirling. After a moment, I go to the chest of drawers and pull on clean underwear and a T-shirt, not bothering with a bra. I find a pair of jeans in the closet, then slip my feet into a pair of flats. The dress I wore to Masque is still in a wad on the floor where Damien tossed it. I glance at it, swallowing as I remember last night. His touch. The way I'd curled against him, warm and safe and satisfied, before drifting off to sleep.

Damien just watches me. When I grab the keys to the Lincoln off the chest of drawers, he stands. "Give me five minutes to get dressed."

"No. I'm going home. We'll get past this—we both know that. But right now, I want to think."

"Nikki. Baby, I—"

I hold up my hand. "I'm not mad. I'm not sure what I am.

All I know is that you should have told me all of that. We talk about trust and secrets, but where Sofia is concerned it never seems to apply. And maybe I understand that there's baggage there. Maybe I get that you're trying to protect me. But, Damien, that's not good enough."

I turn and walk toward the door, half-afraid he's going to follow me, and then a little bit disappointed when he doesn't.

It's not until I'm in the car and exiting the garage that I finally truly believe that he's not coming. I tell myself that's fine; it's what I want. I need time alone. Time to think.

I eschew the highway, taking the long way home and eventually climbing the hill to Mulholland Drive. I have no particular reason to be there, but it's one of my favorite places in the city, and driving that winding route always clears my head. This morning, I want to be clear.

There aren't many other cars on the road, and I'm taking the curves faster than I should when the phone rings. It's Damien, of course, and I punch the button to answer even though I'd be perfectly justified in simply ignoring it. "I told you I'd see you at home."

"Baby, pull over."

His voice is odd, and I frown in confusion. Then even more as I hear the steady *thump-thump* of a nearby helicopter. Around me, the plants blow in the sudden wind, and as a shadow falls over the car, I hit the brakes, careening to a stop as a familiar gray helicopter with *Stark International* printed on the side sets down on the turnaround just ahead of me.

The rear door opens and fear explodes in my chest as Damien climbs down, then runs to my car, his body bent over and his shirt tail flapping in the copter's down draft.

I throw my door open and leap out, my hand shielding my eyes from the dust. "Damien? What the hell?"

"It's Anne," he says as ice fills my veins. "She and Bree have been taken."

18

L   ess than a minute after the helicopter sets down at
      the Malibu house, Damien and I are racing side by
      side up the interior stairs to the third floor.

"Tell me," Damien orders Ryan, who's standing at the
head of a huge table that now fills our third floor living area.
Computers line its perimeter, each one manned by a person
I've never seen before.

"Lara," I cry, looking frantically around the room.
"Where's Lara?"

"With Jamie," Ryan says, closing his hand gently over my
upper arm. "Lara's fine." He looks from me to Damien. "Let's
go into the kitchen and I'll tell you both what I know."

He's speaking calmly, his voice steady and soothing, as if
he's speaking to a child. Any other day, I'd resent it. Today, I
need it. Any emotion from him, and I'll lose it. I'm certain of
that. I need him to be absolutely professional. I need to
believe that he'll get us past this. I need to believe I'll get my
baby back.

I know very little, because Damien knows very little. He
told me in the helicopter that Ryan called and said that we

needed to get home. That Bree and Anne had been abducted, and that they were working on it and to get home as fast as possible. I spent the rest of the flight with my face buried against Damien's chest, my body racked with sobs.

The pilot got us home in record time, and now it's taking all my strength not to scream at the top of my lungs. Instead, I clutch Damien's hand, my bones crushed under the force of his own grip on me.

"Now, Ryan." His voice is dangerously low as we sit at the kitchen table. "Where the fuck is my daughter?"

I've seen Ryan work before, but never on something this personal. This important. And even through my horror and fear, I can recognize and appreciate his cool, professional demeanor. It's calming, in fact, knowing that he's here. That he's watching out for my baby.

"Here's what we know," he says, still standing. "Anne and Bree left this morning for Anne's art class. After class, as they were walking back to the car, someone approached them in another vehicle and ordered them into the back at gunpoint.

I gasp, and Damien's hand tightens in mine.

"How do you know all of this?" Damien asks.

"Moira was here watching Lara. Obviously," he adds, seeing me nod. "Bree told her to expect them back by ten-fifteen. When they hadn't shown up by ten-thirty, Moira assumed they'd stopped to run errands. She texted Bree, asking her to bring back Cheetos as a treat for the girls' lunch. When she didn't get a reply, she got nervous. Five minutes later, she called. No answer, so she called me."

Moira is Ryan's little sister, and knows perfectly well what he does for a living, so her decision to call Ryan makes sense. "But how could Moira know about the car?" I ask. "Or the—the gun?"

"You hacked into a security feed," Damien says, his voice low and tight, trembling on the edge of control.

"Not me. But I hire the best." He meets Damien's eyes, his own deadly serious. "Actually, *you* hire the best. This is why. *Denise*." He lifts his wrist, speaking into some sort of wrist unit. "Send the feed to my tablet."

A moment later, an electronic tablet on the small kitchen table buzzes. Ryan taps it, and Damien and I watch a jerky black and white image.

"There's a bank branch in the same strip mall as Anne's art class," he explains. "You're seeing the feed from the exterior ATM."

For a moment, there's nothing. A few cars leaving the lot. A few moms I recognize from class. Then Anne and Bree step into view. Bree's holding Anne with her left hand, and I can see car keys in her right. Anne clutches a paper bag in her free hand, which explains why they're leaving so much later than the other kids from the class. They'd walked down the sidewalk to the small convenience store.

They pause as Bree looks both ways, then I see them step off the sidewalk and onto the parking lot. They walk toward the Volvo we bought Bree to use when driving the kids around. I can't tell how far away they are when the hatchback pulls in front of them, but Bree tugs Anne tight to her side, keeping her from stepping toward the car. The driver's window comes down, and I see a shadowed face hidden under the rim of a cap.

"We tried to enhance the image, but the perp's wearing a stocking mask. Features distorted. We're pretty sure it's a Caucasian, but even that we can't be one hundred percent on. Not with a black and white image and such poor resolution. And as for male or female … well, the odds are male, but at times like these, I prefer evidence to odds."

I start to nod in understanding, then gasp when I see the barrel of a gun. The kidnapper waves it, and Bree stiffens. I see her look from left to right, obviously trying to assess the situation. Then she hustles Anne into the back seat. The last thing I see before the car drives out of the frame is Bree pulling Anne into her arms.

My vision blurs, and I realize I'm crying. Damien draws me to him, and I cling to his shirt, terrified and helpless.

"What about Bree's phone?" Damien asks. "It's trackable."

"We found it on the street just past the entrance to the parking lot," Ryan says. "Her entire purse was tossed."

I shudder and hold Damien tighter.

"I'm sorry." The voice is soft and gravely. Someone who's been crying so much her voice is raw. I look up, and see Moira standing in the doorway. She has Ryan's chestnut hair, but her eyes are golden brown. Like him, she's slim and athletic, and usually she has an easy smile and a demeanor that suggests a wicked sense of humor.

Right now, she just looks broken.

"I'm so, so sorry," she repeats.

I want to say it's not her fault, but the words get lodged behind the tears in my throat. So instead I stand, and she hurries to me, and we clutch each other, both crying as our legs give out and we sink to the floor together.

"Who?" she asks. "Who would have done this?"

"Sofia," I whisper. Then I pull away from Moira and turn to look at Damien. "Sofia," I repeat.

"No." Damien stands, the horror in his voice palpable. "She wouldn't."

"*Bullshit*." I rise to my feet, my whole body aching, my heart most of all. "She lost it after the miscarriage. The note on my car. The graffiti in my office. She snapped.

Goddammit, she snapped after she lost her baby, and now she wants mine."

I expect Damien to protest again, but all he does is drop back into his chair, his elbows on his knees and his face in his palms. *He believes it.* He really believes that I might be right.

I start to go to him—I want to wrap my arms around him and hold him close, comforting him as he comforts me— but I'm halted by heavy footsteps and a deep, sympathetic voice.

"We need to call the police."

I look over to find Charles Maynard, Damien's attorney, standing near the threshold between the living area and the kitchen. Evelyn stands beside him, and I gulp out a sob. She opens her arms and I run to her, letting her hold me like a child as I cry. As I watch Damien stand and face Charles.

"No police," he says.

"Damien—no." I take a step toward him, but he just shakes his head.

"Not yet," he says, his eyes on me and not Charles. "Trust me. God, Nikki. Trust me."

I draw in a breath and feel Evelyn's hands tighten on my shoulders. Then I nod, just barely. He sees it, and I can almost feel the relief that floods through him.

"I have a team coming in. Experts."

Now it's my turn to feel relief. He means Dallas Sykes, and that means Deliverance. The vigilante group exists to rescue kidnap victims. And while the need for them hammers home the reality of this horror, the fact that they're coming fills me with hope.

Still, they aren't here yet, and I turn to Ryan. "What about *now*. What about finding the car. What about—"

"They're on it," Damien says, and Ryan nods.

"I promise you, my men are all over that area," Ryan assures me. "And we have back door arrangements with several government agencies. I have someone reviewing a traffic camera feed right now. And anything we can't get through cooperation, I promise you we can still manage. I've already given Noah a heads-up," he adds, referring to a friend and former Deliverance tech guru, who I know can hack his way through pretty much anything.

"We'll find them," Ryan promises, his gaze going to both me and Damien.

I lock eyes with Damien, the pain in those dual-colored eyes mirroring the ache in my heart. "I'm going to go see Lara," I say, because right now, I need to hold her close. I need to know that she's still here. That she's still vibrant and real in a world gone completely insane.

"Do you want me to come, too?" Evelyn asks, but I shake my head. "It's okay. Jamie's back there. I won't be alone."

I pause before entering the girls' room. I draw one breath, then another and another. Then I scrub my palms over my face, erasing any sign of tears. I don't want Lara to worry. She's already going to know something is going on. I don't want her having nightmares about her sister disappearing.

I plaster on a big smile, then open the door. "There's my girl," I say, when I see her sitting cross-legged on the bed playing Go Fish with Jamie. "How's my sweet baby?"

I meet Jamie's eyes as Lara turns to me, rolling her big brown ones. "Momm-eee. I'm not a baby. That's Anne."

"Right," I say, my voice tripping over the word. "You're my big girl, and she's my baby." I can't control the shaking in my voice, but Lara doesn't notice. I reach the bed and sit down, then pull her close to me and hug her harder than I intended.

"Mommy! I'm trying to play."

"Oh. So sorry." But I barely let up the pressure of my hug.

Jamie meets my eyes, and I see sympathy and fear. She reaches across and takes my hand, and I blink fiercely, determined not to cry.

We're like that, the three of us together on the bed, when Damien comes in an hour or so later. I turn to look at him, just the sight of him giving me hope, though my head knows that's foolish. He holds out his arms, and Lara runs into them, and I watch as he hugs her tight, pain written all over his strong face.

Then he puts her down and tells her to run to Jamie. "We need to talk," he says to me, then immediately holds up a hand when he sees the arrow of fear strike me. "No, don't worry. We don't have news, good or bad."

I nod, then follow him out of the room with one last glance toward Jamie. And Lara.

"Sofia's here," he says, and I stiffen. "She's downstairs with some of Ryan's men in one of the first floor rooms."

"Why?"

"She's taking a lie detector test."

"She agreed to that?"

He nods. "She understands why we might believe she'd do that."

My mind latches onto the word *we*, and I frown.

He sees it, then shakes his head. "I don't want to think it, but I can't deny you make a good argument. She gets that, too. I figure that's a point in her favor."

I lick my lips. "People can fool lie detector tests."

"I suppose so. More in movies than in real life, I think." His eyes meet mine again. "I need you to be strong."

I nod, then reach for him, but he takes a step back. Just

one casual step, but it sends ice coursing through my veins. "Damien?" I study his face, seeing something horrible and dark and lost there. Seeing fear like I've never seen before.

"We'll get her back," he says. "I'll make sure we get her back. No matter what it takes."

I nod slowly, wanting so much to believe him. I've never doubted Damien. But right now I can't even believe in the reality around me. So how the hell am I supposed to believe in happy endings?

19

"**M**ommy, what's going on?"

I open my eyes to find Lara straddling me, her face scrunched up in question. "Why are all the people here? Are we having a party?"

"No, baby," I say. "It's, um, Daddy's work. Don't bother the people, okay? Just play in your room."

"Okay, Mommy," she says, then turns her attention back to the electronic tablet that's currently showing *The Incredibles*.

I glance at Jamie, who shrugs. "You don't have a TV in the girls' room. And I figured…"

I nod, happy to have Lara distracted today. "I fell asleep?"

She gives me a wry look. "You needed it. Don't worry. They're doing everything they can."

"Is Dallas here yet?"

She nods. "I saw him and Quincy when I stepped out about twenty minutes ago. Riley, too," she adds, referring to Riley Blade, a freelancer who's one of Ryan's best men and does consulting work on Lyle's action movies. "Do you want to go out? Get an update?"

I swallow. I don't want to leave this room. In here, with Lara and Jamie, I can pretend that everything is okay. The moment I step through that door and into what's become the nerve center of the investigation, I'll have to face the harsh reality that my daughter and friend are missing. That I don't know what will happen to them.

That there isn't a thing in the world I can do to change that. And that even Damien can't make it better.

I don't want to go through the door, but I know I have to. And so I draw myself up, kiss Lara's forehead, and walk to the door. Jamie comes up beside me, and I meet her eyes. "You're coming, too?"

She nods. "We'll send Moira in to sit with Lara."

I take her hand and squeeze it. Then I open the door and step out into the chaos.

Right off the bat, I see Dallas Sykes. A playboy billionaire who used to be known as The King of Fuck, he's standing with Damien, his wife Jane beside him. Just seeing him is a relief, because I know there's a hell of a lot more to Dallas than he shows the world. He's the founder of Deliverance, and I have some idea of how many kids he's helped recover. And I also know that he understands the other side. What Anne is going through, because he and Jane were kidnapped together as children.

The thought—*kidnapped*—makes my heart race again. Because although that's undoubtedly what happened, we haven't heard a thing yet from the kidnapper.

I see Riley—a total badass—standing next to Lyle. I'm not entirely sure why Lyle is here since he doesn't actually have the martial arts skills of the characters he portrays on screen. Moral support, I assume when he sends me a reassuring smile. And I'm glad of it.

Ryan is on the phone, and from what I overhear of the conversation, he's talking to Noah, who's still in Austin, doing what he can from his office in Texas.

At loose ends, I pace the room, walking behind the men and women seated at the stations of computers and phones set up around the make-shift conference table. They're all typing or talking on headphones, working hard, focused on finding my daughter and nanny.

And yet with every step, I lose a little bit of hope. All this bluster. All this activity. And still nothing. No word. No hint. No clue.

What if we never get word? What if there is never a clue? A ransom demand?

What if we never see Anne again?

Frantically, I turn around, looking for Damien, but it's Ryan I find in front of me. He reaches for Jamie, who's been my shadow, and brushes his hand over her hair. Then he cocks his head, just slightly, but enough to have her flashing a tiny smile at me.

"I'll be in the kitchen," she says, then squeezes Ryan's hand before heading that direction.

"How are you holding up?" he asks, leading me across the room to the huge glass doors that allow access to the balcony and the view of the ocean. One panel is open, letting in fresh air, and we step over the threshold. It's Monday now, and the Pacific glows in the morning light. A moment later, Quincy Radcliffe joins us, then surprises me by turning back and sliding the door closed behind us.

I look between the two men. "What?" I demand, my fear ratcheting up.

"It's okay," Ryan says. "We don't have bad news. We only want to talk to you."

"Why?" I'm still suspicious. I have a feeling I'm going to be suspicious of everything and everybody for the entire rest of my life.

"It's just—Nikki, you and Damien, you two need to stick together. You don't and it's going to destroy you." Ryan pauses, letting that sink in. "That's what you guys are. You're each other's oxygen."

My head snaps up. "You don't think we're together? Where Anne is concerned?"

"That's not what he means," Quincy says, his accent sounding thicker with the urgency in his voice.

"This is killing him," Ryan says. "You know Damien. He's a man who gets what he wants. He wants his daughter back. And he can't just snap his fingers and make it happen. He's at someone else's mercy. He hates that."

"And you blame him for that? I hate it, too."

"You know that's not what I mean."

"Do I?" I'm being unreasonable, letting my fear morph into anger.

I force myself to take slow, deliberate breaths as I clench my hands into tight fists. I relish the sensation of my nails digging into my palms, and I say nothing until I've formed the words in my head. Words that make me realize how angry I am. How angry I've been all day, and not just about what's happened to Anne. "He let that woman back into our lives. Not openly, which I could have handled. Surreptitiously. After reassuring me for years that she's better, suddenly he's sneaking around at night."

"I know. He told us."

I barely hear him. "We're oxygen, you said? In that case, he's the one who poisoned the goddamn air."

He shoves his hands into the pockets of his slacks, his head lowered. When he lifts it, his eyes are full of determination. "I don't think this was Sofia's doing."

I cross my arms, my posture tense. "Did she pass the polygraph?"

"She did," Quincy says. "I monitored it myself, and believe me when I say I have experience. We're going to do it again, as well. At least two more times."

"But that's not the point," Ryan says. "I don't believe it's in her to hurt Damien like that. Or Damien's child. I don't think you believe it, either. Two years ago, you told Jamie you thought she was doing better."

"Two years ago, she was." I remember the woman who asked permission to hold my eldest daughter. Who was kind and respectful and who apologized to me profusely. "A lot can change in two years. Did Damien tell you that she lost a baby?"

Ryan nods. "Yeah. And that's a factor. I still don't think it's her. And you know she's not the only suspect. Tell me who else it could be. Anyone we should turn our attention to."

I make a face. "Anyone looking to make money."

"You're thinking ransom," Quincy says. "Under the circumstances, who wouldn't be? But even most kidnappings for ransom originate with someone known to the family."

I nod, his words resonating. He's been working with Dallas for years, and in addition to being an MI-6 agent, he watched Dallas being snatched all those years ago. As much as anyone can, Quincy Radcliffe understands what I'm going through. A victim left behind.

"Who else should we look at?" he presses. "Doesn't matter how bloody outrageous you think it is. We have the manpower to investigate. Who's new to your life? Who's said something that felt off? Who has a grudge?"

I look between the two of them. "Have you asked Damien these questions?"

"We have," Quincy answers for both of them. "He's concerned about Marianna Kingsley, of course, and Richard Breckenridge."

I nod. "That sounds about right."

"And?"

I close my eyes, hating that I'd even think it, but they're right. I have to share any suspicions. "Eric, maybe," I say. "He used to work for me, and he's lost the job that he left me for. He's back, and..." I trail off with a shrug, hating that I'm even saying this.

"Anyone else?" Quincy asks me. His voice is gentle, but his words are firm. "No matter how far-fetched."

"I don't know." I drag my fingers through my hair. "I don't know. Carl Rosenfeld? He's held a grudge for a long-time, and then suddenly one of his old employees applied for a job with me."

"Who?" Ryan asks.

"Brian Crane. He's a programmer. I don't really think either of them—"

"Better we dig too deep than not deep enough," Quincy says, and I nod. I'm not going to argue with these guys. Whatever it takes to get Anne and Bree back, I'm on board with it.

"We don't know who's behind this, Nikki," Ryan says. "Or rather, we don't know *yet*. But there is one thing I'm sure of."

"What?" My voice is eager. Intense. Desperate for any scrap of hope.

"One way or another, this is connected to Damien."

The words hit me like a punch. I realize, of course, that he means Damien's money. But the bottom line is the same. My children are in danger because of who their father is.

"He's right," Quincy says. "And Nikki, I'm telling you right now that you're going to have to find a way to come to terms with that."

I nod slowly, numb.

I'm going to have to come to terms with that.

Yes, I am. And so, I think, is Damien.

I nod again, then head for the door, telling them I need to be alone. Except I already am alone. I pass through the living area, so full of people, many of whom were strangers before all of this. I feel shell-shocked, the walking wounded. My daughter is missing. Someone stole her. She's being punished for who her parents are. For her mother falling for Damien. For Damien choosing me.

I see him in the kitchen. He's holding a mug with two hands, his head bowed. I want to go to him—I almost turn that way. But I don't. I stay on my path, moving with purpose to our bedroom. To our massive closet.

There's a ladder like the kind in libraries, and I climb it, then find the old suitcase I'd shoved up there. I pull it down, then open it up to get to the leather case I'd hidden inside. I shouldn't have kept the case—I know that. I should have gotten rid of it. I'd meant to so many times, but each time I thought about it, I pulled it back. Because if the case is in the house and I don't use it, that means I'm strong.

Today, I'm not strong. Today, I'm weak.

Today, I'm going to take what I need.

The case is old, but the leather is polished to a sheen. I unzip it, remembering the horror when Sofia gave it to me. Remembering her taunts. But even then, the instruments were beautiful. Gleaming antique scalpels, lovingly tended, their blades as sharp as possible.

I want this.

This is why I've saved them. Because I knew—somehow, I just knew—that the day would come when I'd need them. When I'd have to cut to survive. When that pain would be the only rope that would get me through because Damien— oh, dear God—because Damien would be lost, too.

Slowly, I choose one of the scalpels. I lift it out from the indention into which it fits. I feel the comforting weight in my hand and I extend my arm.

Then reason grabs me. *Not my arm. They'll see.*

I stand up, then put the case on the island that takes up the middle of my closet. My fingers fumble for the button of my jeans, and I start to shimmy out of them. The denim is tight around my thighs, and I'm pushing the material down when I see my reflection in the full-length mirror.

I'm looking up, meeting my own eyes. And for a moment, I just stare.

Then I gasp, clamping my hand over my mouth before the gasp turns into a yell.

No.

No, no, no.

I don't have to do this.

I have the strength to fight this. Damien may be lost with me right now, but he's given me enough strength over the years. I'm *not* surrendering. I'm *not* doing this.

Wildly, I tug the jeans back up, then fasten them. I put the scalpel back in the case, and I'm about to shove the case into the little suitcase when my phone rings, so I toss the case into my underwear drawer, then pull my phone out from the pocket of my jeans, where it's been all day, a lifeline to Anne.

I race out of the closet and run through the room and into the hall. I'm breathless when I burst into the main living area just as the phone shrieks out a second ring. I look around for Damien, but I don't see him anywhere.

"The phone," I say stupidly as Ryan holds up his hand, not letting me answer just yet. He signals to his team—at all the men and women who will be monitoring this call. Tracing it if they can. My phone. Damien's phone. The house phone. Every phone held by every staff member— Gregory, the cleaning staff, the guards, the grounds folk. Every one of their calls routed through the control center, too.

"Ryan..." My finger hovers, desperate to answer. I don't recognize the number, but today that doesn't matter. I have to answer. I have to know. "*Ryan*. Please."

Denise—blonde and efficient—raises a hand in signal.

"*Go*," Ryan tells me, and I answer the call. "Hello? Hello?"

"Nikki?"

It's Bree. Her voice frantic. Hysterical.

"Bree?" I whisper as my knees go out.

The world turns gray and I start to fall. And for the first time in a long time, it isn't Damien who's there to catch me.

20

"I should have gone with them. Dammit, why the *fuck* didn't I insist on going with them?"

I'm pacing the first floor of the house, my phone out so that I can watch the dot that represents Damien move across the map. They're heading to Mulholland, which I find ironic considering where Damien found me when all of this started.

"Less chance the driver got picked up on a security camera," Dallas explained, before he, Quincy, Damien, and Ryan set out, tracking the burner phone that Bree's oh-so-polite kidnapper had left with her.

"You did insist," Jamie reminds me. "But there was no way that was happening, and we both know it."

"Guess not," I say resentfully. "I'm a grown woman. I'm Bree's employer and her friend, and I'm the mother of a child who's still missing." The pitch of my voice is rising with my hysteria, and I'm having a hell of a time dialing it back. I'm running on fumes. Saturday night, neither Damien nor I got much sleep. I don't even remember when

Sunday turned into Monday, and the sleep I did have was neither long nor restful.

"They're afraid it's a trap," Lyle says. "Damien's protecting you. They all are."

I want to tell him that's bullshit. But Lyle's one of the nicest guys I know, and so I keep my mouth shut and just nod instead, then brush my fingers over my lips as I remember the brush of Damien's goodbye kiss.

Dangerous, I think, and fight back a fresh wave of fear. Surely picking up Bree won't turn out to be dangerous. Surely, there won't be some tragedy that makes this kiss the last.

Riley's downstairs as well, though he's been standing quietly in the open doorway, looking out at the hills of Malibu that surround our property. His phone rings, the sharp sound combined with my lingering fear making me jump.

"Go ahead," he says into his phone, as I look at mine and see that the Damien dot has stopped somewhere on Mulholland near Sepulveda. I hold my breath, watching Riley, who talks in grunts and single syllables. Then he ends the call, looks at me, and says, "They got Bree. She's unharmed."

Jamie grabs my arm, and I go weak with relief, mixed together with my continuing fear for my daughter.

"This is good," Riley says, coming to stand in front of me. "Nikki, look at me."

I do as he orders. "This means we're dealing with someone who's not worried about a freed hostage leading us back to him."

I nod. That makes sense.

"And it also means that the likelihood we're dealing with

someone who snatched them for white trafficking has gone down as well."

"Unless they only traffic children," I say, my voice barely a whisper, as if voicing the fear will make it come true.

"Possible, but doubtful."

I look up at him, trying to decide if he means it, or if he's just trying to make me feel better.

"If that were the case, they'd most likely just kill Bree. Not set her free with a phone."

I nod agreement, because I already know this most likely isn't a trafficking situation. A belief that gives me some small amount of comfort.

From the moment we knew about the kidnapping, Ryan's team—and then later Dallas's people—have been watching the airports and bus stations and docks. Even the border into Mexico. But with the grab seeming to be so specific—and since the victim is Damien Stark's daughter— the assumption from the beginning was a kidnap for ransom. Now, with Bree's release, that seems even more likely.

The house phone rings from where it sits on a pedestal-style table next to the couch in the first floor living area. I glance at it, then hurry that direction. It's a replica of an old-fashioned phone, with a faux rotary dial and the kind of handset that appears to sit on a claw that extends up from the base.

"Wait," Riley says, and I nod, my heart pounding. This is it. This will be the ransom demand.

Riley taps his earpiece. "I need you locked on now, dammit." Then he nods at me, and I rush to answer.

"Hello?"

"Um, hi. This is Rory Claymore. Can I speak to Bree Bernstein, please?"

I frown, meeting Riley's gaze. He motions for me to continue talking. "Rory, it's Nikki Stark."

"Oh, wow. Mrs. Stark. Sorry. I didn't realize you'd answer. Bree gave me this number awhile back. She said her cell phone had crappy service in the kids' playroom."

I nod, numb. He's right about that.

"How can—why are you calling?"

There's a pause, and when he returns to the line, his confusion is clear. "Like I said. I'm trying to reach Bree."

I glance to Riley, who whispers instructions, so soft I'm practically reading his lips. Beside me, Jamie clutches my arm so tight I wince. "I'm sorry, Rory. She's not here."

"Oh." He sounds confused. "Listen, I'm kinda worried about her. We were supposed to watch Casablanca today, then go out after. I bought the tickets like a week ago. But she's not here, and I keep calling her cell, and she's not answering."

I close my eyes, adrenalin flowing out of me. This has nothing to do with the abduction. And all I want to do is hang up.

Instead, I do what Riley instructs. "She's not here," I say. "I'm not sure where she is. She has the day off."

"Oh. Shit."

"Maybe she's lost. If she calls, what theater are you at?"

"The Moviehouse," he says. "That new indie theater on Fairfax. They're doing retro movies all this week. Mrs. Stark, I'm kinda worried. This isn't like her."

"I'm sure she's fine," I say, keeping my voice light. "I'll have her call you the minute I see her."

"Yeah. Okay. Thanks."

I end the call, then look at Riley, who holds up a finger, then nods in response to something someone has said in his ear. "He's there. We have eyes on. He's pacing in front of the theater. Looking at his watch. Expression between worried and pissed."

"What? How?"

"Your husband employs talented people. And there are a lot of security cameras in this city, some of them on a government grid, some of them owned by private business owners. Almost all of them sending a wireless signal."

I swallow and nod, certain that whatever these people have done to get an image of Rory breaks about a dozen laws. And I really don't care.

"You okay?" Jamie asks from beside me.

I nod. I'd thought the call was news, and now that it's turned out to be nothing, I'm feeling hollow.

"What is it?" Riley's asking the question to Jamie, and when I look at her face, I can see why. Her brow is furrowed, and she's clearly considering something.

"He called her cell," Jamie says. "That got me thinking. The kidnapper destroyed her cell phone, right?"

I nod.

"Why give her another one?" She looks between me and Riley, then focuses on Lyle, who's stepped closer. "It's weird, right? Take her cell, but then hand her one. Why?"

Riley starts to answer, but I speak first. "Less chance the press will get involved," I say. "Or the police."

Jamie's brow furrows, and she shakes her head a fraction, clearly not following.

"If they just dump her, she'll knock on a door," I say. "That means explanations. Maybe she'll call the police. Or even if she doesn't, what if someone recognizes her as Damien Stark's nanny? Could end up being gossip. They don't want the press on this anymore than we do."

Jamie nods. "Okay. I get that."

I almost wish she didn't, because now there's just silence.

Silence, and the interminable wait for the men to return with Bree.

I pace the entryway a few more times, and when I can't stand that anymore, I go outside and walk back and forth in front of the house, ending up at the flower garden on the north edge. It's a small plot, but well-tended, filled with colorful flowers that surround a splash of yellow daisies in the middle.

I drop to my knees, then reach out and gently brush the yellow petals. *Ashley.* The flowers were a sympathy gift from Jamie and Ryan after my miscarriage, when I lost the baby that Damien and I had named Ashley, in honor of my sister. It had been Damien's idea to plant the flowers outside where they could thrive in the sunlight, and where we could come sit on the little stone bench and know our baby was at peace.

"Watch over your sister," I whisper, as tears cling to my lashes. "Please, please, let her be safe."

I don't know how long I stay there on my knees, but I don't stand until I hear Jamie calling for me.

"They're here," she says, as I run toward her, watching the black Range Rover pull in past the guard station, then come to a stop in front of the house. Damien's driving, and he kills the engine, then both he and Ryan get out.

The windows are tinted, so I can't see into the back, but a moment later, the doors open and Ryan helps Bree down from the rear passenger seat. Quincy and Dallas get out on the other side, and I run forward, then envelop Bree in a hug, which she enthusiastically returns.

"I'm so sorry," she says. "I'm so, so sorry."

"It's not your fault," I tell her. "It's not."

"I didn't want to leave her." Her face is splotchy, and I

can tell that she's been crying. Now the tears start up again. "He made me leave her."

"I know. I know," I say, looking at Damien as I pull her close. *He*. Does that mean she's certain? Does that mean she saw their abductor clearly?

As if he's read my mind, Damien shakes his head, then comes up beside us. I feel the comforting pressure of his hand sliding over my back as he guides me into the house while Ryan steers Bree through the door in front of us.

"What did she tell you about Anne?" I ask Damien, my voice low. "She's safe? Are they feeding her? Does she know where she was? Can she describe the kidnapper? Does she know when he's going to ask for ransom?"

"As far as she knows, Anne is fine. The rest we'll talk about upstairs." He speaks in a low voice, his tone gentle. But his gaze on Bree's back is hard and cold. And I'm suddenly afraid of what I'm going to hear.

We sit in the living area, Ryan's team still gathered around the conference table as the group that retrieved Bree, plus me, Jamie, Lyle, and Riley, sit on the plush furniture. I stand, occasionally sitting on the armrest of Damien's chair, where he sits straight, like an emperor on a throne.

"Please," Bree says from where she is curled up on the center of the couch, her knees pulled up and her arms wrapped around them. "Can I see Lara before I have to go through it all again?"

"Of course," I say, while Damien says, "Later," at exactly the same time.

"Just a few questions first," Quincy says. "We don't want you to lose any details that might help Anne."

"But we talked in the car."

"We need to go over it again," Quincy says firmly. Bree

nods, her eyes darting to mine. I smile encouragement, willing her to remember something helpful.

"Tell us again what happened," Dallas says.

Bree nods, then tells the story I already know, adding very little to what Ryan extrapolated from the security cameras.

"But you have no idea who grabbed you?" Ryan presses.

She shakes her head. "He wore pantyhose over his face. And makeup. Like really red lipstick and that black eye stuff that football players use. And there were red streaks all over his face. I guess it was supposed to make him even more unrecognizable than just the hose. Oh," she adds, "the ball cap was from Universal Studios, but I guess that's easy enough to get around here."

The men continue their questions, with Ryan and Dallas speaking in calm, soothing tones, and Damien's questions coming harder. Crisper. So much so that I reach over to rest my hand on his wrist. I understand how tense he is, but that can't possibly be helping Bree, who's already endured so much.

Through the questioning, we learn that the kidnapper is probably a male. That he never spoke directly. Everything he said to her was pre-recorded and played back with some sort of voice altering filter.

She and Anne were kept together in a room in what she thinks is a house on a large lot. She heard no neighbors, no traffic. And she believes it was a basement, since there were no windows. If that's so, it could narrow things down, as basements aren't common in Southern California. She thinks it was less than an hour from where they were snatched, but she wouldn't swear to it.

"Could be a wine cellar," Riley suggests.

"Or misdirection," Damien says, though I don't understand what he means.

The room had toys for Anne and a single mattress on the floor. A bathroom was attached, but had no mirror and no door. She thinks a camera was mounted in the ceiling light fixture but isn't certain.

They got food at regular intervals, and always had enough bottled water. He also made Anne drink something that made her drowsy. "I don't think was anything bad, though. And she seemed less scared."

When pressed, she added that the guy had narrow hips and a flat ass, but a broad chest and a large belly. And he favored one leg.

"Could be a disguise," Quincy says. "But everything helps."

As soon as they were snatched, he made Bree cover her face with a sewn-closed ski mask, then used duct tape to tie her hands. He blindfolded Anne and told her it was a game, but he didn't tie her hands as far as Bree knows.

"Thank you, Bree," Dallas says as they wrap up. "I know how hard all this is."

"It's okay. Whatever you need. If it helps Anne, I'll do whatever you need."

"Would you like to see Lara now?" Jamie asks, then leads her to the bedroom where Moira and Lara are tucked away.

I'm sitting on the arm of Damien's chair, my hand in his. But as soon as we hear the door closing, Damien stands up, releasing me. He turns to face me, his expression hard. "This time is for show," he says. "It doesn't happen again."

I stare at him, uncomprehending, then look to Ryan and Dallas to see if they know what he's talking about. From their expressions, it's clear that they do.

I shake my head, my eyes moving among all of them.

Quincy and Riley, too. Everyone, apparently, except me. "What the hell, Damien? What are you talking about?"

"*Her*. I don't want her anywhere near our daughter."

I gape at him, so shocked I slide off the chair and have to catch myself before I hit the floor. "Are you insane? She was kidnapped!"

He captures me with his eyes. "Was she? Or was she part of it?"

I open my mouth to protest, then close it again. I don't want to believe it. I don't want this tragedy to make me think the worst of people I've come to love.

But I trust Damien. I trust his instincts. Even if I desperately hope that he's wrong.

"She stays," Damien says. "But she stays in the guesthouse with a guard watching her twenty-four/seven."

"And if she disagrees?" I ask.

"Then you have to let her walk," Charles says from where he'd been silently taking in everything. "Otherwise it's false imprisonment." His eyes move among all of us. "You can't kidnap someone just because you think they're a kidnapper. If she says no, you either let her leave … or you involve the police. And neither option is ideal."

21

"You don't really think that?" We're standing in the living area, and Bree's voice rises to a frantic pitch as she clutches my hands and looks into my eyes. "I love those little girls. I haven't—I didn't—"

I press my lips together. I don't want to believe it. I don't. But Damien's right. There's a risk. And maybe there were even signs.

"I'm sorry," I say, holding firm. "But you've been acting strange, Bree. I've noticed it for a few weeks."

She shakes her head, her eyes wide, but she doesn't say anything.

"I—I don't want to believe it. But we can't risk our daughter." I draw a deep breath. "Damien and I stand together on this."

"Acting strange." She makes a scoffing noise. "Of course. Isn't that just perfect?"

"What?"

"Doesn't matter. I'm going to my cell." She tilts her head, indicating Ryan's team. "Who's my babysitter?"

Michael, a lanky black guy with a serious expression

and a sleeve of tats stands up. He doesn't say a word, just waits for Bree to head toward the guest house.

She takes a few steps toward the stairs, then stops and turns back. "The irony is that I was acting weird because I love it here so much. I didn't want to leave. But I didn't know how to tell you guys that I wanted to stay instead of going to New York for grad school." Tears stream down her cheeks. "Seemed wrong, somehow, since you guys were so supportive."

I swallow. "Bree..."

"Yeah, well. Whatever." She looks from Michael to Ryan. "Does the prisoner get to use her phone? Can I have guests? Like, can Rory come over? And do me the courtesy of telling me if there are cameras in my bedroom."

"No cameras," I say, then hope I'm not lying. "And you can have guests. You can leave the guest house for the grounds," I add. "But you can't say anything about the kidnapping. That could put Anne in danger."

The fire fades from her eyes, and she nods. "Right. Of course."

Throughout it all, Damien's said nothing. He's simply watched her from where he's now sitting on the sofa. She meets his eyes, and I see her lips press tight together. I know him well enough to see the doubt on his face. But doubt isn't enough to make him back off. Not with Anne's safety on the line.

I doubt, too. But I stand with Damien, just like I told Bree.

"Briefing," Ryan says, his attention on his team. "Everyone not reporting in, go take a ten minute break."

The team scatters, with some leaving for the kitchen or bathrooms, and some coming to the living area where the rest of us are gathered.

Damien rises, then pulls me into his arms. He says nothing, but he holds me close, his arms tight around me, and I melt against him, needing his strength. Right now, though, he feels broken, too, and he clings to me the same way that I cling to him, each of us searching for strength in the other. And I'm afraid, so terribly afraid, that there's not enough between us.

I TRY to focus on the voices as Quincy paces the room, running through what we know, who they've investigated, what they think. But it's too much of a blur. Anne dominates my thoughts, terror cutting through me. Minutes are ticking away, we still haven't had a ransom demand, my nanny may be involved, and I'm helpless. So goddamn helpless.

And Damien is helpless, too.

I'm sitting on the floor, my knees pulled up to my chest. He's standing by the window, looking out at the ocean. He looks tall. Commanding. But it's all an act. I know him too well. There's defeat in his posture. And that terrifies me most of all.

"—with Jeremiah," Charles says, yanking my attention back to the meeting. Jeremiah Stark is Damien and Jackson's father. And I wouldn't put it past him to kidnap his grandchild if he thought there was an upside for him.

Damien turns as well. "What did you say?"

"I said that Jeremiah's had several surreptitious meetings with Richard Breckenridge. My people did some poking around, and it appears that he's invested heavily with Breckenridge."

Damien's face hardens. "Before, you mean. Before Anne was taken?"

"Well before," Charles says, his voice heavy with meaning. "And it was a significant investment."

I'm not sure I understand, but I can see the news disturbs Damien, and I go to him, comforted when he pulls me close.

"So Jeremiah also lost a ton when The Domino fell through for Breckenridge," Ryan says, nodding to himself. "They could be in it together, or either one of them could be acting on his own."

"You really think that Breckenridge could be behind this?" I ask. "For a failed investment?"

Charles looks at Damien. "You didn't tell her?"

I look between them, panic rising. "Tell me what?"

For a moment, there's complete silence in the room. Then Damien shoves his hands into his pockets. He looks first at the floor, then at me. "Breckenridge told me he'd destroy me when I cut him out of The Domino. He said that he'd make sure I got knocked off my pedestal. That he'd hit me where it hurts."

I open my mouth to speak, but it's gone completely dry. I lick my lips and try again. "And you didn't think to tell me that?" My voice sounds far away. Hollow.

"Nikki." There's a plea in his tone as he steps toward me. *Broken,* I think again. *How can Damien be broken*? "Nikki, please."

I realize that I've taken a step backward, my head shaking from side to side. "All your talk about trust," I say. "All your demands." I wrap my arms around myself, thinking about Masque. About trusting him so wholly. So completely. And about him needing that same trust from me.

"How can you not have told me this? If not before, then after we found the notes on my car and graffiti on my walls?

And Anne? Did you just not think about it after our daughter was taken? How the hell could you not tell me?"

I turn in a circle, feeling lost, my hands going into my hair, and I pull on it, as if I can tug the pain free. The loss.

"Nikki, please. I never thought—"

"Damn right," I snap, then lift a hand. "Just stop. Just *stop.*"

Across the room, Jamie's phone rings, and all heads turn to her. She glances at the screen, then looks up at Ryan. "It's Ollie," she says. "Can I answer?"

Ryan nods. Jamie's phone isn't hooked into the network, so she's the only one hearing the conversation. I wish it was on speaker. I want to hear him. I need him. Other than Damien, Jamie and Ollie are my rocks, and although we've drifted apart, now that his call has put him firmly in my mind, I realize how empty I feel without having him here to lean on.

"We can't," Jamie says. Her voice is tight, obviously on the verge of tears. "No—everything's terrible. I'm—yes. I'm at Nikki's. Can you come over?" She nods. "I'll tell you when you get here. See you soon."

She hangs up and looks at me. "Ollie just got to town. He's at Upper Crust. He wanted us to meet him."

I nod. He doesn't know, of course. How could he since we've managed to keep it out of the press? And while I don't want to relive everything that's happened, at the same time, I want my friend beside me.

"You've been working him too hard," Jamie says to Charles, who frowns.

"Ollie hasn't worked for the firm in almost two months," Charles tells her.

"Oh." Jamie frowns, meeting my eyes, as confused as I am. "Well, I just assumed."

"Maybe he was embarrassed to tell us he lost his job?" I direct the question toward Charles, who shakes his head.

"He wasn't terminated. Ollie was doing well."

I'm baffled, and I glance toward Damien out of habit and am surprised by the expression on his face. As if he's puzzling something out. As if pieces are falling into place.

"Damien?"

He lifts his head, his gaze steady on mine. "I'm not sure he was. Doing well, I mean."

I think about his house. What Jamie said about his debt. I swallow. This is one of my best friends we're talking about.

Damien looks at Ryan, who looks miserable. Ryan swallows, then looks between Jamie and me. Then he turns to Quincy, who rubs his chin. It's been a while since he shaved, and I hear the sandpaper-like sound of his hand over the scruff.

"Bloody hell," Quincy says. "Ollie's been in town since yesterday."

"So what?" Jamie says. Then her eyes widen. "Wait, you've been looking at Ollie for the kidnapping? You guys seriously already have Orlando McKee on your suspect list? Like he would ever—*ever*—hurt Nikki. That's bullshit. That is total, fucking bullshit."

I'm glad she's saying it, because I feel too lost to even capture my own thoughts. Like the nightmare is spinning me down into a deep, deep vortex, and there's no one there to throw me a rope. Not even Damien.

"Him saying that he just got into town could mean anything," Jamie continues. "It doesn't mean he's been sneaking around kidnapping children. He's not obligated to ring us the second he gets off a plane."

"He asked me for money," Damien says, and I turn to him in shock. "Fifty grand. About a month ago."

I blink, trying to focus. To understand. "Did you give it to him?"

A moment passes, then another. Then Damien shakes his head. "No."

I sit. "I see." I draw in a breath. "One of my best friends. The friend who got me through all that bullshit with Kurt."

Damien flinches, as does Jamie. They're the only two in the room who know what I'm talking about. How Kurt ripped me apart because of my cutting all those years ago. And how Ollie held me and soothed me and put me back together. He was there for me before Damien was. Hell, if it wasn't for Ollie—and Jamie—I'm not sure I would have Damien now. I'm not sure I'd have anything now.

"My friend asks you for help—for an amount that means *nothing* to you. And not only do you turn him down, but you don't even tell me."

"It's not what you think," he says.

"No," I agree. "It's worse." Everything is piling on. Brick after brick, wearing me down until I feel like I'm going to get hammered right into the ground. Until I'm going to get sucked under and disappear altogether.

"*Nikki*." Damien is in front of me, his hands on my upper arms. "It's not what you think," he says again. "And we will get her back."

I want to believe him, but I'm too lost. Too scared. And instead of speaking, I make a strangled gasping sound, then wrench myself out of his grip. My hand goes over my mouth as I hurry toward the girls' room, only to be intercepted by Evelyn.

"Whoa there, Texas. It's going to be okay."

I wish I could believe her, but all I can do is shake my head. Secrets and lies and obfuscation. It never ends. It just never fucking ends. "I thought I was stronger than this," I say.

"You are," she says. "What you two are going through would break anybody. But you're not broken, Texas," she says. "A little bent, maybe."

I actually smile, and it feels good. A random thought comes into my head, and I tilt my head as I look at Evelyn. "Are you the one keeping the press out of this? Or have we just got lucky that they haven't caught wind of it yet?"

Evelyn Dodge is a powerhouse in this town. She's held every job imaginable, including publicity. Now she works as an agent, representing Lyle and Jamie, among many others. "See? You are lucky. I would have heard if they knew," she said. "So far, crickets. And I'll do my best to keep it that way."

"Good. I figured," I add. "If it was out there, her bosses would have Jamie in front of me with a microphone."

"What? Oh. Yes. Of course, they would."

I watch Evelyn's face, and feel my own crumple. "You, too?" I ask.

She frowns, clearly baffled by my question.

"Everyone's trying to protect me. I hoped you'd be straight. For that matter, considering you're a powerhouse of an agent, I figured you were a better liar. But something's going on with Jamie that you're not telling me."

She snorts. "And that's why I love you, Texas."

"So?"

She looks miserable as she steers me to the relative privacy of the kitchen. "She didn't want you to worry, so you say nothing. You swear?"

I nod, pretty sure I know what's coming. "Lacey Dunlop? They fired Jamie and put in Lacey Dunlop?"

Evelyn shakes her head. Not in denial, but in disbelief.

"Jamie's so much better, but those asshats wouldn't know real talent if it was sucking their collective dicks."

I bite my lip to keep from laughing. Because, honestly, it's not funny at all. "What's she going to do?"

Evelyn waves away my words. "Right now, she's here for you. That's an exact quote, by the way. And after Anne is back and safe and happy, I'll send her out on interviews. She'll end up with a better gig and more money, and fuck them."

"I like that plan." I fear it's too optimistic, though. I know how competitive the market is. And if her station deemed her less appealing than Lacey Dunlop...

I let the thought go. For the time being, at least, my best friend's career is the least of my worries. But, damn, I love her for putting me and my family first.

22

We're all waiting downstairs when the guard escorts Ollie into the house. Naturally skinny, he's filled out since the last time I saw him. His wavy hair is long again, almost brushing his shoulders, and he's pulled it back in a man-bun, which surprisingly suits him.

Beside me, I feel Damien tense, and I reach down, curling my fingers around his wrist. Ollie's brow is furrowed —why wouldn't it be? He's never needed a guard to come inside before—and when his eyes find mine, the spillway opens and I start crying, the tears I've fought off for hours now coming in full force.

"Nikki?" His eyes go to Damien, hard and hot. "What the hell have you done to her?"

It's as if his words have lit a fire, and Damien bursts forward, one hand on Ollie's chest pushing him back against the wall, the other on his throat, holding him there.

"Damien! Stop!" I have no idea how I get across the room, but I'm there before even Quincy or Ryan, and I grab his arm and tug him back. Or I try to. He's like stone.

Seconds later, Ryan wrestles him off, and Damien backs away, his face a mass of fury, Ollie's colored with confusion.

"What the hell?" He looks wildly around at all of us. "Jesus Christ, what the hell is going on?"

"Anne's been kidnapped," I say. The words seem too tame, the syllables too mundane for all the fear that is tied up inside those three little words.

"Oh, God." He reaches back, his hands sliding down the wall as he drops down, ending up splayed on the ground with his legs out in front of him. "Kidnapped? *Kidnapped*? And you don't call the police? You don't pull in the FBI?"

He closes his eyes, his face painted in horror as he draws in deep breaths. "How?" he finally asks. "Who?"

No one says a word, and I watch as Ollie's eyes sweep the room. As realization dawns.

"Oh, *fuck*. Seriously?" His eyes meet mine, then search out Jamie, standing behind me at the base of the stairs. "No way. You two know me. There's no way I'd hurt her. She's my niece. Maybe not by blood, but she's my niece. And you know that," he adds, pointing at Damien. "Whatever differences we've had, you *know* that."

"Damien," I say gently. "Please. Trust me. It's not Ollie."

"Tell you what," Damien says, looking at Ollie, not me. "I'll trust Ollie. If he takes a lie detector test."

"Damien…"

He turns to me. "Why not? Sofia took it. Passed it. Now you feel better about her."

Better is a relative term, but I am at least sure that she didn't take my baby. She's still around, though. Holed up in one of the first floor bedrooms, staying out of the way until this is over. I know Damien has gone down to see her once or twice. I'm content to try and forget she's in the house.

Still, I suppose Damien makes a good argument. "It's

fair," I tell Ollie. "You know I believe you, but just take the polygraph."

I wait, expecting him to sigh and roll his eyes, then complain and agree.

He doesn't. All he says is, "No."

"Ollie. Please."

"Fuck that," he says generally. "And fuck you," he adds to Damien.

"Orlando," Charles says. "You're being unreasonable."

"Maybe. But you're no longer my boss." He draws a breath as he looks around the room full of men, several of whom wear shoulder holsters. "I'm guessing I can't just go back to my hotel."

"Don't worry," Damien says, his voice deceptively calm. "We got plenty of room."

THE HOUSE IS full of people. Friends. Family.

Damien.

Everyone is here. So many people I care about. So many who care about me.

And I still feel completely alone.

It's close to two, and I've spent the last hour in the girls' room playing with Lara while Moira took a break.

Now I'm standing alone on the balcony looking out at the Pacific. I feel numb. I feel raw. And the only thing that changes when Damien comes up behind me and pulls me close is that I no longer feel alone.

I lean back against him, letting his strength flow through me. Wishing he had enough for the both of us. Wishing that he had enough to simply will her to be home again.

How often have I thought that about him? That he commands the universe. That the world bends to his will?

But it's not true. My husband is as mortal as I am, and I'm not sure if that's a comfort or a tragedy.

"We'll get her back." His lips brush my hair as he speaks, his voice rumbling through me. "I promise you, I'll get her back."

I want to believe him, but I can't quite manage. "Why haven't we heard anything? We should have a ransom demand by now."

"I know. I'm worried, too."

I turn in his arms, surprised by the admission, my heart breaking even more from the pain on his face.

"It's been longer than twenty-four hours." It's the first time I've voiced this fear. "I've always heard that—"

He presses a finger to my lips. "We'll get her back."

Our eyes meet and an eternity passes. Then I nod. *We'll get her back.*

"What does Dallas say?"

"He thinks the demand will come today. They released Bree as a show of good faith. Next, they'll demand the money."

"She must be so scared." My voice shakes, reflecting my own terror.

Damien closes his eyes, then silently nods.

His phone buzzes, the tone signaling a call from the guard tower. His brow creases as he takes the call, then he rubs his temples. "Blaine's here to install the painting," he tells me, then tells the guard to let him pass.

"Oh." I blink, uncomfortably reminded of life going on beyond these walls. "We never did say where we want it. Have him take it to the bungalow."

Damien agrees, and we go back inside. I'm prepared to

go down to meet Blaine, but I don't really want to. Apparently, Damien doesn't either, because he signals to Evelyn, who hurries over, still looking put together even though she spent the night in a chair despite our offer of a guest room.

"Would you mind going with Blaine to the bungalow. He's at the guard station right now. He'll be installing a painting."

"Oh." She glances sideways at me, and I'm sure she's thinking about my father. A wave of guilt cuts through me—I haven't told Frank about Anne. But I know he'd come back, and then what? It's not as if he can do anything more than is already being done.

Besides, I tell myself that she'll be back before he could even get on a plane.

I'm not entirely sure where my father and Evelyn are in their relationship. I'm not even sure if there is a relationship. Maybe they're just friends. Maybe Evelyn is just hopeful. Maybe I'm imagining things.

I'm not entirely sure what happened between Blaine and Evelyn, either. Or how they left things. But I can tell by the look in her eye that she misses him.

That look—that small, innocent look—lodges in my gut and brings tears to my eyes, a harsh reminder of the world outside my bubble. A world beyond Anne. A world of intertwined relationships and friendships and love and pain. And while I resent that Evelyn could be thinking about anyone other than my daughter, in that moment, I want her to have love, whether it's with my father or Blaine or someone else entirely.

"Aw, Texas, honey. Come here." She pulls me close, assuming, I'm sure, that my tears are for my daughter. Not realizing that they're for everything. For all the pain. And, yes, for all the hope, too. "It'll be over soon. You'll have your baby back."

I sigh, then release her, my smile wobbly.

"Come with me," Damien says, then leads me past the conference table. Past the clusters of exhausted friends and Stark security personnel. Past the kitchen and the smell of too much coffee and too many sugary donuts. Where Gregory is trying valiantly to keep everyone fed and the place reasonably tidy.

He takes me into our bedroom, then pulls me onto the bed with him. Then he holds me close, my back pressed against him, his lips brushing my hair, his hand on my hip.

I feel like I should protest. To tell him that we have to get up. We have to *do*. But I don't. I relax against him. Because right now, this is what we need. To try and be strong together.

We stay like that for a while, and I'm about to doze off when his low whisper rouses me. "Are you still angry about the painting?"

I frown, then turn in his arms. "You knew about that?"

A smile—albeit a small one—touches his lips. "I wanted the painting. I bought the painting. And you were worried about the kids growing up in a world where they can write a check for anything they want."

"That's not the real world," I say, not sure if I'm pleased or frustrated that I'm so transparent. "But I've thought about it more. And that's not really what you do."

His brows rise. "Isn't it?"

I allow myself a small smile. "Well, maybe a little. But mostly you buy things that mean something to you." I think about the first editions of Ray Bradbury books he has in the library on the mezzanine. I think about the portrait of me that hangs on this floor, and about the one that Blaine's installing right now. A painting that Damien bought to lock in the memory of our first night. Extravagant, maybe. But not foolish. And what does extravagant mean, anyway? God knows Damien can afford those things. It's not as if we'll all go hungry. Maybe extravagance really is relative.

I sigh, trying to organize my thoughts. "I just...I just want us to be better parents than ours were."

He nods. "I know."

Silence lingers, and I know we're both thinking the same thing. We're thinking of Anne.

"Damien, I—"

He shakes his head, cutting me off. "You're wrong, anyway."

I tilt my head, confused. "About what?"

"About what my money can buy. Billions," he says, his voice heavy with disgust. "And I can't get her back." He shifts, propping himself up on his elbow, his expression haunted. "Do you think it doesn't kill me that this is a problem I can't solve with either my mind or my money? That there is nothing—nothing—I can grab onto here. Nothing I can make right. Nothing I can fix. How am I supposed to live with that, Nikki?"

His throat moves as he swallows, the sound wet with unshed tears.

"Nikki," he says as my heart breaks. "I don't think I can—"

"*Yes.*" I reach for him, clutching his hand. I think of the scalpel. Of what I overcame. Of what we've both survived. "Yes," I repeat. "*We* can."

I'm looking into his eyes, and he looks back into me. His eyes are flat at first, and then I see a hint of something. A spark of determination.

"Nikki," he says. And then his mouth is on mine. I twine

my fingers in his hair and tug him closer, our tongues battling in a heated, desperate kiss. We need this. Both of us. Heat. Passion. Wildness.

We need to burn away the fear. To push through the dark shadows. We won't survive this without each other, and we both need to take and take and give.

"I can't wait," he says, breaking apart to tear at my clothes. "Christ, Nikki, I can't wait."

"I know." I push his hands away, my own more nimble, and I strip while he does the same, finally kicking off his jeans with one final, impatient thrust.

I grab his shoulders, pulling him down on top of me as I fall back onto the bed, then pull my knees up to my chest. "Hurry," I beg, because this isn't about making love. This is about sex. Connection.

About need and fear and loss and escape.

Escape. God, yes. Right now, that's what I need from Damien, and I whimper in frustration when he takes his time sliding over me, his cock right there at my entrance, but not inside me. "Please," I beg. "Take me. Take me hard."

For a beat, he looks at me. Then he grabs my hips and tugs me down the bed. I gasp when he flips me over, then orders me onto my knees, my head down, my forehead on the mattress.

He's behind me, his hands on my breasts, gripping me so tight it's almost painful, and I close my eyes, relishing his touch, wanting exactly this. To be used. To be his.

He pulls one hand away long enough to slide his fingers over my core, readying me before thrusting his cock hard and deep inside me. Then he's bent over me, his chest to my back, and he's thrusting hard inside me, the entire bed moving, hitting the wall, probably echoing through the whole damn house. But I don't care.

This is what I need. What I crave.

This. This connection. It's what will give me the strength to survive. I know that. And Damien knows it, too.

His fingers stroke my clit with each thrust, and we're so connected that I can feel every spasm in his body. Every hint of tension as he comes closer and closer to release. To exploding.

"Nikki." He groans my name, his free hand closing around my neck as he pounds into me, harder and harder, until I can't tell where I end and he begins. Until I'm nothing but a volatile mixture of pleasure and pain on the verge of combustion.

And then—oh, dear God, and then—the explosion comes, violent and intense and so damn perfect. My body shakes, my muscles clenching around him, pulling him deeper inside me until I feel his body tighten and hear him cry my name as he explodes inside me, then collapses to the side, pulling me down and holding me tight against him.

I roll over to face him, my breath coming hard, my heart beating fast.

My body starts to cool, my sanity returning.

And as it does, so does reality. These few minutes of forgetfulness swept away as my mind fills again with Anne.

I'm stronger now, but still my mind drifts to everything we have. And to everything I can't bear to lose.

"Damien," I whisper.

"I know," he says. "We'll get—"

He rolls over, diving to the ground as I sit bolt upright, yanked back to full reality by the ringing of his phone.

Damien rips the phone out of the back pocket of his crumpled jeans as someone pounds on our closed door. "Take the call!" Ryan yells as I scramble back into my clothes. "We're set!"

And then, with one sharp look at me, Damien presses the button and puts the caller on speaker.

At first there's nothing. Then the staticky, voice-altered words ring out:

"Do you want your daughter back?"

23

"What do you want?" Damien's voice is ice cold, his words a demand, not a question.

He's in his element now, taking charge. Commanding. If the kidnapper were standing in the room, I have no doubt he'd bend to the force of Damien's will.

But we're not in the same room. And all we have to go on is an altered voice. And whatever information the team can pull from this phone call.

"Two million dollars," the mechanical voice says. "Small bills. Delivered tonight. Seven o'clock."

"It's already almost five," Damien says. "I can't pull that much together that quickly."

"Bullshit. That's chump change for you. I'd bet my own mother's life you've had at least that much pulled and ready to go since this whole party began. Don't play games with me, Mr. Stark. It won't be you or me who loses. It'll be your little girl."

I'm holding Damien's arm, and now my hand tightens. The kidnapper is right about the money. Damien arranged for five million in small bills to be delivered within an hour after we learned what happened. It's been sitting in the utility room ever since.

Damien looks at Dallas, who nods.

"I'll get it," Damien says. "But I want to talk to Anne. I need to know she's unharmed."

"I'll call you back."

And *click*, the line goes dead.

"He's afraid we can trace the call," Quincy says.

"Can we?" I ask.

"Theoretically." Quincy shrugs. "But this isn't theory. So no."

I look to Ryan, wanting an explanation.

"He's undoubtedly calling from a burner phone," Ryan explains. "And he'll call back from another one. If we had the time, we could triangulate the location of the phone, but he's not going to stay on line long enough for us to do that. So—"

"It's doable, but not doable," I say. "I get it."

"Keep the endgame in mind," Dallas says. "This is about getting your daughter back. An exchange of money for the child. There's a difference between information we want and information we need. Right now, we need to talk to Anne. We need to know how the drop's going to go down."

I nod. "And you think he'll really make the exchange? What if he just takes the ransom and disappears. What if—" But I can't finish the thought.

Dallas moves closer, so that he's right in front of me. "This isn't an action movie. And in the real world, there are very few kidnappings for ransom. And most are resolved favorably."

"Meaning?"

"The child is returned."

Warm relief floods me.

"And the kidnapper?"

"Sometimes apprehended, sometimes not. But we're focused on Anne." He points to his eyes, then mine. "That's all we're looking at right now. That little girl."

"Yes," I say, sniffling to hold back the tears that are starting up again. I meet Damien's eyes. "Yes, that's all I want."

The phone rings, and I jump. Ryan holds up a finger, then signals to Damien once the team is set to record and monitor the call. He answers on speaker.

"Mommy?"

My legs fall away, and Jamie rushes to my side.

"Anne, baby. I'm right here. So's Daddy."

"No more Nemo." Her voice sounds drowsy. "Want kitties next time."

I search Damien's face, seeing my own confusion registered there.

Then I remember. "*Aristocats*? Is that what you want?"

"Risto," she says, still sounding loopy. "Please, Mommy."

"Whatever you want, baby." I can barely talk through the tears. "Mommy and Daddy love you."

"Love—"

And the phone goes dead.

"He'll call back," Quincy says. And five seconds later, the phone rings again.

"What did you do to my daughter?" Damien demands without preamble.

"Just making it easier on her. A little Versed to keep her calm. And lots of cartoons. She's fine. You should thank me. She probably won't remember this whole ordeal."

Damien's face goes tight with worry. "You're drugging my daughter? You son-of-a-bitch."

"Hey! I'm being nice. The kid's totally chill, and she's

going to barely remember any of this. You'll have her back soon enough, no harm, no foul. So long as you cooperate."

I see the control it takes for him not to reach through the phone and strangle the guy. I feel the same. He could give her too much of the drug. She could have a reaction. Anything could go wrong and—

"It'll be okay." Jamie stops my pacing, her hands on my arms. I didn't even realize I was moving. "It'll be okay," she repeats, which is ridiculous, because she doesn't know that. But she has to believe it. And so do I.

I concentrate on breathing as Damien comes to me. He draws me close, and I stand with him, our bodies tense, as Anne's tormentor gives the instructions.

"Two million. Two rolling suitcases. Black. No hidden GPS systems. No tracking devices. You take the cases at midnight, and you leave them in the laundry room at the Carousel Inn on Lankershim in North Hollywood. Use a bike lock and lock them to the plumbing pipe. Lock the cases, too. Combination 123. Got it?"

"Got it."

"Then you leave."

"And then?"

"Five minutes. Your final call. Gee, this is exciting, isn't it?"

Once again, the line goes dead.

"No," Quincy says, his eyes hard on Damien before they cut to me. "We're not surveilling. It's too damn risky."

For a moment, I think Damien's going to argue, but he nods, and I exhale in relief.

I pace as we wait for the next call, and when I see Evelyn climb the stairs, I hurry to her side, letting her pull me into the kind of maternal hug I so desperately crave. "How are you holding up, Texas?"

"I don't know," I say. "Right now it feels like I'm learning to walk. We're taking a step, then another, then another."

She gestures to the cluster of men and Jamie. "Bring me up to speed," she's says, then listens as I do. "Quincy's right. Do as the bastard says. This is a payday for him. He wants the money, not Anne."

"I know." I've been telling myself the same thing since this nightmare began.

The phone rings.

Damien waits, gets the signal from the team, and answers on speaker.

"The southwest corner of Ventura and Laurel Canyon. Your wife stands there. She comes alone."

I freeze, my attention glued to the phone.

"Eleven-forty-five to one in the morning. They'll be a sniper on her. I get wind of anybody near the laundry room after the drop—I have even the slightest suspicion that surveilling the laundry or you have thoughts about tracking that money—she gets a bullet in the chest. Everything goes smooth at the laundry, she'll be fine. You'll get your daughter back in the morning. You fuck with me in the laundry room—or you send a female cop to the corner or no one shows at all—you never see your little girl again."

"No." Damien's voice is deceptively calm. "I'll do it. I'll stand there. Goddammit it, you already have my daughter. Not my wife, too."

The line, however, is dead.

He turns to me, his eyes haunted.

"I'm doing it," I say. "What other choice do we have?"

24

"So this is it," Jamie says, hugging herself. "I get dropping the money, obviously, but for Nikki to just stand on the street like a walking target?" A shiver cuts through her, and she wraps the oversized sweater she's been wearing tighter around herself. "That's messed up."

"I'll be fine," I say, and I'm pleased with the fact that my voice doesn't shake. I'm scared, no doubt about that. But not getting Anne back scares me more. So I'm doing this.

I meet Damien's eyes, and although I see my own fear reflected back, I also see determination and acceptance. He knows as well as I do that I have to do this.

"We'll have eyes on the whole time," Quincy says, moving down the length of the conference table to where I'm standing beside Jamie.

Damien's behind Denise, looking down at her computer monitor. I can't see it, but I know she's trying to analyze the voice pattern. Trying to remove the distortion and cut down to the kidnapper's real voice. It's a long shot, and no one expects it to work. But we have to try.

Now, Damien looks up sharply, nailing Quincy with a

long, hard gaze. "Eyes on? The hell we will. He specifically said that Nikki had to come alone."

"She will."

From the opposite end of the table, Ryan taps a monitor. "Traffic cameras. And so far we've hacked into three private security feeds in the area. We're up to about fifty percent coverage of that corner right now. By the drop, I'll get us above ninety. We'll have eyes on you, Nikki. We'll be right there with you."

They won't be, I know. If something happens to me, even with the helicopter and men waiting down the block, they couldn't respond in time. But despite all that, knowing they'll be able to see me gives me some comfort.

Evelyn's been sitting on the edge of the sofa, listening to everything. Now, she stands up slowly, looking more exhausted than I've ever seen her, like she's been turned inside out. She looks, I think, the way I feel.

"This is all good," she says. "But once we have Anne back, how are we going to find the son-of-a-bitch?"

Dallas looks around the room, making eye contact with each of us before answering. "We may not," he says, his voice flat. He drags his fingers through his choppy hair. "We're playing this safe. This op is about getting Anne back. That's the objective. That's the focus. That little girl, safe and unharmed. And to do that, we play by his rules. And his rules are designed to hide his identity."

Quincy nods. "Dallas is right. If the goal were capturing our perp, we'd be playing this differently. Hell, even if the goal were locate and capture. But that's *not* the goal, because that increases the risk. So you all have to live with the possibility that this son-of-a-bitch will walk. We'll do what we can, but I'm not going to lie to you."

I nod. Right now, all I care about is getting Anne. And I

know that once she's home and safe, the entire weight of Damien's determination and resources will rain down on the bastard. If it's possible to find him, he'll be found.

"So now we wait until tonight," I say.

Ryan nods. "Now we wait."

"What about suspects?" The question comes from Moira, who is standing in the archway that leads from the living area to the bedrooms. She cocks her head back toward the room. "Lara's asleep. Gregory is in there with her."

"It's a good question," I say, looking between Damien and Ryan. "What do we know?"

"We're still watching Marianna," Ryan says. "She's sticking close to home, but she bought a burner phone at a drugstore near her place yesterday, and the clerk says she buys them regularly. Not proof. Not even incriminating. But it's suspicious, and we're keeping eyes on her."

"And Eric?" I ask, my stomach in knots. "Anything?"

"We confirmed that he's strapped for cash. The guy's running on financial fumes. So that could be a motive. But he's been in Austin for months, and our perp had time to watch this family and learn routines and habits. So unless he's working with someone—and he might be—he's probably exactly who he says he is—a guy who wants his old job back. But we're not ruling him out yet."

"*Abby*," I say as panic suddenly strikes me. Talk of Eric has reminded me. "The new offices. The interviews. *Shit*."

I move off into the kitchen so I can talk without her overhearing the drama going on around us, and although she's baffled, she agrees to handle the move-in and the interviews by herself, using Travis as necessary. I bite back a smile at that, wondering if working so closely will make things better or worse between them.

"By the way, Brian Crane canceled his interview."

"Oh." I think about Brian. About Carl Rosenfeld. And I wonder if Carl held enough of a grudge against me and Damien that he would go after our daughter. "Thanks for telling me," I say, knowing I'll pass the info on to the team. "And thanks for handling everything."

"That's what partners are for," she says. "To help out in life's little emergencies." She clears her throat. "You can tell me what's going on, you know."

No. I really can't. "I'll give you the whole scoop when I see you," I tell her. *When Anne is back safe and sound.* "Call if you need me." God knows I'll be by a phone.

We end the call, and I head back into command central, then stop short when I see Ollie standing there, leaning casually against the back of the sofa his narrowed gaze skimming over the array of computers and phones and other electronic gadgets.

Jamie's beside him, grinning, and I bound across the room, then hug him close. "You took the polygraph," I say, pulling back. Then I swat him across the shoulder. "You were an idiot not to before, even though I don't think you should have had to in the first place."

"He didn't take the polygraph." Damien is behind me, his hands on my shoulders. He eases closer, then wraps his arms around my waist. It's a silent claim. A show for Ollie to make clear that I belong to Damien.

I smile wryly. I have no idea why he's giving Ollie free rein, but things are definitely getting back to normal.

Then Damien's words hit me, and I turn my head to look at him. "No lie detector? Then why?" I ask the last to Ollie, who shrugs.

"Your husband hasn't told me. God forbid he should ever once loop me into anything important."

"Didn't seem necessary," Damien says. "He didn't refuse the polygraph because he had anything to do with Anne. He refused it because he doesn't want us to know he's working with the FBI."

"What the hell?" Ollie says. "Who says?"

Damien flashes a crooked grin. "You did."

"The hell I did." Ollie pushes away from the sofa, standing up straight. "And what the fuck, anyway? If it was true, it would be a secret. And you're just going to announce it to the room?"

"You announced it," Damien says, heading back into the kitchen.

Ollie looks at me, but I can only shrug, baffled.

"Fuck," he says, then follows Damien. I go, too. As do Jamie, Ryan, Quincy, Dallas, and Charles Maynard.

Damien's in there, calmly pouring a cup of coffee.

"For God's sake, Damien," I say, as he hands the cup to me. "What's gotten into you?"

"Ask your friend."

"I haven't got a clue," Ollie says. "FBI? I never said that, much less announced it to the world."

Damien pours another cup, then goes to sit at the table. He glances down at the newspaper, presumably left there by Gregory. Then he looks up, sips his coffee, and puts the mug down. "You told us when you got here," he says. "When you chastised us for handling a kidnapping without the police or the FBI. How would you know that if you weren't in the middle of it?" He points to the coffeemaker. "Hazelnut. Help yourself."

Ollie sags a little, but goes to the counter and pours himself coffee as Jamie and I stare after him, completely blown away.

"At least I know why you left the firm," Maynard says. "How did this come about?"

"I can't say, so please don't press me." He looks at me as he speaks, and I'm certain that the silent message is that he'll fill me and Jamie in as soon as he can.

"Fair enough," Damien says. "But I assume I'm not on the FBI's radar anymore? And that you're not hurting for cash?"

"Wait," I say. "The FBI was looking at you? Why?"

Damien shrugs. "Ask him. I'm only speculating."

Ollie rubs the bridge of his nose and looks so frustrated that I almost feel sorry for him. Even though it's obvious that he was somehow involved with some investigation that was looking at Damien.

"As far as I know, you're not on anyone's radar at the moment," Ollie says reluctantly. "You're also still an asshole, even if you are a damn smart one."

Damien's expression doesn't change, but I see a hint of a smile touch his eyes. "Good to see you again, too, Ollie."

"Thank you," I say to Damien later, after Jamie and I have pulled Ollie aside for welcome back hugs and a promise not to ask him about his secrets. At least not until Anne is back and things are settled. Now he's with Moira in Lara's room reading her a story, and I'm in the bedroom with Damien.

"I wasn't going to keep him locked in a room once I realized the truth."

He's sitting on the foot of the bed, and I'm standing at the window, looking out at the now-dark sky.

I turn and go to him, straddling him on the bed, then pushing him backward until he's flat on the mattress, my hands holding him down by the wrists. I feel his body shift and tighten under mine—arousal and fear and need all mixed up together. "I love you," I say, then kiss him softly, the touch of my lips against his rousing me further. Making me crave his touch and the forgetfulness I know that it will bring.

"We only have a few hours left," he says, his hands on my face, holding me still. "I don't want you there."

"I'll be fine." But the tremor in my voice betrays my fear.

"You will," he says fiercely. "And so will Anne."

"I'm scared," I admit.

"I know."

I swallow tears. "Make me forget, Damien. Please. For just a little while, make me forget."

And Damien, thank God, pulls me close and makes the world go away.

WITH EVERY CAR that goes by, I wonder if it's the kidnapper driving it.

With every minute that passes, I wonder if he's taken the money from the laundry room. If he's freed my daughter.

I wonder if she's happily watching cartoons. If she's crying for her sister. For her mommy. For Daddy.

I wonder if she has any clue at all what's going on, and I pray that she doesn't. That there's no fear. That there will be no scars. No horrible memories. No nightmares.

Lara believes that Anne is at Aunt Sylvia's, and we were happy to let her believe it for now. We can worry about the truth when it's time to face it.

When she's home.

Please. Please let her be home soon.

I pull my windbreaker tighter around me and pace a tight circle on my corner. It's the middle of the night, but with the ambient light from the nearby buildings, I can see well enough, even with the light rain that has started to fall. I face the traffic cameras and wonder if Damien is looking back at me. I hope he is. He should have dropped the money almost an hour ago. It's almost one now.

Almost time for my vigil to be over.

For a brief time, we'd considered letting me have my phone or an earpiece so that I could communicate. He hadn't forbidden that, after all.

But I rejected the idea, against Damien's wishes. "He wants me helpless," I said. "That's the point. He's not going to want me to be able to talk to my people."

"I want you safe," Damien had countered.

"Anne's the one we're worried about. And we're going to follow the rules. Even rules he forgot to tell us about."

I think he would have argued more, but Quincy had put his hand on Damien's shoulder. "Buck up, mate. She's right. You know she's right."

At the time, I'd felt vindicated. Now, I feel alone.

The kidnapper said I had to stay here until one in the morning, but I'd insisted that Damien stay away until one-fifteen. Just in case.

I glance at my watch. Twelve fifty-seven.

I pace some more, my gaze going to the rooftops around me. Is there really a sniper hiding up there, or is it all a ruse?

I think it's the latter—I really do. But that's not a theory I'm going to test.

A few more steps. Another inspection of my surroundings. Another glance at my watch.

One a.m.

I exhale in relief, then with frustration. Because now that the allotted time has passed, I don't want to be here anymore.

I made the rules, though, and while Damien initially protested, it's clear that he's abiding by my wishes. So I spend fifteen interminable minutes pacing the sidewalk until, finally, I hear the low purr of a Ferrari as it slows to a stop beside me on the damp pavement.

I slide into the car, and he takes my hand, then pulls me into his arms and holds me tight as the wipers move in a steady rhythm. "Any word?" I ask, and feel him shake his head.

"Nothing," he says, releasing me and putting the car into gear. "Dallas and Quincy say we might not hear until tomorrow morning."

I nod, numb, and hug myself. I know we're not in one of Lyle's action movies, but the slow pace and uncertainty is weighing on me.

We're silent during the drive, both lost in our fears. It's almost two by the time we get back, but the inside of the house is still hopping. Jamie is passed out on the sofa, and as I step from the stairs onto the landing, I see Ryan drape a blanket over her.

Damien squeezes my hand, then detours toward the conference table, while I peel off to the right, toward the kitchen. More specifically, toward the coffee.

Someone's brewed a fresh pot, and as I step around the corner, I draw in a deep breath, then end the sound on a sharp gasp as I come to a halt. "*Oh.*"

Sofia looks up at me from where she's filling a tray full of mugs with fresh coffee. "Oh," she says, as if mimicking me.

For a moment, we just stare at each other. She's put on

some weight, and it looks good on her. Before, she was too skinny, as if her problems had eaten away at her. Now, she has curves, and her face glows with health. Her hair is pulled back in a French braid, and a few colorful beads have been woven into the strands. Her eyes are wide, a mixture of fear and shock.

"I—I'm sorry," she says.

I know she doesn't mean for being out of her room. After Damien released Ollie, I told him that he could do the same for Sofia. After all, she'd passed the polygraph. There was no reason to keep her a prisoner. No reason other than to keep her away from me.

"It's okay," I say, more out of politeness than because I really mean it. But the truth is that I'm too tired and too stressed to keep up any pretense. "You were civil to me two years ago when we brought Lara home. Then you start sneaking around? What the hell was I supposed to think? For that matter, what were you thinking?"

She shakes her head. "I don't know. I was just thinking about Damien." She lifts her shoulder. "I needed help. He's where I go."

"He's my husband." I hear the ferocity in my voice.

"He's my friend." There's equal power in hers.

"You tried to hurt me," I snap.

She blinks and a tear runs down her cheek. "That was before. I swear, I'm better now. I was just hurting. The baby. I just..." She swallows. "I was just hurting."

Fuck. I understand pain, especially where a child is concerned. But I also understand fear and self-preservation, and where Sofia is concerned, I will always be wary.

But she's right, too. In some small way, she's right. And I know that a part of Damien will always belong to her, as much as that might pain me.

So I walk to her, take one of the mugs, and then take a single step back. She watches me, wary, but doesn't move.

"Next time, come in through the front door," I say. And then, with my heart pounding in my chest, I turn away from her, and walk back into command central.

25

I'm weighted down with exhaustion, my eyes heavy, my muscles protesting. I've barely slept since this ordeal began, and the few minutes I did grab were fraught with nightmares that gave me no rest.

I'm both hot and cold, my gut clenching, my stomach burning with acid.

I'm the walking dead, barely keeping my shit together, so tired my vision is blurred.

But I can't sleep.

I can't bear to go to my bed, away from the people who are helping to bring back my daughter, away from the call that will tell us where to find her. And though I've tried closing my eyes on the couch in the living area, sleep refuses to come.

"You should take this," Damien says, holding out a small pill. But I only shake my head. I can't risk not waking up when the time comes. I can't miss even one second of news about my baby.

So the night passes like a slow moving troll, heavy and gray and full of danger. And I get no joy from the sunrise that I've watched so often from my balcony as muted colors slowly fill the world. Today, it only means that more time has passed. More danger. More fear.

And a little bit less hope.

"Baby, you need sleep," Damien says when I stumble into the kitchen.

"And you don't?"

Dark shadows ring his eyes, and that gorgeous, sculpted face is haggard with worry.

He nods in acknowledgment, then hands me a cup of coffee. I meet his eyes, but have to look away quickly, afraid I might burst into tears. An arm curls around my shoulder and I look up to find Evelyn. "Come on, Texas. You can't sleep, but maybe you can rest."

She takes me back into the living room, and I lean against her on the couch while Damien paces the length of the conference table, his eyes on the monitors that flash as Ryan's security team—a fresh shift—do their thing.

Charles is gone, though he promised to be back soon. Sofia is asleep in a chaise on the patio. Ollie is hunched over his laptop with Dallas behind him, pointing at something on the screen.

And though they're all so, so busy, there's still no sign of my daughter even though the kidnapper has his money.

I turn my head to speak, but Evelyn strokes my hair. "Shhh," she says. "Close your eyes. Just for a little bit, Texas. Just close your eyes."

I do, then open them again when I hear Ryan's voice. "Nothing," he says, entering the living area from the kitchen. He looks from Quincy to Damien to Dallas. "Fucking rain," he says. I don't know what he means, but I'm too tired to ask.

I'm not sure when morning surrendered to the afternoon, but I do know that when three o'clock rolls around, we've still heard nothing about Anne. And when the clock on the mantle chimes four, I rush to the bathroom and vomit coffee and bile.

Damien hurries in after me, brushing the hair out of my eyes, rocking me. He takes a washcloth and gently cleans my face as I cling to him, helpless and lost, my body wracked with sobs.

"He-he should have c-c-called by now." My words come out mixed with gasps and hiccups. "He won't w-want to hang onto her. It's d-d-dangerous." I close my eyes, trying to block out these horrible thoughts. But they won't stop. They race through my mind, a horror movie on speed. "He's h-h-hurt her. I know it. My baby. Damien, he's hurt our baby girl."

"No," Damien says, forcing my chin up so that I'm looking him in the eye. "No, sweetheart, no." But though his words are firm, I see the fear in his eyes, and it makes my blood run cold.

"Come on," he says, helping me to my feet. Then he lifts me up and I cling to him as he carries me to our bed, then tucks me under the covers. I'd brought one of Anne's toys in here yesterday, a floppy purple bunny, and I curl up with it now, imagining that I can smell her baby scent as I press my face against the soft, plush fur.

The bed shifts as Damien sits beside me, saying nothing as he strokes my hair, his silent ministrations urging me to finally let go and let exhaustion pull me into the welcoming dark.

I'm almost under when I hear the light tap on the door. I want to roll over and see who it is, but nothing feels right. It's as if I'm coming out of anesthesia and I'm hyper aware of my surroundings, but can't move or open my eyes.

"News?" Damien whispers.

"Still no word from him on Anne." I recognize Ryan's voice, barely audible.

"Any luck at the laundry?"

"No. Like we thought, the rain fucked us up. The tech works in liquid, so we thought it would be okay, but after a mile it was too diluted. We couldn't track it."

Couldn't track it.

The words go around and around in my head, getting louder and louder.

Couldn't track it.

Track it.

Track....

The words finally click, and I sit bolt upright. Ryan's gone, but Damien's still in the room, standing by the window, looking out at the ocean beyond.

"What the hell did you do?" My voice is hoarse, and he turns, his brow furrowed, as if he doesn't comprehend my words. "You put in a tracking device? He said not to. He said he'd hurt her."

My fear rises, anger boiling to fury. Fear morphing into terror.

"Not a tracker. A different kind of tech."

"Tech," I say dully. He's speaking calmly, but the words make no sense. I heard what I heard, and Ryan talked about tracking. "What the hell does that mean?"

"That we had a way—a risk free way—to find him. A way to locate the son-of-a-bitch if he didn't release her."

I leap out of bed, pushed into action by the force of the horror that's coursing through me. "That's crazy. Damien, what the hell have you done? Risk free?" The words sound ridiculous. *"Risk free*? If it were risk free she'd be with us. We'd have her."

My legs give out as the real meaning behind my words

hits me. "Oh, God. Damien. Our baby. My Anne. What have you done?" I tilt my head back and look at the man I love. The man I trusted. "What the hell have you done?"

He closes his eyes, and that's when I'm certain that he fears it, too.

"Go," I say.

"Nikki, please."

"Dammit, Damien. I just want to be alone. Please." I hurl the purple bunny at him. "Please, just let me be alone."

He studies me, as if debating the wisdom of going. But then he nods and pulls open the door. "I'm right outside if you need me."

"I won't." My voice is thin. Hollow.

He leaves, and I hurry to the door, then lock it behind him. Then I sink to the floor, my back to the door as I squeeze my eyes shut. I expect tears. A flood of tears. But none come. I'm wrung dry. Empty. My insides scorched from fear and anger and betrayal.

But I need release. Need it like I need to breathe. I'm choking on the pain. Lost in a nightmare. And I don't know the way out. I can't see the path out.

Except I can.

I close my eyes, trying to shut out the truth that is pressing down on me, but I can't. It's so simple. So clean. So easy.

A simple path. A way to bring me back to myself. To take back some of the control in a world that's spinning away. Because if I don't reach out and grab it right now, I may spin so far out that I'll never find my way back.

Frantic now, I scramble to the closet and yank open the door. I pull out my underwear drawer with such force it comes off the track, spilling panties all over the carpeting.

And there, in a puddle of cotton and satin, is the leather case. I'd eschewed it before. Now, it's a lifeline.

Desperately, I open the case, even as a small voice in my head tells me to stop. Tells me that I'll regret it. But I shove the voice down, fighting my way forward, knowing what I need. What I crave.

Knowing what will bring me back.

Breathing hard, I pull the first scalpel free. I changed into yoga pants after my stint on the street, and now I shove them down, then kick them to a corner. I wasn't wearing panties, and now I'm on the floor in only my tank top. I bend my knee, tightening the flesh at my thigh, the ridges of scar tissue now raised and white, with just some lingering pink.

Soon, there will be red.

I take the blade and press the tip to my skin. I hesitate only briefly. I need this. Goddammit, I need this if I'm going to survive what's coming. If I'm going to survive the horrible news about Anne.

Now.

The pressure is familiar, more required to cut flesh than most people think, and there's a satisfaction in making that first incision, a sensual pleasure that comes with the pain, that spirals through me as I draw the blade down giving me that sweet release. The control that comes with having something to cling to.

A quarter inch. A half inch.

I stop, my hand trembling. I tell myself I want more, but I can't stop staring at the thin line of blood. It's white-hot and throbbing now. And I tell myself I want more. I *need* more.

I tell myself that the pain is an anchor. A line back to reality. A secret key that will let me cope.

That's what I tell myself, but it's not working.

It doesn't help.

I gasp in air, because this isn't what I really want. It's not what I really need.

I need Damien, dammit.

But he's not here.

Worse, he's the reason I'm in a closet with a blade in my hand and a wound on my thigh.

I draw a breath and shift my position so that I'm kneeling, then I bend over, my hands resting on the carpet as I sob, my tears falling on my leg, mingling with the blood that's trickling down my thigh.

"Nikki." Damien's voice is so soft I think I'm imagining it. "Nikki." It's louder, and I turn my head to see him standing in the closet doorway. "I'm sorry," he says. "I'm so sorry. You know I'd never do anything to hurt her. To risk her."

I turn to him, my body shifting as I do. I know the moment he sees the blood. The moment he realizes.

His face goes pale. His eyes go hard. "Nikki—oh, God, Nikki. What have you done?"

I open my mouth to speak, to tell him it's okay—that I'm okay. But the words won't come. Then he's at my side, pulling me to my feet. "No, baby, *no*." His hands clutch my upper arms and I can smell the fear on his breath. "Not a blade," he says. "Never a blade. You know that. Nikki, you know that."

I nod, a little numb. I haven't cut since Damien, though I've come damn close. Now, I see the fear on his face.

"You come to me, dammit." His voice is harsh, rough with fear. With pain. "Goddammit, Nikki, when it gets bad you fucking come to me."

He realizes he's shaking me, and he backs off, breathing hard. "We need to bandage that leg."

"I need you," I whisper as he takes a step toward me. "I'm so fucking mad at you, but dammit, Damien, I need you."

With a gasp, I pull him to me, and we both slam back against the island. I close my mouth over his in a hard, brutal kiss that draws blood. And dammit, I want more.

I fumble for the button on his jeans, and he spins me roughly around, and I say a silent thank you as he rips my tank top over my head and tosses it to the floor. "She's okay," he growls. "She's going to be okay."

I nod, tears rolling down my cheeks. "Please," I beg as I spread my legs, as his fingers slide inside me. "Fast," I demand. "Hard," I plead.

He bends me over, the edge of the island hard against my ribs. And when he enters me, hard and fast, I relish the pain that accompanies each thrust. This is what I need. This is what I crave. This claiming. This heat.

Damien.

His fingers tease my clit as my breasts rub the granite top of the island. I feel his body tense, mine rising to meet him, and when he stifles a groan of release, I do as well, my body exploding in time with his, until the tremors stop and he pulls me down to the carpet and wraps me in his arms. I cling to him, then realize that he's shaking.

He's crying silently, and I curl against him, sharing his pain, drawing it in, stronger now, even if just a little. I don't know if he's crying for me or for Anne or if he just needs the release. All I know is that we're together whereas we were apart before. I'm still angry. Hurt. Confused. But I'm better. And so, I think, is he.

His arms tighten around me as he gathers himself, then his eyes bore into mine, his hand tight on my chin as he forces me to look straight at him. "Never again," he says, then rises to pull down the first aid kit. He takes out a small bottle of hydrogen peroxide and cleans the wound, then covers it with a gauze bandage. "Never again."

"Never," I repeat. "Never with a blade."

He studies my face, as if trying to interpret my words. But he knows perfectly well what I mean. I will always need the pain. It's part of who I am. And if I won't turn to a blade, I will turn to Damien.

He nods, then pulls me to him again, holding me close.

We're calm compared to the freneticism of a moment ago. The rawness. The need.

But that doesn't mean all is well. We're still in hell, both of us. But goddammit, at least we're together.

"Nikki!" Jamie's voice blasts through from the hall. She pounds on the door, which Damien must have locked behind him. "Nikki! Damien! She's safe! Come quick! Anne is safe!"

26

I wake to the sun streaming in through the windows, my youngest daughter snuggled between my back and Damien's chest, and the oldest curled up at our feet, where she so often ends up when she sleeps in our bed.

For the first time in what seems like an eternity, I feel refreshed, and I smile as I roll over, then see Damien smiling right back at me.

"She's fine," he says, as if answering a question, though I hadn't said a word.

I run my hand over her tangled yellow locks and nod. "Yes," I say. "She is."

It turns out that she'd been away from the kidnapper's grasp for most of yesterday. At just after eight in the morning, she'd been left at one of the city's many drop-in childcare facilities. He'd said his name was Nicholas Starkey, and that he would need to leave her all day in order to attend a series of business meetings.

The facility has security cameras, but they'd walked up, so there was no identifying vehicle in the parking lot. He wore a ball cap, which hid most of his face. The security cameras revealed a mustache and beard, but those were likely stage makeup. The angle of the cameras provided a particularly useless view.

The facility reported that Anne seemed groggy at first—something we later confirmed as the lingering effect of the Versed. She perked up later, but called frequently for her mommy, daddy, and sister.

Eventually, closing time arrived, with no bearded man there to pick her up. That was when they checked the paperwork and called the number. Our number. Ryan answered, and we all raced to get her.

The facility will be receiving a very large donation later today.

Our pediatrician had met us at the facility and confirmed that she was absolutely fine, and there were no lingering effects from the Versed. As far as we can tell, Anne remembers nothing. Well, nothing except Nemo.

Now, she stirs in her sleep, and I reach over her for Damien. He glances down, relief so obvious he practically glows with it. But when he looks up at me, his eyes are haunted.

"I'm sorry," he whispers.

I shake my head. "I'm the one who cut."

"And I'm the reason."

I prop myself up on my elbow. "You should have told me. Whatever that tracking thing you did, you should have told me the truth." But then I shake my head and sigh with frustration. "But maybe … oh, hell. I don't know. He let her go. Whatever you did, it didn't make him keep her or harm her. So I don't know."

"I wanted—*want*—to kill the son-of-a-bitch. I wanted to find him for you. To destroy him for us. For Anne. And I justified doing whatever it took to find him. It was a risk I shouldn't have taken." He looks down, to where my leg is hidden under the covers. "Anne may be fine, but you're not. You cut because of me. All this time, and I'm the reason you took a blade to your skin."

"Don't," I say. "I did this. Not you. You don't blame me for my weaknesses. It really doesn't make sense to blame yourself."

"Oh, I think it does."

"Damien. Don't."

I think he's going to argue, but then he nods. "You're amazing."

I laugh without much humor. "Apparently I'm a mess."

"An amazing mess."

Now, I roll my eyes. "What I am, is yours. Always. No matter what."

"And thank God for that."

He leans over to kiss me, then gets a little fist in his face when Anne stretches. We both laugh, which wakes her up, which makes us laugh some more.

"Breakfast," he says, and I nod in agreement.

I expect to find the house empty, but Ryan and Quincy are still there. Dallas had to fly back to New York, and Ryan sent his staff home to their beds. Evelyn and Ollie both left word that they'd be by later, Jamie is still asleep in one of the guest rooms, and Sofia went back to her hotel. The last of which makes me happier than I want to admit.

"We need to tell Bree it's over," I say, but Damien's face tightens. "What?" I press. "You don't still think she's involved?"

"She was released. The kidnapper knew her schedule. Let's just say the jury's still out."

"I don't believe it," I say. "I trust her." But do I? If I really trusted her, wouldn't I have pressed Damien harder to let her go?

Damien, I notice, is frowning, too.

"What is it?" I ask.

He shakes his head, then tells me to get the girls dressed while he takes care of breakfast.

I do, herding them to their room and helping them into their clothes, and giving Anne so many hugs and tickles that it's a wonder she's not running from me.

When I come back, I find out that my husband's been cheating on me, and I put my hands on my hips and stare him down.

He and Ryan are standing behind Quincy at one of the computers, and he lifts his hands in surrender. "I only enlisted Gregory to cook breakfast because I had a flash of brilliance."

I cock my head. "Only a flash, Mr. Stark? You're slipping." But I tell the girls to go in the kitchen and Mr. G will feed them. Since Gregory spoils them rotten, I hear no complaints as they scamper that direction.

"Okay. Tell."

"Your husband's not exaggerating," Quincy says, focusing intently on his computer screen even though he's speaking to me. "The bastard's a bloody genius. Even if he was a little slow on the uptake."

"Weren't we all?" Damien says. "And we may be wrong."

"We're not," Ryan says, then grins at Damien. "And thanks to you, we'll be able to prove it."

"Prove what?" Jamie asks, walking into the room in a pair of pajamas that were obviously bought for Ryan. She rubs sleep out of her eyes as she looks at me. "What did I miss?"

"No idea, and I've been standing right here."

"I started thinking more about Bree," Damien tells me. "About the kidnapper knowing her schedule." He points to the computer. "Take a look."

Quincy waves us over, and Jamie and I get closer so we can both see his screen. "Know what this is?"

Jamie and I exchange a shrug. "A guy standing on a sidewalk."

"Look closer." He manipulates the mouse and zooms in. It's Rory, no doubt about it. Then he pulls back, and the Moviehouse behind him comes into focus.

"That's the theater on Fairfax," I say. "The one where he was meeting Bree for *Casablanca.*"

"Oh, yes it is," Quincy says. "And I'm quite fascinated by the extremely large number of wireless security cameras in that particular area. I believe I caught him from no less than eighteen different setups."

"Is that bad?" I ask.

"Actually, it's good. Here's what's truly interesting." He taps more keys, the tape scrolls forward, and Rory's walking away from the theater.

"Um, so?" Jamie sounds as confused as I feel.

"Check the time stamp. It's two minutes until the show starts. You're expecting a date. Worried. And you don't give her two extra minutes?"

I'm not sure that's a smoking gun, but I nod, urging him to continue.

"Got this from a traffic cam about three blocks from your daughter's art class. See? We can make out the license plate. Jerrol and Elsbeth Colgate."

"Doesn't ring a bell."

"Not surprised as they live in Hawaii," Ryan says. "But they visit their children in Big Bear, Santa Barbara, and

Long Beach three or four times a year. So they keep a car garaged."

"I made an inquiry based on Damien's theory," Quincy says, "and learned that they do significant business with Franklin & Youngman."

I start to shake my head, then remember the name. "Financial advisors."

"No way," Jamie says. "Is that where Rory works?"

"It is," Damien says.

"Oh, God." I stumble into the chair next to Quincy, then look up at Damien. "And Bree?"

"I think he targeted her because she was our nanny."

I remember what Ryan said at the Foundation brunch. That Rory looked like a guy who hadn't grown up. A guy, I'm assuming, who expected a Stark grant to be his golden ticket. And when he didn't make it big right off the bat, he decided to take a shortcut.

"That's the theory," Damien says, when I spell it all out for him.

"But that's not proof. If we want to nail this guy, there has to be proof."

All three men look at each other, and then Ryan speaks. "Yeah, well, that's where some kickass Stark tech comes into play."

"The tracker? But I thought the rain messed that up."

"Just the exterior tracking," Damien says. "With luck, he'll have opened the cases."

"With more luck, he hasn't already skipped town," Quincy says.

"He's here." Damien's face is hard as stone. "Right now, I'm feeling very, very lucky."

27

A s soon as Damien finishes running down the Rory theory once again, Bree crosses her arms over her chest, then looks at me and Damien in turn, ignoring everyone else around the conference table. "So is this where you officially fire me or is it where you arrest me?"

"Neither," he says. "This is where I apologize. And where I ask for your help."

"Apologize?" Her brow furrows as she looks at me. "Is he serious?"

I nod, but say nothing.

"You passed the polygraph," I tell her, glancing at Quincy, who administered it less than an hour ago.

"He set me up," Bree says, her voice hard. "He made it so it looked like I could just as easily be his partner as his victim."

Damien nods.

I see her throat move as tears form in her eyes. "I didn't know it was Rory. He made me put that mask on whenever he was in the room. And the only time I saw him was when he grabbed us, and he was wearing that stocking."

She hiccups, her chest shuddering from her tears. "I didn't want to leave her. I never would have left Anne alone. I didn't have a choice. I swear."

"I know," I assure her. "And Damien and I are both sorry. We should have had more faith."

"No." She takes a deep breath. "I get it. Those two sweet babies. You can't take chances." She rubs her eyes. "So what exactly are we doing here? Are you giving me my job back?"

"If you want it," Damien says. "But right now, there's another job we want to talk to you about."

"Um. Okay."

"Good," Damien says, then takes the seat next to her. "Are you familiar with nano-technology?"

From the look on her face, she's even less familiar with it than I was an hour ago. I'd at least heard of it. But Bree's expression makes it clear that she's certain that Damien is talking science fiction when he describes the crystalline quantum dots—dust, really—that can be seen only through a certain type of lenses.

"You're serious," she says, then adds, "Wow," when Damien nods.

"It's tech we've been developing for the military and the intelligence community, and it's had limited, successful field testing."

"So, what does this have to do with Rory?"

"The particles are suspended in a liquid—that way they can be sprayed on a suspected terrorist, for example, and then certain field glasses can be used to track the suspect back to his base."

She nods, apparently watching an action movie in her head. "So you sprayed Rory?"

"We didn't get close to Rory. We sprayed the money. And we sprayed the outside of the case."

"Oh. *Oh*. I get it. So when he moves the case, some of the dust is left behind."

"That was the idea," Ryan said. "Had the weather been clear, we should have been able to track the particles back to him. And, we hoped, to Anne. But it rained. It diluted the particles, washed some away."

"In other words, we were screwed," Damien says.

"So what now?"

"Now we want you to reach out to him. Tell him we've finally let you out of your cell. That you miss him and can't believe we kept you here like a prisoner when you'd been kidnapped, too. That you're annoyed with us for not trusting you. Tell him you have to get out to clear your head. That you want to see him."

I watch her face as she processes all of that. "You want me to get into his place. And when I do, I'm going to be looking for the quantum thingies."

"Exactly," Damien says. "If he opened the case and handled the money, there should be dust onsite. Even if he didn't, we might get lucky. There might be some latent dust from when he handled the exterior of the cases. Some minute amount the rain didn't wash away."

She nods slowly, processing everything. "I wear glasses sometimes."

Damien smiles. "Yeah," he says. "We know."

I HADN'T REALLY BELIEVED he'd still be in town, but when Bree reached out to Rory with the concocted story, he told her how sorry he was that her boss was an asshole and invited her over to his place.

"The money won't be there," Damien says from where we sit in a nearby van, the team monitoring the situation with a variety of gadgets. "He's smart enough not to raise suspicion by leaving town right away. That means he's smart enough not to have the bulk of the money on his person. But I'm betting he couldn't resist pocketing a little, and that means we should see the quantum residue."

"So if Bree doesn't see the dots, we're out of luck."

"Not out of luck," Riley says. "Just on to plan B."

Riley had gone back to his house last night, but Ryan called him back for this operation because of his hand-to-hand combat skills. We're all hoping Riley's going to be bored silly. But better to have him around just in case.

Charles Maynard is also in the van, along with a LAPD detective he's worked with before.

"How much longer?" I ask, my nerves getting the better of me. "Why the hell didn't we wire her? We need to know what's going on in there."

Beside me, Damien calmly twines his fingers with mine. "We couldn't risk him finding a wire. They're dating, remember. Whether it was real to him or a ruse, he'll keep up pretenses. We can't risk him pulling her close."

"I know. I know. I just hate the waiting. I'm terrified for her."

He squeezes my hand. "She'll be fine," he says, but I know he's just placating me. He's worried, too.

Minutes tick by, and my stomach twists into knots as I turn my phone over and over in my hand. "Isn't it time yet?"

"One more minute," Quincy says. "No point in calling too soon. She needs to look around."

I know that, of course. I just want this over with. So I sit while the clock ticks down until finally—*finally*—Ryan signals for me to make the call.

I draw a breath, dial the number of her new phone, then close my eyes until she answers.

"What do you need, Nikki," she says in the overly-polite voice we discussed. As far as Rory's concerned, she's still irritated as hell with me and Damien.

"I'm trying to find Lara's pink party dress. Have you seen it?" It's a pre-planned question in case he's listening in.

"It's hanging on the outside of her closet, as plain as the nose on your face."

I almost sag with relief, as everyone in the van shifts to attention.

"Oh, hell," I say. "I see it now. Sorry to bother you."

"No problem." As she ends the call, I hear her say, "Honestly!" to Rory, and decide that Bree deserves a bonus based solely on her acting abilities.

"That's it," the detective says, picking up his radio to call the uniformed backup he has waiting. "We're going in."

28

"Damien actually punched the guy?" Sylvia looks between me and Jamie and Bree. It's Saturday, and days have passed since the arrest. Now we're on the bungalow's rooftop patio, sipping wine around the table, taking a little bit of girl time before the house is inundated with little kids, arriving to help celebrate my girls' birthdays.

Jamie just shrugs. "Don't look at me. I wasn't there."

"It was beautiful," Bree says. "I said I needed to get something out of my car, and when I opened the door, the cops burst in, Damien with them. And he punched that bastard right in the mouth."

"You were great," I tell her. "Thank you."

Her smile is a little tearful, but genuine, and she reaches for my hand. "We're good," she says, for what feels like the millionth time.

"You saw it?" Syl asks me, and I shake my head.

"But I heard it through Damien's mike. Rory went down like a little baby. And I'm so jealous that I didn't get to punch the guy myself I can't even begin to tell you."

"I'm never going on vacation again," Sylvia says. "I can't believe you didn't call us. We would have come right back."

I smile ruefully. "That's why we didn't call. What could you have done except worry, too?"

"I could have worried with you," she says gently. "So everything's over? Rory's in jail? They found the money?"

"They found all of it," I tell her. "Including five hundred of the ransom in his wallet. Damien's people had recorded the serial numbers."

"When's the trial?"

"He confessed to everything," Jamie says.

"He acted entirely on his own. Sought Bree out like we suspected."

"Fucker," Bree snarls.

"And the motive was what Ryan guessed," Jamie adds. "That he's a self-involved prick who believed he was entitled to a silver platter and blamed Damien when one didn't come his way."

"The sentencing hearing is in a week," I say. "Meanwhile, he's in custody. And he'll stay locked up for a long time."

"And the girls?"

"They're great," I say, once again feeling that wash of relief that overwhelms me every time I think about how bad it could have been. How we could have lost Anne or she could have been returned traumatized. As it is, she really doesn't seem to remember much other than a constant stream of cartoons. Versed is a drug they use to chill kids out before surgery. I recall that when they gave it to Lara, she remembered as much about the pre-op time as she did about the operation. In other words, exactly nothing.

I could kill Rory Claymore for what he did to my little girl, but for that one small thing, I'm grateful.

Bree stands up. "I need to get back to the girls. They're bubbling over about the party, and I should help Moira keep them occupied until the guests start to arrive."

"Thanks," I say, meaning more than about today's birthday party, which has turned in to a much bigger celebration. "I need to hit Jamie up about something, and then I'll be out." I check my watch. "Sally's supposed to be here in an hour with all the cupcake stuff, so let's meet in the first floor kitchen when she gets here." The party will be by the pool, so the rarely-used first floor kitchen is the best staging area for today's extravaganza.

She gives me a thumbs-up, and Sylvia stands. "I'll walk back to the house with you. I want to find Jackson and compare notes." She winks, and I know she's purposefully trying to make me laugh. Because Damien is undoubtedly telling Jackson the entire story, too.

"Did you ever find out who vandalized your office?" Jamie asks me after they've both left.

"I wish. I'm guessing Marianna Kingsley, but I may never know for sure."

She makes a face. "Sorry."

I shrug. "All things considered, nasty words on my wall are no big thing."

"No, but that was a factor. Not a big one, but a factor."

I nod, not meeting her eyes. I told her that I'd cut, and other than Damien, she's the only one who knows. Not even Ollie who, years ago, I might have told even before Jamie. But I can't deny that things have changed between us. He has his secrets. And I have mine.

"Nik," she says gently. "You should talk about it."

"I know. And I will." I've already called the counselor I saw before we adopted Lara. I wanted no secrets that might come out and prevent the agency or the Chinese government from approving our application. "Damien suggested it, too. But it won't happen again." I meet her eyes, mine hard. "Nothing like that will ever happen again."

She nods, and I know she understands that I'm talking about the kidnapping as much as the cutting.

"You're really okay?"

"I am," I say. "A little rough around the edges, but I think that's fair, don't you?"

"I'd be surprised if you weren't."

We're silent for a bit, then she runs her finger over the rim of her glass. "How's Damien?" she asks.

I sit back, because isn't that a loaded question?

"He's ... hurting," I say. "But he's trying not to show it. Anne's a lot of it, but we got her back, and in large part because of him. Who he is and what he does."

"Magic dust," Jamie says. "Gotta give the guy props."

I know she's trying to make me laugh, but all I can manage is a tiny smile.

"It's you," she says. "Because you cut."

"I think he blames himself for the kidnapping. Like he's supposed to sprinkle that magic dust all over our lives and keep us in a safe box or something. It's stupid, because he can't protect us like that. No one can. But it's Damien." I manage a smile, and Jamie nods. *It's Damien.* And that pretty much says it all.

The press found out, too, which has made it doubly hard. Because every time we turn around, we're reminded of what happened. So far, we've avoided interviews. But I know from Evelyn that they've been calling day and night. Damien's repeatedly turned down their requests for even two or three minutes on the air, even though the press has treated him—and the entire team—like the brilliant heroes they are.

"And even though he gets a lot of the credit for getting her back, he knows that you cut because of the kidnapping." She nods, considering. "Yeah, I can see that messing with him. Hell, it's messing with me. I don't have any good advice, though. I wish I did. If I had a brilliant idea, I'd totally tell you."

"I know. And I've got an idea. Maybe not brilliant," I admit. "But I think it's a start. And to do it, I need your help."

TWO HOURS LATER, I find Damien in the second floor library, his favorite place in the house, but also the place he goes when he's feeling the most melancholy. He's standing over the display case that holds the first editions of the Ray Bradbury and other sci-fi books he loves. Recently, we added pictures of the girls to the case, and I have a feeling that in a few years, their favorite baby books will go in there as well.

"Hey," I say, coming up behind him and putting my arms around him.

He turns, then pulls me close, and when I tilt my head back, he closes his mouth over mine, claiming me with one long, deep, heated kiss. The kind that makes me think of naughty uses for the wooden desk behind us, then makes me regret the fact that we'll have guests arriving in under an hour.

"Hey, yourself," he says when we finally break the kiss.

"Is that a tease? Or a promise for later?"

"Both," he says, cupping my chin and brushing his thumb over my lips. He's smiling at me, and that kiss just about melted me. Anyone looking at us would think that everything was perfect. But I know better. I know that things have shifted slightly off-kilter. There's a hesitancy with me now. A gentleness that's sweet and tender and that any other woman wouldn't complain about. But I know Damien like I know myself, and I know when something is off.

I cut, and he blames himself. And though he probably doesn't mean to, he's holding back, his guilt like a wall rising up between us.

And all I want to do is climb over it.

"I know it's the girls' birthday party," I tell him. "But I have a present for you." I take his hand and lead him toward the back of the mezzanine where there is a small couch in front of a flat screen television.

"A present?" he says when I turn on the television, then punch buttons until it's set up to broadcast a video from my phone.

"Not so much a present as a possibility. I want to give this to Evelyn," I say. "I want her to release it to the press for us."

His expression is both confused and wary, but he nods when I ask if he's ready. The screen blips and shakes, then goes steady on an image of me and Jamie sitting side by side on a love seat inside the bungalow. It's a tight image, one single shot since we did it ourselves, and my phone was on a tripod.

It's Jamie's interview of me. And although this may turn out to be only for Damien's eyes, if he agrees to release it to the press, then it will also be a feather in Jamie's cap and a kick in Lacey Dunlap's ass. Because this will be the only interview about our daughter's kidnapping that the press ever sees.

I sit hand-in-hand with Damien as we watch the screen. As Jamie introduces me, and I tell—slowly and haltingly— the story about how Anne was abducted. About our terror and about our investigation. I don't reveal too many details and I don't talk about the team, but the point of the interview was never the details. It was the emotion. The fear.

Ultimately, this interview is about me, and when we get to the part where the ransom had been delivered but our daughter hadn't been returned, I take Jamie's hand, and I look at the camera, and I tell the world that I am a cutter. Not only that, but I talk about how I locked myself in my bedroom that afternoon, and how I pulled out a blade.

"It's a battle I've fought since I was a teenager," I say. "My husband knows that. He's known from before our marriage. And throughout our relationship, I drew on Damien's strength to help me battle that horrible urge. One of the reasons I was able to fight, even through the rough times, was the knowledge that he was beside me. And more than that, I knew that he didn't judge me."

"When Anne wasn't returned, the urge to cut must have been overwhelming," Jamie says, exactly as we'd planned.

"It was. Too much for me to resist. And I gave in to that need." On screen, I wait a beat.

On the couch, beside me, Damien sits perfectly still, his hand tight around mine.

"I'm not proud of myself. Just the opposite. After so many years of managing not to cut, I felt ashamed. Disappointed in myself. And I was so afraid that Damien would think less of me. That the strong woman he'd seen fight the urge to cut had suddenly disappeared before his eyes."

"Is that what happened?"

I shake my head. "No. No, because Damien was there for me. Not just in the moment, but *there*. He understands me, and he's strong for me. I had our entire relationship to bolster me. Everything he's said and done. Every way in which he's supported me as I've fought this battle over and over."

I watch my image blink rapidly, and I remember the way tears stung my eyes. "He's told me repeatedly that everyone breaks sometime. And that the thing to remember is that it doesn't make you weak. Just wounded."

On the couch, I draw in a breath, thinking once again of the way those words have always made me feel.

"Most of all," my screen image continues, "he's promised me time and again that he will always—always—be there to help me heal."

A tear trickles down my cheek, both on the screen and on the couch.

"Damien is the reason I survived this ordeal. He's the reason I'm not wallowing in self-loathing for having backpedalled. He's strong," I repeat. "And he shares that strength. And part of what makes him strong is that he doesn't stand alone. I need him more than anything, but he needs me too. Together, we were strong enough to survive. Both the kidnapping and my cutting."

"He played a significant role in finding the kidnapper, too, didn't he?"

"A huge role," I confirm, then slide into the final part of the interview where I talk about the unspecified tech that Damien used to track Rory down.

We chat a bit about how well Anne is doing. How she remembers hardly anything, and that we are hopeful the ordeal won't scar her emotionally.

Jamie wraps by asking if there's anything I want to add. I nod, then look straight at the camera. "As many people are aware, my husband founded the Stark Children's Foundation many years ago to help abused and underprivileged kids. More recently, the foundation created the role of Stark Youth Advocate. These advocates are adults—celebrities or others in the spotlight—who have overcome a harsh past or some sort of personal trauma. Something that adds a level of empathy to their relationship with the kids."

I hesitate just briefly, remembering how I'd choked at the brunch. But I'm not going to choke now. "I'm proud to say that I'm joining their ranks, and I hope that my experience with cutting—and my continuing struggle to fight that urge—will help at least some of the foundation's kids."

Jamie thanks me, then wraps up the interview with, "I'm Jamie Archer here with Nikki Fairchild Stark in an exclusive interview following the horrific kidnapping of Nikki and Damien Stark's youngest daughter, Anne."

In front of us, the television screen goes dark. Beside me, Damien sits perfectly still.

"I'd like to release it," I say. "Jamie and Evelyn can figure out what outlet would be best."

"Nikki." His voice is thick. Raw. "Are you sure?"

I nod, understanding that he doesn't just mean releasing the tape. He's talking about everything.

I slide off the couch, then kneel in front of him so that I can look up and see his face. "Don't you know?" I ask. "Don't you understand that every word I said was the truth? Don't blame yourself for what I did, Damien. But do know that you're the reason I'm still standing despite everything."

His throat moves, and though he says, *baby*, no sound actually comes out.

Then he's reaching for me, pulling me up into his arms, his lips closing over mine for a wild, delicious kiss. "The guests," I say as he yanks my skirt up.

"Fuck the guests," he retorts, and I laugh. Both in joy at my victory and at the imagery. Because this is one part of the party to which the guests are most definitely not welcome.

"Fast," I say, straddling him as the echo of the doorbell rings out. "And quietly."

He doesn't disappoint, and soon I'm riding him, his hands on my ass as we move together, hard and deep, until I feel him explode inside of me. I start to cry out with my own release, unable to hold back, but he silences me with his mouth, pulling me close and holding me tight until my body quits shaking and I'm loose and boneless in his arms.

He brushes a kiss over my lips, then grins. "You need to pull yourself together, Mrs. Stark. We have guests in the house."

"Funny." I climb off him and clean myself up, then make a quick turn in front of the mirror by the elevator. Damien takes my hand, and I smile up at him.

"Ready to go see our girls?"

"Always," I say, as we step onto the elevator and head down together for Anne and Lara's birthday celebration.

EPILOGUE

D amien Stark stood in the doorway of his master bedroom, his gaze fixed on his sleeping family. On the woman he loved with every fiber of his being. Who was the reason he drew breath in the morning. The love of his life, and the mother of his children. The woman who loved him back with equal ferocity, seeing past his faults, his fears, his flaws.

As far as he was concerned, Nikki was the biggest miracle of his life, and to this day he didn't know how he'd been so lucky as to not only find her, but to keep her.

And dear God, those precious little girls.

As much as he loved Nikki, he hadn't truly understood how full his heart could be until he'd held Lara in his arms for the first time. And though he hadn't expected it was possible, his heart had expanded even more when he watched Anne's birth and saw her draw that first breath.

Every day his daughters looked up at him with wide, trusting eyes, and every day, he felt that punch in the gut. A fear that he couldn't live up to the trust he saw there. That somehow, someway, he would fail them. Not in the way his own father had failed him. But in some other, fundamental way.

And it had happened.

He'd let his guard down. He hadn't been prepared. Everything he'd done to keep his family safe, it hadn't been enough.

He had one job as a father. One job as a husband. To protect his family.

One job, and he'd failed.

He thought of Rory. Of Nikki, huddled in the closet with a blade, blood streaming down her fair skin.

Anne, alone and scared.

They'd gotten Anne back, and he knew in his gut that Nikki was strong enough to survive this. But that didn't change the simple, basic fact.

He'd failed.

Roughly, he massaged his palms over his face, then looked again at his girls, curled up together, safe and asleep.

Safe.

For now, at least...

But for the first time in a long time, Damien wasn't looking fearlessly at the future. Instead, he saw the shadows. The dangers.

But he had resources. He had means.

Most of all, he had the determination and resolve that came from years of experience and success.

He was fucking Damien Stark.

And, goddammit, he would protect his family.

The End

Want more Damien Stark ...
told for the first time
from Damien's point of view?
Don't miss **DAMIEN**, coming January 2019

Haven't met **Lyle Tarpin** yet?
Grab your copy of Wicked Dirty now!

Crave more **Jamie & Ryan**?
Dive into Tame Me & Tempt Me!

DAMIEN

I am Damien Stark. From the outside, I have a perfect life. A billionaire with a beautiful family. But if you could see inside my head, you'd know I'm as f-ed up as a person can be. Now more than ever.

I'm driven, relentless, and successful, but all of that means nothing without my wife and daughters. They're my entire world, and I failed them. Now I can barely look at them without drowning in an abyss of self-recrimination.

Only one thing keeps me sane—losing myself in my wife's silken caresses where I can pour all my pain into the one thing I know I can give her. Pleasure.

But the threats against my family are real, and I won't let anything happen to them ever again. I'll do whatever it takes to keep them safe—pay any price, embrace any darkness. They are mine.

I am Damien Stark. Do you want to see inside my head? Careful what you wish for.

Grab your copy of **DAMIEN** now!

Wicked Dirty

Excerpt

Don't miss Lyle's story, *Wicked Dirty*, part of this scorching new series of fast-paced, provocative novels centering around the ambitious, wealthy, and powerful men who work in and around the glamorous and exciting world of the Stark International conglomerate … and the sexy and passionate women who bring them to their knees.

It seemed like the perfect plan. Let a guy into my bed. Let him touch me. Let him fuck me.

Why not?

I was desperate, after all. And you know what they say about desperate times.

Besides, it's not as if I was going to fall for one of my clients. I'm not one of those prissy girls who loses her heart at a kind word or a soft touch.

I'm not a woman who falls at all. Not for a man. Not for anybody.

I've been screwed far too many times. And if I'm going to get screwed anyway, I might as well get something out of it.

That was what I thought, anyway.

Then he *walked in, with his beautiful face and his haunted eyes. Eyes that hinted at secrets at least as painful as my own.*

He touched me—and despite all my defenses, I fell.

And now …

Well, now I can only hope that when I hit the ground, I won't shatter into a million pieces. And that maybe—just maybe—he'll be there to catch me.

Chapter One

The setting sun cast a warm glow over the Hollywood Hills as nearly naked waitresses glided through the crowd with a rainbow-like array of test tube shots. Or, for the more traditional guests, highball glasses of premium vodka and bourbon.

The liquor flowed, the guests laughed and gossiped, the hottest new band in Los Angeles shook the roof, and entertainment reporters took photographs and videos, all of which they shared on social media.

In other words, the lavish party at Reach, the hip, new rooftop hotspot, was a dead-on perfect publicity event.

The purpose, of course, was to officially announce that Lyle Tarpin, one of Hollywood's fastest rising stars, had joined the cast of *M. Sterious,* next year's installment in the wildly popular Blue Zenith movie franchise.

The script was solid, the action pulse-pounding, and Lyle still couldn't believe that he'd been cast, much less that he was set to play the eponymous M, an emotionally wounded antihero.

It was a role that could catapult him from the A-list to over-the-moon, transforming him into a Hollywood megastar with his choice of meaty roles and the kind of multimillion dollar paydays that had only been a glimmer of a dream when he'd started this Hollywood journey.

In other words, this was an opportunity he didn't intend to fuck up.

Which was why he forced himself not to wince and turn away when Frannie caught his eye and smiled. She tossed her head, making her auburn locks bounce as she walked toward him, her sequined cocktail dress revealing a mile of toned legs ending in a pair of strappy sandals that showed off a perfect pedicure.

One of Hollywood's most bankable stars, Francesca

Muratti was set to play Lyle's love interest—the Blue Zenith agent who turns M from his dark ways and recruits him to the side of justice—both saving him and, hopefully, adding another long-running hero to the franchise.

"Hello, lover," she said, sliding her arms around his neck and pressing her body against his. Frannie had a reputation for being a wild child who made it a point to sleep with almost every one of her male co-stars, and she'd made no secret that she wanted Lyle to join that little fraternity.

Honestly, Lyle didn't know if she was insecure, overly horny, or simply into method acting. All he knew was that he wasn't interested. Which, considering the damage a pissed-off Francesca could do to his career, was ten kinds of inconvenient.

"Kiss me like you mean it," she murmured, then leaned in, preparing to make the demand a reality, but he angled back, taking her chin in his hand and holding her steady as her eyes flashed with irritation.

"Anticipation, Frannie." He bent close so that she shivered from the feel of his breath on her ear. "If we give them what they want now, why would they come to the movie?"

"Fuck the fans," she whispered back, her hand sliding down to grab his crotch. "This is what I want."

And goddamn him all to hell, he felt himself start to grow hard. Not from desire for her, but in response to a familiar, baser need. A dark room. A willing woman. Just once—hard enough and hot enough that it wore him out. Soothed his guilt and his pain. Quieted the ghosts of his past, the horror of his mistakes.

Enough to tide him over until the next time. The next woman.

And to maybe, if he was lucky, chip away at the wall he'd built around his heart.

His thoughts churned wildly, and he imagined the feel of a woman's soft skin under his fingers. A woman who wouldn't look at him with Jennifer's eyes. Who wouldn't remind him of where he'd run from or what he'd done. A woman who'd give herself to him. Who wouldn't care about his flaws as he let himself just go, hard and hot and desperate, into the wild, dark bliss of anonymity.

"Mmm, I don't know, Lyle," Frannie murmured, her hand pressed firmly against his now rock-hard erection. "Here's evidence that suggests our onscreen chemistry is real. Give me a chance and I bet we can really raise that flag."

"I like you fine, Frannie," he said, taking a step back and cursing himself for giving into fantasy. "But I'm not fucking you."

From the glint in her eye, he was certain her famous temper was about to flare, but an editor he recognized from *Variety* walked up, and Frannie downshifted to charming.

Lyle hung around long enough to greet the guy and answer a few questions about the role, then made his escape when the conversation shifted to Frannie's new endorsement deal.

He grabbed a bourbon from a passing waiter and sipped it as he crossed to the edge of the roof. He didn't like heights, which was why he sought them out. Hell, it was why his apartment was on the thirtieth floor of a Century City high rise, and the reason he'd spent countless hours getting his pilot's license. When something bothered him, he conquered it; he didn't succumb to it.

And that's part of why this bullshit with Frannie irritated him so much.

"You never struck me as the stupid type."

Lyle recognized the throaty, feminine voice and turned

to face his agent, Evelyn Dodge. An attractive woman in her mid-fifties, Evelyn had been in the industry for ages, knew everyone worth knowing, and was as tough as nails. She also never took shit from anybody.

Lyle studied her face, trying to get a bead on what she was thinking. No luck. His agent was a blank slate. Good when negotiating deals. Not so good when he was trying to gauge a reaction.

"That girl's got more power than you think," she continued when he stayed silent. "You want the quick and dirty route to Career-in-the-Toilet Town? Because that path runs straight through your pretty co-star. You piss Frannie off and suddenly Garreth Todd will be playing M and you'll be lucky if you can get a walk-on in a local commercial for a used car lot."

"Thanks for giving it to me straight," he said dryly.

"You think I'm exaggerating? I thought you knew your ass from a hole in the wall. Or have I been misreading you all this time?"

"Christ, Evelyn. I'm not naive. But I'm not sleeping with Frannie just to make things nice on the set. Are you honestly saying I should?"

"Hell no, Iowa," she said, using his home state as a nickname. "I'm telling you that you need to be smart. As long as you're single, she's not going to let it drop." She sighed. "You've worked damn hard to get where you are, and you're flying high. But let me remind you in case you think that makes you invincible — the higher you are, the more painful it is when you crash back down to earth."

"I'm not going to screw anything up, Evelyn."

"You don't know Frannie the way I do. She's destroyed careers more established than yours—and that was before she had a hefty gold statue on her mantle."

Fuck. He ran his fingers through his hair.

"How long have we worked together?" she asked, obviously not expecting an answer. "Two, three years? And never during all that time have I seen you date. A few women on your arm at a party, but you go stag more often than you go with a woman."

"What the hell, Evelyn?" He knew he sounded defensive, but she was coming dangerously close to pushing buttons he didn't want pushed, and to peering into dark corners that were better left in the shadows.

"You told me once you weren't gay, and that's fine. Thousands of teenage girls across the country sleep easier knowing you're on the market."

"Is there a point to this?" He tried—and failed—to keep the irritation out of his voice.

She cast a sharp glance at his face. "I'm just saying that if you have a girlfriend tucked away in an attic somewhere, now's the time to pull her out and dust her off. Because our girl Frannie is like a dog with a bone. A very pampered, well-groomed dog, who has one hell of a bite when she doesn't get her own way. But she doesn't mess with married men."

"So, what? I'm supposed to trot off to Vegas and make a showgirl my bride?"

"Just be smart. And if you do have a girlfriend hidden away, then bring her to a party or two. And if you don't, then get one."

"It's bullshit," he said mildly. "But I'll take it under advisement."

"Good. Now let's go mingle."

With a sigh, he glanced around the set-up. At the free-flowing alcohol and never-ending stream of finger foods offered by waitresses in outfits that were just a little too skimpy to be decent, but which covered a little too much to be obscene. At the napkins and stemware that displayed the series' logo, and at the band in the corner that was playing a never-ending stream of music from the franchise, while on the opposite side of the roof, clips from the previous movies played in a continuous loop on a giant screen.

It was opulent, ridiculous, and completely over the top.

Jennifer would have loved it.

She would have swept into Hollywood and conquered it, making Francesca Muratti look like an amateur in the process.

Go big or go home. Wasn't that what she'd always told him? Jennifer? With her innocent eyes and her not-so-innocent mouth?

But she'd never gotten the chance.

And now here he was, thirteen years to the day since that goddamned hellish night. And Jenny was dead, and he was standing in a spotlight wearing Armani and living her dream.

How fucked up was that?

"I lost you somewhere," Evelyn said. "Let's head to the bar. I think you could use another drink."

Damn right he could, but he shook his head. "I was just thinking." He gestured with his hand, indicating the whole area, including the city beyond the rooftop. "This really is where dreams come true."

But only an unlucky few—like Lyle—knew how many nightmares hid inside those bright, shiny dreams.

He forced a smile for Evelyn's sake. "It's past seven. I've been here for almost two hours. I've been effusive and charming and a team player. I've done everything they've asked. Officially, anyway," he added, thinking of Frannie's overtures. "That should at least earn me a cookie, don't you think?"

She crossed her arms, shifting her weight as she looked at him. "Depends on what kind of cookie you're looking for."

"I'm leaving—"

"Dammit, Lyle."

"Do I ever cause you problems? Do you have to run interference for me? Do I not live up to my damned golden boy reputation?"

She said nothing.

"Make an excuse for me. Anything. I don't care." For just a moment, he let his mask down. The innocent Iowa boy who'd been discovered at seventeen, plucked out of obscurity to ride to fame on his Midwestern good looks and piercing blue eyes. He'd thrown himself into the work, scrambling up through television and indie films to where he was today. A genuinely nice guy, untarnished by Hollywood's bullshit.

Except that was all just a part, too. And for a flicker of a moment, he let Evelyn see the pain underneath. The loss. The darkness. And all the goddamn guilt.

Then he was the movie star again, and she was looking at him, her brows knit with an almost maternal concern.

"Please," he added, his voice low and a little hoarse. "It's not a good day. I need—"

What? A drink? A fuck? Magic powers so he could change the past?

"—to go. I just need to go."

"Do you want company?"

Hell, yes.

He shook his head. "No. I'm fine. But thanks."

But he did want company. Just not the kind that Evelyn

was offering. He wanted the kind of company that was raw. That was dirty and fast and anonymous. With complete discretion. And absolutely no fucking strings.

Wanted? No, he didn't want it. Not really.

But he damn sure needed it.

Needed to open the valve and release the pressure. To erase the guilt, even if only for a few glorious minutes. To escape the ghosts and the memories and all the shit that he tried so hard to keep buried. That he never let anyone see.

That's what he needed, because without that release, his mask really would start to crack, and the whole world would learn that the clean-cut Lyle Tarpin was nothing more than a goddamn fraud.

Grab *Wicked Dirty* Now!

Charismatic. Dangerous. Sexy as hell.
Meet the men of Stark Security.
Coming in 2019

Stark Security, a high-end, high-tech, no-holds barred security firm founded by billionaire Damien Stark and security specialist Ryan Hunter has one mission: Do whatever it takes to protect the innocent. Only the best in the business are good enough for Stark Security.

Men with dangerous skills.

Men with something to prove.

Brilliant, charismatic, sexy as hell, they have no time for softness—they work hard and they play harder. They'll take any risk to get the job done.

But what they won't do is lose their hearts.

Shattered With You
Broken With You
Ruined With You

ABOUT THE AUTHOR

J. Kenner (aka Julie Kenner) is the *New York Times*, *USA Today*, *Publishers Weekly*, *Wall Street Journal* and #1 International bestselling author of over one hundred novels, novellas and short stories in a variety of genres.

 JK has been praised by *Publishers Weekly* as an author with a "flair for dialogue and eccentric characterizations" and by *RT Bookclub* for having "cornered the market on sinfully attractive, dominant antiheroes and the women who swoon for them." A five-time finalist for Romance Writers of America's prestigious RITA award, JK took home the first RITA trophy awarded in the category of erotic romance in 2014 for her novel, *Claim Me* (book 2 of her Stark Trilogy) and the RITA trophy for *Wicked Dirty* in the same category in 2017.

In her previous career as an attorney, JK worked as a lawyer in Southern California and Texas. She currently lives in Central Texas, with her husband, two daughters, and two rather spastic cats.

Visit her website at www.juliekenner.com to learn more and to connect with JK through social media!

Printed in Poland
by Amazon Fulfillment
Poland Sp. z o.o., Wrocław